Dirty Deeds

Dirty Deeds

By Megan Erickson

Mechanics of Love series
Dirty Deeds
Dirty Talk
Dirty Thoughts

Bowler University series
Make It Last
Make It Right
Make It Count

Dirty Deeds

A MECHANICS OF LOVE NOVEL

MEGAN ERICKSON

AVONIMPULSE
An Imprint of HarperCollinsPublishers

Excerpt from *Dirty Talk* copyright © 2015 by Megan Erickson.
Excerpt from *Dirty Thoughts* copyright © 2015 by Megan Erickson.

Excerpt from *Guarding Sophie* copyright © 2015 by Julie Revell Benjamin.
Excerpt from *The Idea of You* copyright © 2015 by Darcy Burke.
Excerpt from *One Tempting Proposal* copyright © 2015 by Christy Carlyle.
Excerpt from *No Groom at the Inn* copyright © 2015 by Megan Frampton.

EPub Edition DECEMBER 2015 ISBN: 9780062407771
Print Edition ISBN: 9780062407788

AM 10 9 8 7 6 5 4 3 2 1

This book is dedicated to loving yourself first.

Acknowledgments

THIS SERIES HAS been such a blessing to me. I've loved writing every word, every character. It's been my happy place. And I have the readers to thank for that. You asked for a story about the Payton brothers, and that's why this series exists.

And because of that, you gave me a chance to write Alex Dawn, a woman who's stronger than she thinks. I'm so proud of her and this book. And Spencer is a true hero.

Thank you to Amanda Bergeron, my editor at Avon, who gave me the chance to write this series. And thank you so much for pushing me to make every book as perfect as possible. I'm proud of all these characters and I always felt like you were proud of them too.

Thank you to Marisa Corvisiero, my agent, my friend. You do so much for me, and you are my biggest cheerleader. I couldn't do this without you!

Thank you to my critique partners—AJ Pine, Natalie Blitt, and Lia Riley. I know that we don't always have time to read each other's work before publication anymore. But you are still my partners in this business in every way. We get each other through every day, and I wouldn't want anyone else by my side.

Thank you to all the readers and bloggers who've been with me on the dirty journey of this series. It's been a blast, and I am so grateful for each and every one of you.

Thank you to my family, who deals with my crazy life. My husband has had to put up with a lot this year—all the times I've had to disappear to write or edit. He's been such a great support, and I am so blessed to have him.

And last but not least, to Andi. You'll never be one of the "little people."

Chapter One

ALEX DAWN GROWLED as she tightened the hubcap with the tire iron and thought, for the fifth time, that she should have gone home an hour ago.

But that meant going home to an empty house, which she didn't think she'd hate but had learned to her supreme horror that she did, in fact, hate living alone.

She'd never lived alone, not ever. First she'd lived with her mom and sister, Ivy, and then...*him*...and then again with Ivy and her daughter, Violet. She liked living with Ivy and V, but now they had moved in with Ivy's boyfriend, so Alex was alone. In that apartment that used to be filled with Ivy's clothes and Violet's coloring books.

Alex banged the tool on the rubber of the tire. The *thunk* was comforting. She did it again, and again, wondering why she was doing this, but couldn't deny it felt good as hell to get some anger out. Because that's all she seemed to have lately. Anger. Anger at *him* and at her life and anger at the fact that she couldn't seem to be fucking happy.

It was a shitty cycle.

Therapy was helping, a little, but it dredged up old wounds she'd tried to bury for so long. She hated being unhappy. But the more she dwelled on it, the less *happy* seemed to be within reach. She did like her job, though, so that was something. Working at Payton and Sons Automotive as a mechanic was more home than that empty apartment.

Her phone rang, and she glanced at the caller ID before tucking her phone in between her ear and shoulder. "Hey."

"What're you doing?" Ivy's voice was soothing.

"Working," Alex answered.

There was a pause, as if Ivy was checking the time. "You're still at work."

"Tell her to go the fuck home!" yelled a male voice in the background. Brent Payton. Ivy's boyfriend and Alex's coworker.

"Stop swearing," Ivy muttered, but there was no heat to her words.

Alex smiled. "Tell him I'd stop working if I didn't have to pick up his slack."

There was a rustle on the phone and then Brent's voice was clear. "Seriously, why are you still there?"

Alex shrugged, even though she knew no one could see her. "Why do you care? I'm getting stuff done so you have less to do tomorrow." It was Friday and Alex was off the next day, but Brent was on the Saturday shift.

"Alex." Brent sighed. "Go home."

Where was home? she wanted to ask. But instead she traced an oil spot on the concrete with her boot. "Yeah, okay. Just so you know, this Jeep here—"

"I've been drinking. Leave me a fucking note."

Alex rolled her eyes. "Fine. Take care of my sister for me."

"Always do."

Alex was about to hang up when Ivy's voice came back on the line. There was a giggle, and Alex was happy for her sister at the same time a pang of envy sliced into her heart. "Alex?"

"Yup."

"Want to come over or something?"

"Nah, that's okay. You guys have a nice family night or whatever."

"Alex, you're family too."

She was, but Ivy was starting a new family, a nice, perfect nuclear family, and there wasn't room in that house for a clingy sister. "I know, but I'm cool. Gonna go home and crash." She'd been reading Ivy's romance books she'd left behind too.

"Okay, but if you change your mind…"

"Thanks, honey, but I'm fine."

Ivy sighed. " 'K, love you."

"Love you too."

Alex shoved her phone back into her pocket and glanced around the garage. She really should go home. The sun was setting, painting the fall sky in streaks of pink and orange. Hooking her thumbs in her pockets, she walked to the front of the garage, leaned against the side of the open bay, and gazed at the sky and the Friday night traffic on Main Street in Tory, Maryland.

She tapped the tire iron against her jean-clad thigh, enjoying the breeze on her heated skin and through the thin fabric of her tank top.

Her nerves were jittery, and sometimes she still had the urge to run. To flee. To be far away from *him* and her past as best as she could. But if she'd learned anything since she moved to Tory, it was that she couldn't keep running. So she stayed here, where Ivy found the love of her life and where Alex had a good job and could see her niece grow.

She'd given up hope long ago she'd get the fairy tale that seemed to happen for everyone else. And that was okay. She'd hardened and carried a chip on her shoulder that was like an old friend now.

She was about to turn around and close up shop when the sound of a rattling exhaust caught her attention. She turned her head to see a red Mercedes—the source of the sound—making its way down the street. The car turned into the parking lot of Payton and Sons and Alex waited as it parked in front of her and the driver turned off the engine, which thankfully killed the noise.

Alex glanced at her watch. It was after seven now. Technically the shop closed an hour ago, but she waited for the driver to get out of the car, because it wasn't like she was in a hurry.

The door opened. A man's black dress shoe planted on the ground of the parking lot, attached to a gray-panted leg. That leg just…kept going. The man had to be tall as hell, and when he emerged from the car, Alex swallowed. Yes, he was tall. Very tall, probably close to six-four. He wore a gray suit with a white shirt that was unbuttoned at the top and a dark blue tie, loosened so the knot hung off to one side. He slammed the car door shut with a little bit of anger, and Alex jolted at the sound and the force, her body stiffening.

She hated herself a little at her knee-jerk reaction to a big man who was angry.

She squared her shoulders and gripped the tire iron, watching the tall man with dark hair glare at his car with his hands on his lean hips, broad shoulders rising and falling with a heavy sigh.

He speared his fingers through his hair and turned to Alex, opening his mouth to say something but stopping abruptly at the sight of her. He blinked.

She blinked back.

He was about ten feet away, and even from here she could see the brilliant blue of his eyes, the long dark lashes framing them. The little bit of silver peppering his hair at his temples.

He was gorgeous in a clean-cut, serious businessman way. The effortlessly wavy hair, the square jaw, the lips that threatened to open any minute and spit out such words like *merger* and *acquisition* and *accounts payable*. He looked like he didn't smile, but scowled from under a heavy brow.

The type of man who'd always looked down his nose at all the Dawn women. Called them *easy* and *white trash* under his breath. Yeah, she was judging, but her defense was to judge first. Better to size up whom she was dealing with quickly than be caught off guard.

Basically, Mercedes Man was the exact opposite of Alex's type.

She placed the tire iron she was holding on the ground and crossed her arms over her chest. With a raised eyebrow, she said, "Having some trouble?"

He blinked again, his hand frozen in his hair. Then he dropped it at his side, the other still on his hip. "Bloody car."

It was Alex's turn to be surprised. The guy was British. She'd never met anyone who was British, and she really only heard British accents on TV shows like *Game of Thrones* and *Spartacus*, when all the actors had these vague European accents in order to appear exotic. She grew up in Indiana. Not a hotbed of diversity.

"You guys really say 'bloody'? Like that's actually a thing?" she asked—and immediately clamped her hand over her mouth, because the man's dark eyebrows dipped in a scowl, which still did nothing to lessen his attractiveness.

"Do you Americans really say 'yee-haw'?" he shot back at her, the last word morphing into what Alex assumed was an attempt at a southern accent.

"You've officially said that word more than I have in my whole life," she answered drily.

He paused, like he wasn't sure whether to laugh or glare. In the end, he went with a glare, along with a muttered, "Well, then, I'll be sure not to blurt that out at random times."

"That might be a good rule." She took a step forward and jerked her chin in the direction of his car. "Need some help?"

"Your bloody roads," he said. "Can't go a hundred meters without hitting a pothole, and it's done a number on my car." His eyes took in a sweep of the shop. Alex tried not to look at it through this man's eyes. Everything about him, from his clothes to his car, was sleek and clean and put together. The shop behind her was an older building, with a few—okay, several—cosmetic issues. It smelled like grease, oil, gas, and rubber, and she loved every fucking inch of Payton and Sons. So this guy could sneer at it all he wanted. It was home to her. When that arresting blue gaze returned to hers, his eyes were unreadable. "Can you service a Mercedes?"

Oh, for fuck's sake. "Uh, yeah, we can service a Mercedes."

He didn't flinch at her dry tone or her looks-could-kill laser eyes. The man was made of steel. "I see. Well, then, can you look at it, or do I need to speak to a manager?"

She kinda wanted to punch the guy. "No."

He stared. "No…you can't look at it, or no, I don't need to speak to a manager?"

"Neither." She gestured toward the unlit sign in the window of the office. "We're closed." Maybe she would have stayed open if anyone but this guy had pulled into the parking lot.

He sighed and ran his hands over his face and up into his hair, tugging on the dark strands before dropping his arms to his sides. "Fuck," he muttered, turning his glare back onto the car.

She stuck her hands in her pockets. "Look, I'll make sure the guys coming in tomorrow look at it, but that's all I can promise."

After a silent thirty seconds, he nodded. "That'll have to do then."

She took a step forward. "I'm Alex, by the way."

His gaze dipped down her body for one minute before locking eyes with her. "Spencer."

That name. So British and posh and everything Alex wasn't. "Do you need a ride somewhere?" She should just make him figure it out on his own since he was kind of a jerk, but she could always use some karma points. And it wasn't like Tory had a taxi service.

"I'm at the Tory Inn."

"I know where that is. I can give you a ride, if you want."

He studied her again, and she wondered what he thought of her. She was dirty after a long day at work, but she always wore a full face of makeup and red lipstick. *He* had hated it, but she didn't wear it for him.

"Okay, yes," Spencer said with a nod, his tone brusque. "I'd like that. Thank you." His last two words were tacked on, like an afterthought.

Don't hurt yourself thanking me. "I'm going to close up the shop, so you can get your things and I'll meet you at my truck." She pointed to her old Ford in the corner of the lot. His eyes followed her finger, and then he gave a short nod.

"Give me ten," she said.

It really only took her five minutes to close up the shop, but she needed some time to gain her bearings. She could feel his judgment of her and her workplace on her skin like ants. She wanted to get home and shower and forget about this uppity Brit. Why had she offered him a ride home? Stupid, stupid Alex.

Also, why did he have to be hot?

When she approached her truck, he was standing by the passenger door, head bent, a lock of dark hair falling onto his forehead as he tapped away at his phone. As her footsteps approached, he looked up. He held a fancy-looking bag, the strap crossed over his chest.

"That all you have?" she asked.

He nodded and his head swiveled as he looked up and down Main Street. He sighed, and for the first time since she'd met him, his severe face softened. "Look, I'm sorry. I've had a shite day, and I was an arse. Can I buy you dinner or a drink to make up for it?"

Alex hesitated. *No, no, just say no.* But he was looking at her with a somewhat eager expression, and she was starving. A free meal. While looking at a hot guy. Hopefully he kept his mouth shut. "There's a little place down the street, serves burgers and beer."

"Lovely."

As they got into the truck and she put on her seat belt, she said, "But you don't have to pay—"

"Please, Alex."

She tried not to think about how she liked the way he said her name, drawing out the first syllable and emphasizing the *x*. "Sure, okay," she said as she backed out of the parking lot, glancing at him as she did.

He smiled then. A smile that transformed his surly face into...something gorgeous. Spectacular. Like he belonged in some period film with a cravat, sipping champagne. She tried not to think about how his smile made her feel, even as the warmth spread down to her toes. He was just a hot guy, and she'd been around hot dudes before. Hell, she worked with some. So why couldn't she quit perving on this one? Especially because he'd already shown he could be an asshole. God, was that who she was? A woman who was doomed to always want to bone jerks?

Spencer's name was probably something like Spencer Addington IV, and he probably had a distant relative of royalty. Surely, his family played polo or cricket or whatever they did over there in Britain.

Either way, despite the way his eyes lingered on her lips and the way his long tapered fingers rested on his thigh, he wasn't her type.

Hell, she didn't have a type anymore.

Being alone was lonely, but at least it was safe.

SPENCER HAD BEEN a right prick.

He knew it, and the peculiar woman sitting beside him driving this old truck knew it.

And he wished he could take it back. He knew he'd insulted her. And in a way, he'd wanted to at first. This town and this garage reminded him too much of where he came from, and that was definitely not what he wanted to really ever be reminded of.

He couldn't wait to get out of here. Fucking car. As soon as it was fixed, he was gone, back to his flat in New York, where he'd barricade the door for a couple of days and binge on *Shark Tank*.

His Prick Act was polished and impenetrable, and he liked it that way. Everyone maintained a distance from him and respected him for how well he did his job and didn't ask him questions or, God forbid, try to get to know him.

But Alex hadn't backed down despite his English ire, and maybe that was why he'd caved. Apologized. Offered to buy her dinner. He wasn't sure what to make of the woman driving this old truck he now sat in. She wore oversized jeans and big boots and a tight white tank top. Everything was a little worn, but did nothing to hide the enticingly curvy figure beneath all the clothes.

He'd nearly swallowed his tongue when he'd turned around in the parking lot. He'd expected a man with a potbelly and receding hairline—his father, basically. Instead, he'd seen the dark-haired sprite with red lips, bright blue eyes, and a tire iron.

The sight of her gripping the metal, her stance slightly challenging, had made him a little hard, which was disturbing.

He really should have just gone to the hotel and ordered a pizza or something. Socializing with a female American mechanic had never been on his bucket list, so he wasn't sure what had made him want to spend more time with her. He didn't want to think it was just so he could look at her for longer, because that was shallow.

Maybe it was the flash of caution that had crept into her expression as he had turned to her with anger still in his eyes over his car.

Her little hand had regripped the tire iron, and it'd been something of beauty to watch her steel herself to address him.

But it was just a dinner, a way to pay her for the ride to the hotel, because he hadn't seen any taxis around. So he'd eat and be polite and that would be the end of it.

Her truck was old, the engine a little loud. But it was clean. When she lowered the visor to shield her eyes from the sun, he spotted a picture tucked into a pocket there. A woman and a little girl. The woman looked a lot like Alex, so she was either her sister or Alex was a lesbian who preferred women who looked a lot like her.

Spencer really needed to get it together and quit making up shite about the woman beside him.

Good Christ.

Her hands gripped the steering wheel, her fingernails stained from the work she did every day on vehicles. Spencer had done everything he could—scratched, kicked, and clawed—to rise out of his life where those would have been his hands. Where that garage would have been his life.

They pulled into a nondescript brick building and as Spencer stepped out of the truck, he eyed the dozen motorcycles in the parking lot. This was…what did they call it…a biker bar? He couldn't be sure, but he felt incredibly out of place in his suit and tie. Of course Alex would take him somewhere like this—her turf. She was striding toward the door now and looked over her shoulder at him with a raised eyebrow. "You coming, Posh?"

"Posh?"

She gestured to him with a limp hand. "All dressed up with that accent."

He cocked his head. "So I'm automatically a stuck-up snob because I'm British?"

Without missing a beat, she said, "And because of the way you turned up your nose at my shop. Now come inside and let's eat, then I'll send you on your posh way, *Spencer.*" She said his name with a little derision and he wondered what she would say if she knew his whole name.

"Calm down, Sprite," he said in response as he took off his jacket and tie and threw it into the seat of the truck. He slammed the door and walked toward her, the gravel of the lot crunching under his shoes. He rolled up the sleeves of his shirt to his elbows as she stared at him.

"Sprite?" she asked.

Those blue eyes. Did she know how round and bright and utterly bewitching they were? "Yes, Sprite."

"What does that mean?"

"You're…" He held out his hands and gestured up and down her body. "Small. Petite."

She stared at him.

"Erm, like a little truck-driving, car-fixing fairy, I would say." He sounded half-mad.

She must have thought so too, because she hadn't moved. She was a contradiction, this short little thing with her bright red lips, eyes dark with makeup, nearly black hair pulled up into a severe ponytail.

"You're weird," was all she said before licking her lips and continuing toward the door of the pub. He followed, thinking this night was what was weird.

IT'D BEEN A long time since he'd had some drinks and maybe it was his nerves or whatever, but after a half hour, he looked at the bottom of his empty pint and wondered how many he'd had. Because he was already slightly pissed and good Christ, when had he not been able to hold his liquor?

They sat close together at a high-top bar table. The conversation between him and Alex was stilted at first, the tension from their parking lot altercation lingering.

Why are you in town?

For business. Do you like working at the repair shop?

Yes.

But now that they were both well lubed, Alex's cheeks were rosy and Spencer's blood was thrumming in his veins and the assortment of greasy pub food they'd ordered sat between them mostly untouched.

Which should have been the first sign that his night was going to end up fucked.

And now, Spencer wasn't hungry anymore. At least, not for food. All he could think about was Alex's knee pressed against his under the table, the way her bare arm brushed the hair on his forearm. The way she leaned close, those red lips wet and tempting.

She reminded him a little of the women back home, the ones he grew up with. A little rough around the edges, where lately, he'd dated nothing but smooth.

Alex, though...well, he wasn't sure she was like any woman he'd ever met, even the ones he knew in England all those years ago. She had this inner sexual confidence radiating from her, a promise that she'd be the best he'd had in a long time, if not ever.

He tried to remember why he was here, why it was important to keep his mind on his work, but it was bloody difficult with the alcohol coursing through him, fuzzing his head, and the heat of Alex's body next to his.

"How long you in town?" Alex asked.

"I leave tomorrow. Been here several days."

She tilted her head. "And then where's home?"

"New York."

Alex hummed under her breath. "Of course Posh is from the city. I bet you live in a penthouse with a pet tiger and a baby grand piano."

Her assumptions were so hyperbolic that he knew she was taking the piss. "Leopard."

"Excuse me?"

"My pet is a leopard. Leopold the leopard."

She paused for a minute as what he said soaked through her own alcohol haze, then she threw back her head and laughed. "Gold leash?"

"Nothing less than twenty-four karat."

"I don't even have a fish. Well, I used to, but then my niece thought it needed a burger. I think it tried to eat it and choked and died. Sad day."

The picture in the truck must have been her sister and niece then. He appreciated the bread crumbs that were helping him form the whole picture of his sprite.

"I'm sorry about your fish." He could feel his London accent slipping a little with the alcohol, his Manchester roots showing as he drew out his vowels a bit more than usual. This always happened when he didn't have the mental capacity to keep up the ruse of a more posh accent, which was why he tended not to drink and excused himself from company before he grew too tired. But he didn't think Alex would notice—or care.

And maybe, the thin glass of Leslie Michael Spencer's façade was starting to crack.

Alex drained the rest of her beer and met his gaze steadily. She hadn't moved away when he said he was leaving tomorrow. If anything, she had drawn closer, as if the time limit was exactly what she wanted.

And really, why not? Why the fuck not, if they were both offering and they both knew the score?

No heavy feelings, no complications, just heavy breathing and fun.

Sitting in this bar with this intriguing woman, he wondered when the last time was he'd done anything he could classify as fun.

Chapter Two

SOMETHING WAS HAPPENING, and Alex wasn't even sure what it was. But Posh had settled a bit, his accent changing slightly as the beer in his glass had been drained.

She couldn't stop staring at his hands. Right now, one was resting casually on the scarred tabletop, tapping along with the classic rock from the old jukebox in the corner. His other hand was rubbing his full lower lip back and forth. Back and forth.

She wanted that finger to be hers. She wanted to feel those lips on the pad of her thumb, on her own lips.

The last time she'd been with a man was…well, not too incredibly long ago. Ever since *him*, she relegated herself to casual, one-time hookups. Because while she liked the intimacy, she preferred it stay purely physical. She'd entwined her life with another man's to the point it'd nearly broken her. She wasn't the Alex she'd been before, and she knew now that she never would be. But she was okay with who she was now.

And never again would she let a man change that.

But this…this was perfect. Spencer's voice was deep, and he was drawing out his words now, almost to the point she didn't understand what he was saying, but what did it matter? He was here for one more night.

She'd only ever been with men who were just like her—worked with their hands, wore jeans and boots to work. Rough around the edges. Posh wasn't rough. He was smooth and slightly untouchable with his pressed suit and shiny shoes and silver watch that probably cost more than her truck.

But he was looking at her like he'd pawn his watch in a second to get into her pants. Well, he wasn't going to have to pawn anything, because she wanted him just as much as he wanted her.

He paid for her dinner—even though she barely ate anything—as a thank-you, and she let him, watching those long tapered fingers flick a credit card out of his wallet and the efficient way he scribbled his name on the receipt. There were a couple of looped scratchings, then a big S followed by a squiggly line.

"What's your name?" She craned her neck and squinted at his signature, which was more like a doodle.

He lifted his eyebrows at her. "Spencer."

"Yeah, but you got some chicken scratches before that big S there."

"I go by Spencer."

"Is that a British thing to go by your last name? Because—"

"The initials are L. M. For my first and middle name." He was slipping into Haughty Posh, but she wasn't intimidated.

She cocked her head. "What does L. M. stand for?"

He hesitated. "Leslie Michael."

She made a strangled sound in her throat, trying not to laugh. "Leslie."

His scowl held no heat. "Leslie is a perfectly proper British name—"

"I picture a little redheaded girl with pigtails and freckles when I hear the name *Leslie*."

He turned in his chair. "Are you quite done making fun of my name?"

"Why do you go by Spencer?" She was poking him like a sore tooth, but she wanted to know just a little bit about the man she planned to get on her knees for. If he let her.

His tongue snaked out to the corner of his mouth. "I'm not fond of Leslie."

"Good call, Posh." She drained her beer. "Let's go with Spencer. Not sure I could let a dude named Leslie stick his hand up my shirt." She stood up, ignoring his widened eyes. "Ready?"

He followed her outside, the clack of his expensive shoes a contrast to the clomp of her boots. She was hyper-aware of his gaze on her back, like fingers down her spine. When they got to her truck, she reached out to open the door but the next second, a hand spun her around and a body pressed her up against the side of her truck.

She looked up, up into the face of one turned-on Brit. Her knees nearly buckled.

When they'd arrived at the bar, the sun was still setting, so she hadn't thought to worry about where she parked. Now she realized she'd chosen a spot that the dim lights outside the bar didn't reach. They were mostly in darkness, and she probably should have been afraid. Spencer was much taller than her, broader. His forearms were muscular, and she could see the roundness of his biceps under his shirt.

But for some reason, she wasn't worried. The only part of him that touched her was his chest brushing along hers. She'd worn a push-up bra today, and she cursed the padding that was separating her from rubbing her hardened nipples against him.

His hand was braced on the side of the truck, the other hanging at his side in a loose fist. His entire body was tense as he stared down into her eyes.

Slowly, very slowly, he lifted the hand at his side and settled it on her hip. Her tank top had ridden up so a strip of skin was bared between it and the top of her jeans. He ran his thumb along that strip of skin, watching her face. She got the impression he was waiting for her to say stop, or keep going, and she appreciated that.

Although what did she expect from a man named Leslie Michael Spencer?

She curled her tongue around her top teeth and lifted her chin. "You too posh to take what you want?" she whispered.

He barked out a laugh. "I have to make the first move, do I?"

She swallowed. "I'm pretty sure my invitation to stick your hand up my shirt was the first move." She was proud of her chest, always had been. Dawn girls were blessed in the boob department, that was for sure, despite their small statures.

His eyes dipped to her chest, then back up. "Hmm, I guess you're right."

"Your move, then, Posh."

"This *was* my move. Not letting you get in the car, pressing my body to yours, showing you that I want you." He emphasized that with a slight roll of his hips. "So, actually, it's now your move, Sprite."

There were a lot of things about a man's body Alex liked. Hands were one. Legs and asses were others. She'd seen glimpses of the muscles in his thighs flexing in his pants, the perfect shape of his ass, so now she decided she needed to feel too. She reached down with both hands, running her fingers up the back of his thighs, then cupped his ass. She pressed his hips to her, and he exhaled roughly. "Your move now," she whispered.

And move he did. His head descended and their foreheads bumped, his hair tickling her skin. And then she couldn't feel anything, really, but both of his hands on her hips, his fingers digging into her skin and then his lips on hers. Those full lips that curled around his English words and called her "Sprite."

The man could kiss. His mouth opened on hers and his tongue was inside her, tasting her. He made a soft groaning sound in his throat and then he was pressing against her harder, the thick bulge in his pants rubbing along her belly, their height differences making this standing make-out session difficult. But Alex didn't care, not when he was devouring her, not when she had the freedom to focus on the pleasure without the relationship—a relationship where she constantly wondered what would come next, what words *he* would use to hurt her, make her feel less than.

With Spencer, this was all there was, and it was better than it'd ever been as she ran her hands up through that thick hair, threading her fingers in it, and angling her face so she could kiss him more, deeper, just *more*.

She didn't want to be standing anymore. She wanted to be somewhere she could spread her legs and welcome him between them. Where she could grind herself into that erection that was growing steadily, pressed up against her stomach.

Damn this public parking lot.

She pulled away, breathing hard, staring into his blue eyes. His lips were wet, glistening in the light of the moon. A fall breeze blew over her heated skin and she shivered.

He raised his hands and ran them over the goose bumps on her arms, as if he wanted to warm her up. His eyes didn't leave hers. "Who are you, little Alex the mechanic?"

He drew out the *a* in mechanic, making it a long vowel instead of a short one. She wanted to say that she wasn't sure who she was anymore, that she was still learning who she was now since leaving the old Alex behind. All she did was shake her head and press her hands to the cool metal of the truck behind her.

"It's your move now," he said.

She licked her lips. "I've been meaning to see what the hotel rooms are like at the Tory Inn."

He smiled, and she thought they'd both played pretty strategically.

ALEX LET HIM off at the lobby of the hotel and went to park her truck, so that by the time she was striding through the front doors, he had a key in hand and had already pressed the button to take them up the lift to the fifth floor.

And by the time they reached his door, he was uncomfortably hard and all too aware of Alex at his back, the heat of her skin, the sound of her breath.

The way those blue eyes never strayed from him.

He dropped his bags beside the closet and turned around to face Alex as the door clicked shut behind her.

She'd let down her hair, so now it fell around her shoulders in a mass of dark brown waves. A few strands caught in her eyelashes and she blinked them away. She stood the exact same way she had outside the garage—feet braced apart, hands loose at her sides. Her eyes were a challenge, not demure. She wasn't playing coy or pretending to be an ingénue.

No, they both knew if she was in his hotel room right now, she wasn't that. Instead of seductive, her posture was powerful, confident, and fuck if that didn't turn him on more than anything he'd ever seen.

She licked her lips, the crimson stain still in place. "Whose move is it now?" she whispered.

"Game's over," he said, drawing out the *o* on purpose.

Alex smirked, then they each took a step forward and met in a crash of limbs and skin and clothes that needed to *go* right the fuck now.

The taste of her was even better than it had been against her truck, because he didn't have to hold back now. He gripped her head and tilted it back with his thumbs along her jaw. She let him as she dug her fingernails in the skin of his wrists, like, *you may be in charge now, but that could change*.

She was tiny against his body, yet warm and coiled tight, like a spring.

He coasted his hands down her arms and then rucked up her shirt beneath her breasts so he could get at the soft skin of her stomach. She sucked in a breath as his fingers skimmed along her ribs, across her belly, and around her navel.

Her hands were on him too, working deftly at the buttons on his shirt. She made a frustrated sound in her throat then stepped back, whipping off her shirt to reveal a red lace bra. Her breasts were heaving, spilling over the cups, and then she was back against him, tugging his shirt over his shoulders and down his arms.

In the next minute they were on the bed, him on top shirtless, her writhing below him, thrusting her hips into his. Her boots were off, somehow, and he toed his shoes off quickly as her fingers began to fiddle with his belt.

He pulled down the cup of her bra to expose her breasts. She was well-endowed, more than a handful, and his mouth watered at the sight of her peaked nipple. He didn't know what to do first. This was a buffet, and he was starving and everything looked so damn good that he was frozen in place. "Tell me what you like," he whispered, sucking on the skin of her neck as he thumbed her nipple.

She gasped. "I like men."

He huffed a laugh as his lips skimmed her shoulder. "I sure hope so."

She didn't say anything else as she managed to unhook his belt.

"Come on," he prodded. "Tell me what you like."

She stopped moving for a minute and stared at him. Her dark hair was spread out on the white comforter, her lipstick smeared, her cheeks flushed. She blinked for a minute, then seemed to gather her strength. "I like…" She bit her lip and spit out one word. "Hands."

Spencer rested his hand on her breast. "Okay."

"I like to watch a man…touch me." She seemed to be gaining courage now.

He wondered if a man ever asked her what she wanted. A surge of anger washed over him at the thought no one had. And then Spencer focused back on her. He lifted a hand to her face and ran the pad of his middle finger over her lips. "How do you want me to touch you?"

"Why are you asking me this?" she demanded.

"So I can do what you want," he shot back.

She stared, as if caught off guard. Then she swallowed. When her voice came, it held a bit of a challenge. "I want you to lay on your back in this bed. I want to take off your pants. I want to suck your cock until you're…begging. And then I want to climb on top and ride you. That's exactly what I want."

That's what he wanted to, everything that she said, every word that spilled from those kiss-swollen lips.

So he rolled off her onto his back on the bed and bent his elbows, lacing his hands behind his head. "Then you have at it, and get the rubber from my kit while you're at it."

ALEX PAWED THROUGH Spencer's things, finally finding the condom even though she could barely see through the haze of…what were these? Tears?

Why was she crying? There was no crying during one-night stands.

So she blinked them away, not wanting to dwell on how much it had affected her that he'd asked what she wanted. Because she hadn't known how much it meant to hear that question. She was used to taking what she wanted. But she'd never been *asked*. She'd never been forced to vocalize it for the pure reason that a man wanted to make her feel good. That he wanted to do what she liked.

It made her a little angry too, that this stranger was the first one to do it. What was wrong with her that men she'd loved and thought loved her back hadn't ever done that?

When she turned back to the bed, Spencer hadn't moved. He was still there, lying on his back, arms behind his head, blue eyes watching her every move. He had a tattoo on his left pectoral, something large and furry.

Flipping open the fly of her jeans, she unzipped them and let them drop to the floor. She stood before him then, in her red bra and matching panties. That was her indulgence, her big fuck-you to everyone who treated her like dirt because of what she did for a living. Knowing she wore sexy underwear made her feel empowered. She'd never worn them for *him*. It had always been for her.

But now, with Spencer's gaze raking over her body, she was glad she had these. That she had something to give this man.

She stepped toward him, pulled his socks off, then his pants. He wore a pair of plaid boxer briefs, and she smiled at the thick ridge showing beneath the cotton.

He didn't move as she lowered the waistband to reveal his cock. She was startled at first because he wasn't cut. She'd never seen an uncut cock in person. He reached down and gave himself a couple of strokes, so the head of his cock peeked through the foreskin.

She loved giving blow jobs. Really, really loved it. Or at least, she used to. *He'd* made it about power after a while, refusing to do anything but stand while she kneeled at his feet. She'd hated that, his hand on her head, gripping her hair. Well, she'd pretended he did it out of love, but she knew now it hadn't had anything to do with love.

With Spencer on his back, she didn't feel like something lesser. She felt like she had the power, and so she bent down and took his big, thick cock in her mouth to the root and then pulled off.

Spencer hissed out a sound between his teeth. His hips jerked but he didn't fuck her mouth or press a hand to the back of her head. His hands were fisting the sheets, the blue of his eyes visible only through thin slits as he stared down at her with his mouth open.

She smiled at him, then began to get to work.

He was thick, thicker than she was used to, especially because she was out of practice, but God, she forgot how good this felt, to make a man feel this good, to have the power to do this.

When his thighs tensed, she pulled off and he made a whimper sound in his throat. She laughed as he looked at her like she'd kicked his puppy.

"You stopped," he gasped.

She smiled as she took off her bra, and he must have forgotten his pain, because his eyes zeroed in on her breasts. "Fuck, you're gorgeous."

She slithered out of her panties, then ripped open the condom packet and rolled it onto him. Straddling his waist, she leaned down, bracing her hands on each side of his head. Her hair fell in a dark curtain around them and his eyes shone even brighter somehow. "You ready?"

"Take it away, Sprite," he said.

She rose and lowered herself onto his cock.

It'd been maybe six months since she'd had sex, and even then it had been quick and she'd been a little drunk.

She wasn't drunk anymore. Anything that had been pulsing through her system had been pushed out with the all-consuming arousal pounding through her veins.

His cock inside her was perfect, and she felt full, so damn full. He was inside her to the hilt, and she threw her head back, swiveling her hips as his hands coasted up her thighs and gripped her waist.

She wasn't ready to move yet, wasn't ready to start because then it'd be over, so instead she relished the feel of him. She lifted one hand to cup a breast and lowered another to press against her engorged clit.

"Christ," he whispered.

Alex opened her eyes to see Spencer's gaze honed in on her hand and where he had entered her body. He reached out and pressed her clit where her finger was, his gaze lifting to hers as he began to swirl it. "That? Right there?"

She nodded, unable to speak as every nerve in her body was centered right where he was touching her.

So she began to move. Slowly at first, loving the slow drag of his cock in and out of her body. He rolled his hips slightly but let her set the pace, watching her face as he continued to focus on her clit, working to make her feel as good as he could.

She picked up the pace then, until she was slamming herself onto him, the sounds of slapping skin filling the room, harsh pants and groans and curses.

Falling forward, she braced herself on the bed and he reached up, tugging her face to his and breathing against her lips. His thumb hadn't stopped circling her clit and God, she was close. So close.

"Come for me, Alex, my little sprite," he said.

She groaned and he answered it with one of his own.

"I…"

"Come on."

"Coming…" she gasped.

"Yes," he whispered. "This is where you belong, riding me."

And that was really all it took, that heavily accented voice telling her what she knew to be true. That's how her orgasm rocketed through her, as she stared into his eyes, breaths mingled, his thumb still helping her to chase her pleasure.

He came a minute later, thrusting up into her and moaning into her mouth.

When his hips stopped jerking, Alex realized they were kissing. Both of Spencer's hands gripped her hair, holding her to him as his tongue slowly licked into her mouth.

She didn't roll off, she didn't move, knowing it'd be a while before she had this intimacy again.

Spencer's hands drifted down her back, his blunt nails raising goose bumps along her skin. She tucked her head into his neck, sighing against the hair curling at its nape, enjoying his smell, his heat, his hands on her body.

He'd held her like this. At the beginning. Then it was like he knew how much she craved the closeness, the cuddling, and denied it.

Bastard.

Maybe Spencer noticed the sudden tension in her body because he made a soothing sound and pressed a kiss to her temple, his hand squeezing the muscles of her shoulders.

Then his hand rested on her hip, as if it belonged there. And no matter what he'd said during sex, she didn't belong here.

Which is what made her lift herself off his warm body and climb off his lap.

She picked her underwear off the floor and began to dress slowly, methodically. The bed creaked but she didn't look up, not until she was completely dressed, her hair tied back into a ponytail.

When she turned around, Spencer had slipped his boxers back on and sat at the end of the bed, elbows on his knees, watching her.

She gave herself a minute to look at his lush lips, those blue eyes, the dark hair peppered with streaks of silver. The light freckles dotting his nose, cheekbones, and the top of his shoulders and back.

He wasn't bulky, but he was nicely toned. A very attractive man. She wondered if he had a girlfriend at home. Maybe even a wife. Alex wondered if she'd be a huge regret.

She could have asked but instead she stepped between his legs, touching his hair and the concentration of gray at his temples. "I need to go."

He nodded, and Alex searched his eyes for regret. It was there, in the wrinkled skin of his forehead.

She felt regret too. Regret that she hadn't met Spencer before she'd been broken by *him*.

"Will you be at the shop tomorrow when I go about my car?" he asked.

She shook her head. "I'll call in the morning, tell them about it."

" 'Preciate that," he said, his voice thick.

She needed to leave, now. Before she tore off her clothes and climbed between the sheets for round two. So she leaned down and pressed a chaste kiss to his lips. "Thanks for a great night. Have a safe trip back to New York."

His gaze searched hers. She didn't know what he was looking for. "I will."

She nodded and stepped away from him, letting her arms drop to her sides. Before she thought too long about it, she pulled out her keys and tugged a keychain off the ring. She set it on the desk near his laptop, her fingers lingering over the plastic logo of Payton and Sons.

Spencer watched her movements silently. Her hand was on the handle of the door when he spoke again. "Sprite?"

She looked over her shoulder to where he hadn't moved from the foot of the bed. "Yeah?"

"Thanks."

She smiled. "We take hospitality seriously here in Tory."

Then she walked out to the sound of his husky laugh behind her.

Chapter Three

HONEYBEAR LOWERED HER shoulders, paws stretched out in front of her, butt in the air, keeping her eyes on Violet as she waggled the Frisbee in front of the dog's nose.

"Go, girl!" she shouted and tossed the Frisbee as far across the park lawn as she could.

Alex squinted with her hand over her eyes as the dog took off, her niece waiting with her hands clasped together to see if the dog would catch it midair.

They'd decided to spend some time that morning at the park before Ivy had to go into work. The fall air had begun to creep into Tory, and they wanted to enjoy it before winter made it less fun to be outside.

Honeybear made a running leap and snatched the Frisbee between her jaws. Violet whooped. "Did you see that, Mom?"

"Yep," Ivy answered. She turned to Alex and nudged her with her shoulder. "What's up? You've been quiet today."

Alex stared down at her feet, wiggling her toes in her red Chucks. They sat on a blanket in the park, bottles of water and a bag of pretzels between them. Violet was crooning to Honeybear, who'd returned happily with the Frisbee. "I thought the silence was nice. What do you want me to talk about?"

Ivy rolled her eyes. "Fine, be evasive."

"I'm not being evasive."

"Well, you're being…something. Forget it."

"I will," Alex huffed. Truthfully, she'd slept like shit. After the evening in Spencer's hotel room, she'd gone home and tossed and turned. Usually after a round of fantastic sex, she slept like the dead, but not this time. Not with the feel of Spencer's hands on her, his whispered words, *tell me what you like.*

She'd liked what he did. That was basically it. And no other man had done it for her like that in her life.

"Mom?" Violet called.

"Yeah?"

"I gotta go to the bathroom."

Ivy stood up and smoothed down her sundress. "No problem, honey."

Alex whistled to Honeybear. "Stay with me, girl." The dog dutifully trotted over to Alex and plopped down on the blanket. She kept her head up, though, tongue out, watching as her two humans walked toward the brick building that housed the bathroom. Alex reached out and scratched Honeybear's head.

Honeybear was Brent's dog first, a stray from the shelter gifted to him by his brother, but the canine had attached to Ivy and Violet pretty quickly. The dog was spoiled despite her stupid name, which Brent insisted was given to her by previous owners. Apparently she wouldn't respond to anything else.

Alex leaned back and closed her eyes, the sun hot on her lids. She'd been so sure of her life when they moved to Tory. No men. None. No way would she let a man rip her apart like *he* had. *Robby.*

When she'd first met Robby, he'd been good to her. Treated her well, saved her the corner brownies, and asked her to move in. She'd grown up with a single mom and Ivy, and Alex was self-aware enough to know she'd craved male attention her whole life because of the lack of a father figure. Robby had given her attention and made her feel beautiful and loved until…he didn't anymore.

Once she began to live with him and he'd done an effective job of isolating her from friends, he'd shown who he really was. He'd never raised a hand to her, but his words were weapons. It didn't matter if he yelled them or whispered them or hissed them in her ear—they all hurt.

They all pierced holes in her flesh until she couldn't breathe, until she didn't even recognize herself anymore.

It wasn't until Ivy and Violet came to live with Alex and Robby that Alex began to see just how bad it had gotten. So they'd picked up and left one day while Robby was at work. Alex couldn't imagine how much the man had raged when he came home to an empty apartment.

They'd moved to Tory and although there'd been some growing pains, they'd settled in. Alex was working a job she loved, where she could still be close to her sister and watch her niece grow.

Ivy hadn't had that much luck with men either. Violet's father had abandoned her as soon as she got pregnant. They'd both been committed to a spinster lifestyle until Brent came charging in and stole her sister's heart.

But that was okay, because Ivy was happy and loved, and Violet had a great father figure in her life now.

Alex had thought she'd be okay by herself, and she had been until last night, when one too-gorgeous-for-his-own-good Brit had shown her that there was more out there.

She shook her head and opened her eyes, fisting her hand in the fur at Honeybear's neck. It had just been sex. She needed to get over it, especially because she'd never see the man again.

Ivy and Violet were on their way back, so Alex tried to relax her face. She didn't smile, because that probably would have alarmed Ivy if Alex all of a sudden got cheerful, but she didn't want to look angry. Honeybear hopped to her feet and trotted toward Violet, who'd picked up the Frisbee again.

Ivy sat back down on the blanket and stuck a pretzel in her mouth.

Alex looked at her younger sister, the way her dark, wavy hair spilled around her shoulders, the way her blue eyes looked bright even in the sunlight. Some people used to think they were twins, until Ivy decided she liked clothes and makeup and Alex decided she liked boots and engines.

Ivy turned to Alex and met her gaze.

Alex glanced at Violet, ensuring she was out of earshot, then licked her lips. "I, uh, met someone last night."

Ivy's chewing slowed, then she swallowed. "Okay."

"It was…different. Shook me up is all."

Ivy's eyes narrowed. "Did he hurt you?"

Alex held up a hand. "No, no. Calm down, tiger. He was…just different. And not because he had a British accent"—Ivy's eyebrows shot up—"but because he treated me…well. Really well. For a one-night stand. So I'm quiet because I'm dealing with the aftermath of a hookup that affected me in a way hookups never do, okay?"

Ivy blinked at her. "You hooked up with a British guy?"

"Yeah."

"Did he say 'bloody'? Please tell me he said something like, 'I can't be arsed, but that's bloody brilliant.'"

Alex stared at her.

Ivy shrugged. "I watch the BBC sometimes. They have good miniseries."

Alex laughed. "Uh, well, he didn't say that phrase, but he did say 'bloody.'"

"Wow," Ivy muttered.

"And he was hot, and had the most stuck-up name. He wore a suit. I mean…he was the opposite of what I'm normally attracted to, but he had great hands and hair I wanted to run my fingers through, so I went for it."

Ivy nibbled her lip. "How did you meet him?"

"His car was acting up. He pulled into the shop after we were closed. I offered to drive him to his hotel, but he wanted to buy me dinner as a thank-you. And, well, dinner was great and then I didn't exactly drop him off at his hotel."

"Will you see him again?"

Alex shook her head. "Nah, he was only in town for business and he said he'd be leaving today. They'll probably fix his car and then he'll be gone."

"And are you okay with that?"

"Of course I'm okay with that." Her voice came out sharper than she'd intended.

Ivy didn't back down. "You don't have to snap at me."

Alex heaved a sigh. "I don't even know him. Hell, he could have a girlfriend back in New York or London. He could be royalty or some shit. I don't know. I was an easy American who he met on a business trip."

Ivy frowned. "Don't talk about yourself like that."

Alex blew out a breath and grinned. "Hey, he was easy too."

Ivy pursed her lips to hide a smile. "You're awful."

"Look, it's not a big deal. But you wanted to know why I was quiet, and there it is. We don't keep secrets, remember?"

Ivy's eyes lowered. When she'd been dating Brent, she'd kept it from Alex, afraid that Alex would be upset that she'd gotten involved with a man when they'd both sworn them off. But Alex was more angry that she'd kept it from her than that she'd found a man to love. "Yeah, no secrets."

"I didn't say that to make you feel guilty or anything."

Ivy watched her daughter wrestle Honeybear to the ground. "I know."

"Anyway, it's fine, it's over. I have work to concentrate on. They're giving Gabe more hours, and he's a pain in my ass."

Ivy laughed. "Aw, he can't be that bad."

Alex rolled her eyes. "He stares at my boobs like all the time. I can't even bend over or he's ogling my ass. Kid is a walking hormone."

"He's not a kid. Maybe if you and Cal quit calling him kid, he'd grow up."

Alex huffed. Her sister had a point. "Well, I'm just trying to lead him right. He's already scared of Jack, so I don't want the guy to have more reasons to yell at Gabe." Jack was Brent and Cal's father, the owner of Payton and Sons. Gruff as hell, but he had a big heart, even if it took a lot of digging to get there.

"Fine, so I'll forget about your hot British guy. But I'm glad you told me. And if you need to talk about it anymore—"

Alex waved a hand. "Yeah, yeah, you're there for me. You love me. I'm the best sister of all time, yadda."

Ivy laughed, shoving Alex's shoulder. And Alex tried her very best to push that intoxicating, accented male voice to the back of her mind so she could enjoy the day with her family.

SPENCER STARED AT the two men, who were clearly brothers or at least close relatives. They both had gray-blue eyes. One stood with a cocked head, grinning. The other was scowling.

Spencer didn't prefer the grin or the scowl. He preferred his car fixed so he could go home. He rubbed his temples, wishing he had more caffeine, but he'd woken up in his hotel room feeling like he needed to get the hell out of this town. It'd been fortunate the hotel had a car service that drove him to the garage.

The man who was grinning stepped forward with his hand out. "I'm Brent Payton."

Ah, so he must own it, if the sign on the front of the building meant anything. Spencer extended his hand. "Leslie Spencer. Erm, I go by Spencer."

For some reason, that made Brent grin harder.

The other man grunted out one syllable. "Cow."

"I'm sorry?" Spencer asked.

The man blinked those steel eyes at him. "Cow."

Spencer frowned. "Cow? Like moo cow?"

Brent began to laugh and the other man's face didn't change. He spoke slowly this time, drawing out the word. "Cal. My name is Cal."

Christ, these fucking people. "Oh, okay, pleasure to meet you, Cal."

"I told you that you mumble," Brent said, elbowing his brother. "Enunciate like a human."

"I'll enunciate you," Cal growled.

Spencer thought he looked a little scary, but Brent only laughed in his face.

These were the men Alex worked with?

A teenager emerged from the back room, sipping from a Starbucks cup. The kid wore black Converse shoes with skulls on them, a pair of cutoff denim shorts, a tank top that exposed most of his chest, and his hair was…green. Bright green.

Spencer's father's shop in Manchester consisted of three middle-aged men who rarely discussed anything that didn't have to do with vehicles. Payton and Sons was clearly not his father's shop.

The kid stopped next to Cal and peered up at Spencer with big brown eyes.

Spencer nodded at him and then turned to Cal. When the man stared back at him impassively, Spencer cleared his throat and turned to Brent instead. "So I'm here about the Mercedes there." He pointed to his red sedan in the parking lot. "Alex said she'd leave some sort of note?"

"Oh, he's British!" the teenager shouted. Spencer flinched, and a headache began to form at his temples.

"Yeah, we're all aware, Asher," Brent said.

"Do you live in London?" the kid asked.

It was like most Americans thought the entire United Kingdom was made up of London. "Um, no, I live in New York."

"Oooh." Asher's eyes were big.

"Anyway," Brent said. "We'll take care of your car. You wanna wait around until it's done or you need a ride somewhere?"

A ride. Spencer gritted his teeth against unbidden thoughts of last night. When his sprite had managed to dismantle him one moan at a time. "I'll work in your waiting room while you work. That all right?"

Brent nodded. "Fine by us."

It was Saturday, but Spencer's work never stopped. He spent a couple of hours sitting in Payton and Sons answering e-mails, trying to ignore Brent's less-than-stellar singing as he crooned along with the radio.

Asher came in every once in a while to straighten up the counter, but Spencer got the impression the teenager wanted to stare at him and get a chance to hear him speak again.

Spencer wasn't in the mood to be a sideshow.

This town, this shop, these people were a little too much like what he moved away from. What he tried to hide when he suppressed his Manchester accent.

Spencer left England when he was eighteen and had gone to college in New York for a degree in business and hotel management. He'd been a hotel manager for years until his friend Penny plucked him from that job and convinced her father, CEO of Royalty Suites, that Spencer's skills would be better used as a location scout. He'd been in his current position for close to seven years now—a job that allowed him to travel. He liked that, since nowhere was really home anymore. Not Britain, not New York.

It was a little lone wolf, but that suited him. At thirty-five, he was officially a confirmed bachelor. His mother passed away when he was ten, and his father didn't care about grandchildren.

So jet-setting businessman he was.

The past week, he'd evaluated whether Tory could support a hotel and which locations would be best for a new six-floor Royalty Suites. Spencer was urging his company to go forward with the plans to build there. He thought the town could support it with business travelers. The current hotel, which was where he was staying, was older and small.

There were several places he'd been tasked to research—one was the land behind Payton and Sons, although he wasn't recommending that one. Tory sat right off a major highway and not far from the state's main airport, so the need for a hotel for business travelers—like him—was evident. The location Spencer was recommending was on the outskirts of town, near the large MacMillan Investments office building. There was easier access from the highway and fewer back roads to get into the main part of town.

He placed a couple of finishing touches on his report, which wasn't due until Monday, and sent it off to his bosses.

Spencer stretched, his back cracking. He rubbed his neck and as he shifted in the hard chair, his keys in his pocket jingled.

After Alex had left last night, he'd stared at the keychain she'd left on his desk, running his fingers over the smooth surface. It was clearly something they had printed for the shop, a ring attached to a plastic tab that bore the shop's logo and contact information.

He wondered why she left it, but was glad to have the memento. He resisted taking it out of his pocket to look at again, and instead thought about how he should get up and walk around a bit. If not, he'd have to find a chiropractor in town before driving back. He was accustomed to sleeping in different beds in hotel rooms, but he couldn't remember a bed that had been less comfortable than the one he was in now. He gazed across the street and a sign caught his eye. *Delilah's Drawers.*

"What is Delilah's Drawers?" he asked Asher, who was pretending to type on the computer.

The teenager blinked at him. "What?"

He pointed. "That sign says Delilah's Drawers. What kind of shop is that?"

"Oh, it's, um, a high-end consignment shop. Women's clothes, jewelry, accessories, stuff like that."

He shut his laptop and winced at the crick in his back. "I can walk there, yes?"

Asher nodded. "It's set back off the road a bit."

He could bring something home for Penny's daughter, Claudia. She loved consignment shops, digging through the jewelry until she found some hidden gem of costume jewelry. He placed his laptop in his bag and stood up. "May I leave this here while I run across the street?"

"Sure." Asher came out from around the counter and took the bag from him. "I'll just place this behind the desk."

"Thank you."

THE SHOP WAS tucked among some trees, with the signage visible from the road. Spencer pushed the door open and a bell rattled. He stopped abruptly inside the door, gazing around at the neat racks of clothes, the long glass counter with displayed jewelry, the large bookcase full of purses.

Claudia would love it here. So would Penny.

A small Asian woman appeared from a back room. She seemed surprised to see a man in her store, then quickly flashed a bright smile. Her red lips reminded him of Alex's. "Hello, I'm Delilah. Can I help you with anything?"

"Just browsing," he answered.

Her eyes lifted for a minute. "Great, well, let me know if you need help."

"Will do, thank you."

He fingered a couple of dresses on a rack, but there wasn't anything in Claudia's size. He thought for a minute about picking something out for Penny, but her second husband hated Spencer enough as it was. Probably best not to rock the boat even more.

He moved on to the jewelry and had picked up a long gold necklace when a pair of pink nails clicked the counter in front of him. He looked up and dropped the necklace with a clatter.

Recovering as quickly as he could, he picked up the necklace and placed it back, but he couldn't stop staring at the women in front of him, who looked so much like Alex, he did a double take.

But she wasn't Alex. Her hair was longer and not pulled up into a severe ponytail. She wore a dress and pink lipstick. Everything about her was softer, less harsh.

It was a surprise to him that he preferred harsh.

This was Alex's sister, though, no doubt about it. He recognized her from the picture in Alex's truck.

Well, this was awkward. Did she know? He wasn't sure, because her expression was schooled. Was he imagining the cold look in her eyes?

He cleared his throat. "Uh, I'm looking for a gift."

"For a girlfriend?" The sister's voice wasn't anything like Alex's. She also said "girlfriend" with an edge. Oh God, she probably knew. And Spencer stood there like a wanker, this knowledge of what he'd done last night all around them like smoke.

But still he bristled, because what right did this woman have to interrogate him? Alex had walked out on him. No strings. He didn't owe anyone an explanation. "A friend," he answered coolly and noncommittally. A very good friend, who was married with two children.

The silence stretched between them. He felt the woman's eyes on him as he bent his head to fiddle with the jewelry again. The eyes were the same as Alex's, that startling blue. And why was he still thinking about Alex? They'd both gotten what they wanted last night and then she'd left. Which was probably for the best.

He could barely see anymore, so he held up the necklace to the sister. "I'd like to purchase this, please."

She nodded curtly and rung him up efficiently. He handed over the credit card, which she glanced at. The lines around her mouth tightened as she swiped it through her machine. He was glad this wasn't a place that served food or she'd probably spit into his coffee.

How small was this damn town? Would he run into the niece next? That would just be his luck.

While they waited for the credit card machine to approve him, he stuck his hand in his pockets. "So, uh, this is a nice little shop. How do you manage to pull in such nice things?"

She stared at him.

Bloody hell, what did he say wrong? "I just mean, it's a small town, just wondered how you were able to collect this much high-end merchandise." He sounded like a pretentious prick and needed to stop talking right now.

Ivy ripped off his credit card receipt with a thin-lipped smile. "It *is* amazing, since most of us can only afford Walmart."

"That's not—"

"Have a good day."

He figured the best course of action was not to talk anymore, so he nodded, took his bag, and left quickly. As he jogged across the street, back to the safety of Payton and Sons' waiting room, he thought it was good he was leaving. Clearly everyone here thought he was some *posh* rich guy from the city. Which was only half-true. Sure, he had money now. But posh he was not, especially if they'd seen how he grew up.

He hoped like hell that his car would be done today because he wasn't sure he could take another weekend here.

Chapter Four

ALEX LOVED TO watch her girls dance.

Ivy spun so that her dress flared out around her thighs. Delilah shimmied her hips, her black hair shining in the lights above the dance floor.

Jenna was laughing, her head back, her arms out, as she twisted her hips and rolled her head back and forth, long hair flying.

Alex stood with her elbows on the bar behind her, a foot cocked on the lower rung, an empty shot glass dangling in her hand. She placed it on the bar top and kept watching her friends.

She lived for girls' night out. Nothing but her friends and some booze and a whole lot of forgetting about all the reasons Alex's life wasn't at all like she thought it'd be.

But that was okay, because her skin was warm from dancing and her head was buzzing from the alcohol and there were a lot of guys in here looking to blow off steam.

Just like her.

Steam that had been building up all week because she couldn't get that damn fancy-pants man with the accent out of her head. It'd been only one night, but that one night had thoroughly messed with her head.

Just thinking about him made her eyes fall shut, her lower belly heat up. She didn't want to admit it when she was sober, but now that she was half-lit, she could concede she craved him a little.

She loved how hyper focused he'd been on her. When she'd had his attention, she'd had his *full* attention. He'd made her feel so damn wanted, even sweaty after a day's work. He hadn't cared. He'd wanted her. And her forwardness hadn't seemed to make him question his self-esteem. He didn't have to be top dog; he wanted her however she was willing to give herself.

Dammit, she needed another shot.

Something brushed her elbow and she turned her head. A man with a ball cap pulled low over his brow met her eyes. He was big—broad shoulders, work-roughened hands. He smelled like cigarette smoke and beer, and a short beard surrounded his full lips.

He was giving her that look, his gaze lingering on her mouth and her breasts.

A month ago, she would have smiled. Flirted. Let him take her home.

She would have ripped off her clothes and torn off his and tumbled onto the couch or in bed or wherever was closest.

She would have lost herself in the feeling of a man's hands on her, his lips wetting her skin, his cock inside her.

And she would have left immediately afterward.

It would have been fine. She was happy then. Except now she wasn't. Because all she could hear was Spencer's voice, and she craved that in her ear and his hands on her skin.

Not this guy next to her who looked like he would be up for a rough ride.

So she didn't smile, and she donned her effective resting bitch face, and turned away.

The man snorted, ordered his beer, and walked off.

She closed her eyes, listening to the beat of the music, and dropped her head between her shoulders. She jerked when a hand landed on her arm, but when she looked up, it was only Ivy. Her smile was soft, her cheeks flushed. She squeezed Alex's shoulder. "Come on, it's girls' night and you're hanging out at the bar like a weirdo."

"That's what people do, ya know, at bars. Hang out near them and drink."

Ivy tugged on her hand. "Delilah wants to dance with you."

Alex squinted at her sister. "How drunk can I get?"

"Pretty drunk. Brent is picking us up, and Vi is sleeping over at Cal's."

Alex nodded, ordered another shot, and downed it in one gulp. She slammed the empty glass on the bar. "All right, let's dance."

By the second song, the alcohol was burning a fiery path through Alex's body. Her limbs were loose, and her head was spinning a little. She knew she was on her way to the not-cute drunk stage, but she wasn't trying to impress anyone.

When they took a drink break, a water was placed in front of her. She glared at Ivy, who blinked at her innocently. Alex grumbled and sipped the liquid through her straw.

"So," Delilah said. "I heard you're training Gabe."

Alex used a napkin to mop up a spilled drop of water. "Yeah, I am."

"How's that going?"

Alex shrugged. "It's okay when he's not staring at my boobs."

Delilah opened her mouth but Jenna cut her off. "I thought the rule was that we don't talk about boys on girls' night out."

"I'm not talking about boys," Delilah protested.

"Gabe's a boy." Ivy stated the obvious.

"He's a boy, yes," Delilah said. "But he's not...you know...a *boy*. I'm asking Alex about her job."

Jenna raised her eyebrows.

Delilah threw up her hands. "Don't look at me like that."

"I'm not looking at you like anything. I just think that was a sneaky way to ask about a boy. I'm disappointed in you, Delilah." Jenna wiped away an imaginary tear.

"I'm not interested in Gabe," Delilah said through gritted teeth. "He's like, a teenager."

"He's twenty-two."

"Too young for me."

"You're thirty, not seventy-five."

Delilah stared at her drink and crossed her arms over her chest. "I like them older, okay? More experienced."

"Don't pout," Jenna said.

"He is kind of cute," Ivy said.

Delilah glared. "I don't go for cute."

Alex smacked her palm on the table. "There are no boys, and there is no fighting on girls' night out."

Delilah ducked her head, Jenna picked at her nails, and Ivy nodded as she said, "Except when they are our designated drivers and pick us up."

Alex snorted. "Yeah, except for that."

Ivy smiled, Delilah and Jenna started giggling, and then Alex joined in until they started getting looks from other customers.

An hour later, they were all sufficiently drunk. Delilah and Alex were hiding out in a booth. Delilah had pulled her sunglasses over her eyes, so Alex wasn't sure how she could see. And she sipped her water slowly from a straw.

At least, Alex thought it was water. It could have been vodka.

"I like his handwriting," Delilah mumbled.

"Who?" Alex asked, craning her neck around the bar.

Delilah smacked her arm. "He's not here."

"Who?" Alex asked again.

"Davis."

Alex was starting to think it was vodka, and her mouth opened in an O. Davis was Brent's neighbor, a former fire-fighter who was now in a wheelchair after an accident at work. Alex liked him; he was gruff and no-nonsense and fit well into the family. She didn't, however, think Delilah had even noticed the guy, let alone what his handwriting looked like.

"When did you see his handwriting?" She didn't bother reminding Delilah it was girls' night out and they weren't supposed to talk about boys.

Delilah rattled her drink. "He came into the shop, looking for a present for his sister. He wanted something a specific style, and I couldn't figure out what he meant so he drew it. With words. I got a little turned on."

Yep, it was vodka. "You got turned on by a guy's handwriting? Am I hearing this right?"

"It was all soft lines and capital letters and hot, okay? Shut up. Quit judging me."

"I'm not judging—"

"I don't know. Whatever. He thinks I'm a shallow flake."

Alex was going to protest, but then decided not to. Maybe Davis did think that. She barely talked to the guy.

"Why couldn't his handwriting suck? Look like a pre-schooler's? Then I wouldn't have conflicting feelings."

Alex was having trouble following this conversation. "Are you attracted to his handwriting or him?"

Delilah rolled her eyes. "Him too, of course. And his voice. And sometimes his eyes when he's not scowling. Oh, who am I kidding? I love when he scowls."

"Does he know you...think this about him?"

"Hell no." Delilah violently turned in her chair to face Alex. "Everything I said just now was in a cone of silence. I meant to declare that first but then I forgot. So. Retroactive cone of silence." She made a weird hand motion around them, like she was encasing them in something.

Alex wondered at this point who was more drunk, because she was nodding vigorously in agreement.

And then she started thinking about how she hadn't seen Spencer's handwriting. Then she started thinking about his hands again, and his voice, and that magnificent ass.

Shit, why was she thinking about Spencer? "I need a drink."

"Me too," Delilah said, draining her glass. "But first, tell me about the British guy."

Alex's body stiffened. "What?"

Delilah pushed out her lips. "Shit."

Alex elbowed her. "How do you know about the British guy?"

"I noticed Ivy giving this British guy in our store the cold shoulder. He was hot too, so I asked her what the hell that was about. And she told me you two hooked up."

Alex knew her hackles were raised, but she wasn't sure why. In the past, when she'd found a hookup for a night, she never kept it secret, like it was shameful. She was up-front about it to her friends. So Ivy telling Delilah that Alex had hooked up with the guy shouldn't have mattered.

Not at all.

So why did it?

"Why was she giving him the cold shoulder?"

Delilah didn't meet her eyes. "Uh…"

There would be no reason for Ivy to do that, unless Spencer had adopted his snobby attitude. Which wasn't unlikely. "Did he say something?"

Delilah pretended not to hear her question.

"Look, I'll never see him again, so it's not a big deal. Just tell me what happened." She should get up and walk away. Why did she give a shit?

Delilah turned to her. "He was buying a necklace. For a friend." She said the last word with her fingers crooked in air quotes.

Alex swallowed, and she gripped the bench so hard, her fingers went numb. "Okay."

"Shit, I have a big mouth," Delilah said. "I'm sorry, I—"

"It doesn't matter." Alex hadn't seen a ring. The knowledge she could be an "other woman" sat like acid in her gut, but she couldn't do anything about it now. She hadn't seduced him. That had been a team effort, what they did. "Okay, I'm going to go get that drink now."

Delilah placed a hand on her arm. "Are you mad?"

"Why would I be mad?"

She shrugged.

Alex shook her head. "No, not mad. Just…really thirsty, okay?"

Delilah bit her lip and nodded. Alex rose and walked to the bar, with one purpose in mind: to get really drunk and forget all about stupid Spencer.

"I'm sorry?" Spencer leaned forward in his chair and cocked his head. "What did you say?"

Richard Moore, CEO of Royalty Suites, repeated himself, speaking slower this time. "You weren't the only one in Tory, Maryland, evaluating a location for a new hotel."

Spencer blinked. "I'm still confused."

"Look, Spencer, as you know, Cody Aldridge is stepping down as head of the new development team. And you applied."

Spencer was unsure what that had to do with Tory. "Okay."

"Well, you aren't the only one who wants the job. The other employee who I think is as capable as you applied as well. So we sent Nick Paultino to Tory a couple of weeks ago as well, and he submitted his own report."

Spencer's stomach twisted painfully in his gut. "You...we're essentially competing?"

Richard nodded. "Yes, we will be evaluating both reports. Yes, your previous job history speaks for itself, but we also wanted something where we could compare you directly."

Spencer didn't know what to say, so he said nothing.

"I'm sorry if you feel—"

"Duped?" Spencer said, speaking through gritted teeth as he gazed at the New York City skyline out the window behind his boss's desk.

The man sighed. "This is tough for me, Spencer. I've known you since you were a freshman in college. And Nick is my...son-in-law. I have to make sure I'm making an unbiased decision here."

Spencer fisted his hands on his thighs and willed himself to keep his face impassive. Penny, as the vice president, would have known. She would have known that her father was deciding between Spencer and her *own husband* for this job.

She hadn't said a word.

Objectively, Spencer knew she wouldn't have been able to, but she was his best friend, dammit. Although, he had to admit, Nick—as her husband—would likely be more furious.

They could use some new blood among the higher-ups at Royalty.

"Spencer?"

He got himself under control enough to meet his boss's eyes. "Yes?"

"Are you still interested in the job?"

It would mean a little less traveling, and it would be a raise. And really…wasn't that what Spencer was supposed to do? Keep moving up in his company. He should want the better, higher-paying job, right?

So he nodded. "Yes."

Richard drummed his fingers on his desk. "We'll be taking a look at your reports. It's possible we'll send you back to Tory if we need further information."

Spencer tamped down the flare of alarm. "Sure."

The man nodded. "Great, then that's all I need from you today. Any questions?"

"Not at this time."

Richard smiled tightly at him, in the cool professional way he had.

Spencer walked back to his office quickly, thankful it was the end of the day because all he wanted to do was go back to his apartment and be alone.

Except when he got to his office to gather his things, Penny was there.

And for once, she looked less than put together. Her blonde hair was a little tousled, her pink lipstick on her teeth from where she bit her lip. "Spencer."

He gathered his suit jacket from the back of his chair and slipped his arms into it. "Pen."

"Are you mad at me?"

He wasn't. He understood he didn't have the right to be. "Frustrated? Yes, but not at you. Definitely not mad."

"Nick's kinda mad."

He pressed his lips together to prevent himself from saying less than desirable things about Nick. He didn't keep much from Penny, but his complete disdain for her second husband was one of them. Well, she knew he wasn't fond of Nick, but she wasn't aware how deep his irritation went.

She sighed. "You want to say something mean about Nick, don't you?"

Spencer dropped his bag onto his desk and slipped his laptop into it. "I said it in my head."

She laughed softly at that. He looked up at her and grinned.

Penny had been one of the first people he'd met as a fish-out-of-water freshman at NYU. He'd come over on a student visa, with a thick Manchester accent and no money. Penelope Moore had been outgoing and friendly and immediately reeled him in with her charming hook once they realized they had most of the same classes.

They'd never dated. They'd never even kissed. They'd hugged when they graduated and when Penny divorced her first husband, but she'd always been a friend. She was beautiful, and Spencer cared about her more than he cared for just about anyone other than his father. But they'd never been compelled to take their friendship in the direction of a nonplatonic relationship.

Maybe because Spencer didn't do relationships. Or maybe because he'd always been so scared of messing up the one real friendship in his life.

Either way, it didn't matter.

"Claudia loves the necklace you bought," Penny said. "Thanks for that."

He smiled. He was fond of her children, an older girl and a younger boy from her first marriage. "Of course, happy to do it."

She tapped her pink-tipped fingernails on his desk. "We'll have to visit the shop if we go back."

Spencer ducked his head, fiddling with the clasp of his bag. He hadn't told Penny about…well, about Alex. He could barely even believe it had happened himself, like it was all one giant hallucination.

Except alone, in his apartment, he could do nothing but think about Alex. About her body and the way she talked and the way she moaned when he was inside her.

Shit, he was going to get hard in his office in front of Penny.

He sniffed and hauled his bag over his shoulder. "Sure, Pen."

"So, I'm sorry but obviously I couldn't tell either of you."

"I know."

"And Nick already thinks…"

"That he's competing with me for your affections?" Spencer asked.

She fiddled with her ring. "It's a new marriage—"

"Five years isn't that new—"

"And he's threatened about the fact that you came first."

"He should get over it," Spencer said, leading her out his office door as he turned out the lights.

"I know," Penny said, walking beside him through Royalty Suites' mostly empty headquarters. "But you know how he gets."

He huffed under his breath.

She smacked him. "Stop."

As they walked, he thought again of his meeting with his boss. "Have you seen Nick's report?"

She shook her head.

He frowned at the floor, running the other locations in Tory through his head. There weren't many. There was the one Spencer was recommending. Then the one by the old lumberyard. Then...the one near Payton and Sons. Spencer took a deep breath so he didn't work himself into a frenzy. What if Nick chose that one? There'd been some attractive traits about it. But they'd probably have to work to buy some of the auto shop's land...or all of it.

Alex, despite sleeping with him, thought he was a posh asshole. What would she think if he swooped in after shagging her and tried to take her business out from under her feet?

She'd hate him.

He shook his head and pressed the button for the lift. Penny was still standing next to him, lost in thought herself. She shook her head. "Anyway, you want company tonight? You can come over and we'll all get pizza."

"I'm sure I'm the last person Nick wants to see today."

"He can separate my friend from his work colleague."

Spencer raised an eyebrow.

"Okay, maybe not," Penny muttered.

Spencer bumped her with his shoulder. "You have a nice night with your husband."

"Penny," a voice called.

They turned around to see Nick standing in the hallway, a frown on his face.

Spencer took a step away from Penny, then cursed himself for his reaction, because he shouldn't feel guilty for talking to his friend. He hated Nick a little for that.

Nick was blond and blue-eyed—an attractive man who'd wooed Penny after he was hired at Royalty. Spencer could tell he loved her very much, but sometimes his possessiveness and competitiveness was off-putting. Penny chalked it up to alpha males butting heads in the workplace, but Spencer thought it ran a little deeper than that.

Just because Nick was married to Penny didn't mean Spencer had to like the guy, who always seemed to try too hard. He went out of his way to buy Penny elaborate gifts and flowers. He kissed his father-in-law's ass so hard, Spencer was surprised his lips weren't in a permanent pucker.

Spencer sometimes wondered what Nick did for himself, or if he just spent his entire life trying to impress others.

And it seemed Nick knew Spencer didn't care for him, and returned the sentiment.

Spencer lifted his hand as the door to the lift opened with a ding. Nick didn't move and Penny waved as she walked backward toward her husband. "Have a good weekend, Spencer!" she called.

He grunted as the doors closed.

BACK IN HIS apartment, Spencer quickly undressed and slipped on a pair of sweatpants and a T-shirt. He found leftover Chinese food in the fridge and heated it up in the microwave, then ate sitting on his couch, watching the news.

It'd been about a week since he came back from Tory.

A week since he'd worked very, very hard to forget about Alex.

But he couldn't, especially when he looked at his keys every day and saw that damn keychain that he refused to get rid of.

His hookups with women had dwindled the older he got. He was set in his ways now and accustomed to being on his own. Penny had told him to use a dating app, but they were all either too focused on hookups or too…desperate. Either way, they didn't work for him, despite their happy pictures of smiling couples.

Before Alex, it'd been…God, too long since he'd been with a woman. Maybe that was why his head was spinning, why he couldn't forget about her.

He needed to, though. He was up for a promotion, one that he'd had his eye on since before Cody ever announced his retirement.

He walked to his kitchen to wash his plate and load it in the dishwasher.

A maid came in twice a week and cleaned his apartment. He wasn't here much anyway, so the biweekly cleaning left it rather sparkling. His black countertops gleamed. His tiled floor sparkled.

He ran his bare foot over the floor as he leaned back on his kitchen island.

He wondered where Alex lived, what she did in her spare time. She clearly had a loving sister, a niece, men she worked with who cared about her.

He hadn't been surrounded by family like that…well, ever. He'd grown up with a distant, workaholic father. His mother had died when he was ten, so his life had been a small flat in Manchester while his father worked on cars all day, then came home and drank beer all night. Spencer guessed he parented as best as he could.

His relationship with Penny had been rocky at first as Spencer wasn't quite sure…how to do it. The friend thing. The *I rely on you and you can rely on me* thing. Which was why he was loath to expand his circle wider. It'd taken years to get his friendship with Penny to this point.

He wondered, though, what kind of friend Alex was. What kind of girlfriend. How would it feel to be loved by her?

He shook his head and pushed off the island. He should just go to bed. This wallowing and thinking was just putting him in a shitty mood.

And he really, really needed to get Alex out of his head.

Chapter Five

Two weeks later...

PENNY STOOD IN the parking lot of the Tory Inn, hands on her hips. Her nose wrinkled as she gazed up at the hotel. "Not a Royalty Suites, is it?"

Spencer rolled his eyes as he hauled his suitcase out of the boot of his car. "Don't expect chocolates on your pillow."

Nick laid his arm across her shoulders. "I told you that you didn't have to come, Penelope."

She leveled a glare at him. "My father wants me to check out the sites. I'm an employee, just like you are."

"Yes, and you never let anyone forget it," Nick muttered as he set their luggage on the cracked concrete.

"You two about done?" Spencer asked.

Penny smiled at him brightly. "Just your average marital bickering. Totally normal. You wouldn't know, Mr. Lone Wolf."

"I'm not a lone wolf," Spencer huffed.

Penny made a howling noise and walked ahead of them into the hotel, her heels clicking smartly.

Spencer sighed and glanced at Nick, whose brows were furrowed in irritation.

Spencer wanted to ask him what *he* was so uptight about. Spencer was the one who was sweating through his shirt thinking about being back in Tory, Maryland, for the indefinite future.

He'd see Alex again. This town was too small and apparently her family and friends were everywhere. He wondered if she'd be angry. What they had was clearly meant to be one-time. He wasn't invited to get to know her any more than he'd invited her.

He could maybe hole himself up in his hotel room for the duration of his stay, but that would defeat the purpose of why he was here.

Which was to work.

Plus, Penny would never let them stay inside. She'd never been to Maryland, and she wanted what she called "the full experience."

He reminded her this was a business trip, that they were making the final decision on where to build another Royalty, but Penny said they could mix business with pleasure.

He'd nearly swallowed his tongue. Last time he was in town, he'd done just that and all it had gotten him were wet dreams. And a keychain.

Christ, he needed to get a grip.

Penny handled checking them in while Spencer and Nick stood awkwardly in the lobby surrounded by luggage.

"So, the drive was okay for you?" Spencer asked.

"The roads in Pennsylvania are shit," Nick grumbled. "What the hell do those people do to their roads? Penny read the whole time. She should have ridden with you. I'm sure she would have enjoyed it more."

Spencer kept quiet, which was usually the way his conversations with Nick went. But it was getting harder and harder for Spencer to ignore Nick's remarks. Spencer also worried about Penny. Her first marriage had not been a good one. Her first husband and father of her children was a man who seemed to want a strong woman on his arm but yet wasn't willing to stand aside as that strong woman stood on her own. Spencer didn't know how to approach Penny about Nick, how to caution her on his behavior and ask if their marriage was okay behind closed doors. Was it any of his business?

And it wasn't that he thought Nick didn't treat Penny well, because Nick did try. It was that he didn't think Nick was the man for her. Which sounded incredibly pompous when he thought about it. Who was he to know what was best for Penny? But Nick seemed vaguely threatened by everything, from Penny's position at Royalty to her friendship with Spencer.

For now, Spencer kept his mouth shut and pulled out his cell phone, tapping aimlessly until Penny walked to where they were standing, key cards in her hand.

They were on the same floor, a couple of rooms apart, and Spencer was finally able to breathe when he was behind the closed door by himself. He unpacked his clothes and opened his laptop on the small desk. But he stared at his backdrop and eventually his gaze drew to the window in his room. His view was the pool, which was closed for the season.

Nick was also a scout for Royalty. That was how he and Penny had met. Spencer didn't care much about impressing Richard Moore. He worked because he liked it. He loved fulfilling a need in a town for excellent lodging. He loved the site of a freshly built hotel, the air still smelling of cooling asphalt.

The past two weeks, the team in New York had narrowed down the site for a new hotel to two locations—the one Spencer recommended, and the land behind Payton and Sons Automotive. That…had not been his recommendation. At all. For some reason, Nick had thought that location was more attractive, except he wanted more. He wanted the land the auto repair shop sat on too. Which meant…he wanted to buy out the Paytons.

That made Spencer want to puke, but he didn't want to think about that, couldn't entertain the thought that Nick's recommendation would be chosen over his. So his job while in town was to convince Penny his recommendation was best, while Nick would…well, he'd do what he did, which was flit around like a fly and annoy everyone. Or maybe just Spencer.

Spencer had confidence he could convince the company that he was correct.

He knew his emotions weren't swaying him. He'd chosen to recommend the first property before he'd ever laid eyes on Alex. But now, he was even more determined. He didn't know a lot about his sprite, but he knew she loved her job and she loved that garage. It was evident in her posture when she stood in the shop and in her voice when she talked about her work.

Spencer shut the lid to his laptop and paced the room restlessly. He'd always loved being alone. He needed the time to recharge his batteries, to keep all his armor in place so he could continue to be the carefully crafted L. M. Spencer.

But the past two weeks, his skin had felt too tight, his chest heavy. Like there was something else he should be doing, something he was missing.

Thoughts of Alex had eased him and shortened his breath all at the same time. When Penny's father had instructed the three of them to return to Tory, Spencer had gone home and gotten drunk. On the hundred-year-old Scotch he'd been keeping for a special occasion.

He'd woken up on his living room floor wearing his robe. It had been unsettling.

He didn't know what he would say when he saw Alex again. How would she react? They'd both been safe under the presumption they'd never see each other again after that night in his hotel room. That had been their safety net, and now he'd poked a big ol' hole in it.

He got the impression Alex didn't like surprises.

Yeah, well, he wasn't too fond of them either.

He undressed and got in the shower, thinking maybe he'd sleep because come tomorrow, he'd have to unleash Penny and Nick in Tory.

And he wasn't quite sure this would end well for anyone.

BELLINI'S HAD GOOD crab cakes. And that was the only reason Alex had let herself be talked into a fancy dinner on Friday night.

Brent didn't seem too happy either, but he'd do anything for his girls. Ivy and Violet had gone all out, dressed up with hair and makeup and heels to celebrate Ivy's birthday.

Okay, so Alex was at this fancy dinner for the crab cakes *and* her sister.

She was even in a dress, although it was black with a bright-red cherry print. She'd spent a good twenty minutes going through her lipstick stash to find the perfect shade to match. Her eye makeup was on point, dramatic winged eyeliner and smoky eye shadow.

Hey, if she was asked to dress up, she was going to do it her way.

Didn't stop her from wearing lace-up boots, though. Because heels were the devil.

She took a sip of her wine and watched Violet carefully pick up the correct utensil to eat her fancy salad. Alex thought it looked like rabbit food, but clearly she wasn't the clientele for a place like this. Ivy loved it and that was all that mattered.

Her sister looked radiant, wearing a purple dress, her hair loose around her shoulders. Her happiness was a tangible thing, floating in the air like a feather. Alex wanted to snatch it and tuck it behind her ear, save a little for herself.

She stared at her nails, which were painted dark blue, the polish chipping. She picked at a thumbnail, trying not to let her mind wander and think about Spencer.

His nickname for her had made her give up the clear soda for life. She wondered if he thought about her at all, if he regretted their time.

If he still had that keychain.

That had been dumb, to give it to him. No way would he keep something like that while he was cruising around New York, saying hello to his doorman and sitting in his fancy office.

Buying necklaces for women that weren't her. She shouldn't be bothered by that, because she'd agreed to the one-night rule. Hell, she'd wanted it. So what right did she have to be angry he slept with her the night before and bought a necklace for another woman the next day?

She didn't have any rights to his life. She wasn't willing to give him any rights to hers.

She shook her head as the waiter placed their plates in front of them. Alex dug into her crab cake right away, while Ivy tutted over the gorgeous "presentation" of her dish.

As they ate, Ivy was moaning about the tenderness of her fillet while Violet was talking about a boy at school.

Brent was—predictably—frowning at the idea of a boy paying attention to Violet.

"He told me my hair is the color of poop," Violet said. "It was really mean."

"That kid is a, a—"

Ivy looked up at Brent sharply with big eyes.

"Is an…awkward boy," Brent said, cringing.

Alex hid her smile behind her napkin.

Brent's glare told her she hadn't hid her giggle well. "Anyway," he said, focusing back on Violet, who was listening intently. "Your hair is beautiful. So's your mom's and so's your aunt's." He grinned and ran a hand through his hair. "Mine is great too, right?"

Violet nodded.

"You like your hair?"

"I love my hair," Violet said, twirling a strand.

"Then don't let a boy make you feel differently about it," he said. "And if he bugs you too much, tell a teacher."

"Okay," Violet said.

Alex wasn't grinning anymore. How she wished she'd had someone like Brent when she was a little girl. Then maybe she wouldn't have let Robby change how she viewed herself. Maybe she would have been strong enough...

She took another sip of wine, and excused herself to head to the bathroom. Despite eating most of her crab cake, she probably shouldn't have had so much wine beforehand. She was a little unsteady and even more grateful she hadn't worn heels.

In the bathroom she stared at herself in the mirror, fixing her lipstick and wiping a smudge of eyeliner below her eye. Her hair was down, which was rare for her, and a little huge. It had rained earlier and the humidity had wreaked havoc on her mane, so it cascaded all around her like she was in a bad '90s sitcom.

She huffed and did her best to tame it down before she walked out of the bathroom.

She weaved her way through the tables and was close to reaching her family when a feminine laugh caught her attention.

It wasn't the owner of the laugh who stopped Alex in her tracks. It was whom the woman sat with. Alex remembered that suit jacket. Those shoulders. That hair that was a little on the longer side now, curling around his ears and brushing the collar of his shirt.

She couldn't understand what he said, but she'd remember that deep rumble anywhere. His head was turned slightly, so she could see his profile.

Spencer.

Leslie Michael Fucking Spencer was back in town.

And he was sitting with a woman who looked like she'd stepped out of a New York socialite magazine. Large earrings dangled from her ears and she wore a necklace that sparkled in the candlelight on the table. Her dress was a deep purple color, something classy, and her makeup was understated yet clearly done with care.

She was everything Alex wasn't.

And Alex was okay with that, dammit. She'd always been okay with that until fucking Robby had made her feel like that wasn't enough, like that would never be enough, until she didn't know what was right anymore.

All she knew was that the man she couldn't get out of her head was sitting with a gorgeous woman, and they were smiling at each other and drinking wine. This was the woman he belonged with. That he'd marry.

Alex had known all along, of course, that she wasn't anything special to him. What they had was simply a hookup, but to see Spencer's future with her own eyes wasn't a good feeling. She thought she'd never see him again, and maybe it was a little irrational, and maybe they hadn't made promises, but she was a little angry with him for violating this unspoken pact.

Something rolled in Alex's gut and she placed a hand over her mouth. Oh God, the last thing she needed was to throw up in the dining room of Bellini's.

So she put her head down and walked briskly to her table, hoping Spencer didn't see her.

When she sat down, she gulped the rest of her wine as Ivy stared at her. "You okay?"

Alex set her glass down harder than she meant to. The centerpiece rattled. "Uh, yup."

Ivy frowned. "You sure?"

"Never been better."

Ivy opened her mouth to say more, but Brent—God bless the irritating bastard—began talking about the Halloween costumes he planned for this year, and Alex thanked him silently for the reprieve.

She pretended to listen while her brain could do nothing but focus back on that table. Spencer was here. He was back. In Tory.

The questions rattled around and around—questions she didn't think she'd ever get answers for, because she intended to do everything she could to keep from running into Spencer again. He must have lied too. He had a woman. She was there, right across from him, with her perfect hair and white smile and class.

She ate dessert methodically, not really tasting it, while Ivy gave her odd looks in between bites of her crème brûlée.

Brent paid the check and everything was going swimmingly as they stood up from their table until Brent scanned the restaurant.

His eyes lit up.

And Alex knew at that moment she was a little doomed.

"Hey, it's the English guy!" he said. "Babe, hold on, I wanna say hi." He bent down. "Vi, you wanna meet someone from Britain?"

Violet nodded enthusiastically as Alex looked at her sister in horror.

Ivy pulled on Brent's arm. "Honey, he's having dinner, maybe we shouldn't interrupt—"

"Nah, it's cool." He grabbed Violet's hand and began walking toward Spencer's table.

Alex didn't move, just stayed where she was standing, because how the hell would this end well?

Brent arrived at their table, and Spencer's dining companion looked up at Brent, smiling radiantly, and then Ivy was all possessive girlfriend, stalking haughtily over to the table and slipping her arm in the crook of Brent's elbow.

Alex rolled her eyes and followed slowly, fingering the hem of her skirt and watching the table from under her lashes.

Spencer looked up at Brent and Ivy, his face going momentarily pale before he craned his neck around them, looking for...And then his gaze met hers.

He'd been looking for her.

His expression didn't change as she arrived at the table and stood behind Violet. His gaze didn't leave her face, though, until Brent drew his attention.

"Good to see you, man. You back in town for work?"

Spencer's gaze flitted from Brent to Alex before settling back on Brent. "Um, yes. I am actually."

"What do you do?"

"Royalty Suites."

"The hotel chain?"

"Yes, and we're looking here in Tory for locations to build one."

"Huh." Brent scratched his head. "Would create more jobs in the area, so that's good. We can support another hotel?"

Spencer smiled and nodded. "Yes, it's why we're here. You aren't far from the airport and your highway is a main thoroughfare for business travelers."

"Cool." Brent nodded, but his interest seemed to have waned. "So, how's the car?"

"It's running fine, thank you."

"Great, great. Well, hey, this is my girlfriend, Ivy, and our daughter, Violet. And you met Alex, right? She works at the shop too."

Spencer swallowed and shifted in his seat. "Yes, we've met. I actually met your girlfriend too, at Delilah's."

"I like your accent," Violet said and giggled.

And Spencer smiled. "Well, I like yours."

Ivy's eyes were narrowed as she stared at the woman at the table. "Did you like the necklace?"

Alex's knees buckled and she braced a hand on Violet's shoulder to steady herself. Could this get any more awkward?

The woman was smiling big now, holding out a delicate hand to Brent. "I'm Penny." Her accent was American. "And that necklace was for my daughter. She does love it."

Alex worked hard on breathing properly. Damn, it was worse. He had kids.

Brent stared at her hand like he didn't know what to do with it, then he enclosed it in the grasp of his big hand and shook it gently. "Nice to meet you, Penny."

"Lovely town you have here," she said, her tone not condescending, which made Alex angrier. She wanted this woman to be a stone-cold bitch. But she wasn't. Her smile was genuine, her eyes warm.

"Spencer bring you for a vacation?" Ivy asked, her voice even.

Penny's perfectly sculpted eyebrows lifted. "A vacation? Oh no, I work with Spencer. But maybe we'll take some time off and enjoy all the sites Maryland has to offer, right, Spence?"

Spence. She called him Spence.

Alex curled her hand at her side into a fist.

Spencer's gaze was back on Alex and he muttered, "Sure."

And Alex had never been good at keeping her mouth shut. "I hope hospitality on this visit is just as nice as it was on your first visit."

Spencer's eyes widened slightly. Ivy's head whipped to Alex, and Brent's brows furrowed.

"What does *hospitality* mean?" Violet asked.

Alex knew her face was red, that her voice had been bitter. Penny's gaze was ping-ponging between Spencer and Alex, something like understanding dawning on her face.

It was time for this to be over.

"Well, we should be going—"

A man arriving at the table cut her off. He bent down and kissed Penny's cheek, then sat down at an empty chair Alex hadn't even noticed was at the table.

Penny laid a hand on his shoulder. "This is my husband, Nick. Nick, these are some Tory residents Spencer met when he was here."

The man took a sip of his water. "Nice to meet you."

Penny was married. To a man who wasn't Spencer. Which meant her daughter was…not Spencer's? Alex shifted her gaze to Spencer, who was watching her steadily, if a little smugly. She wanted to wipe that look off his face.

Instead, she tugged on Ivy's arm, then Ivy pulled on Brent. "Well," he said, "I gotta get my girls home. Good to see you again, man. Let me know if you have any more car issues."

Spencer nodded and Brent slung his arm around Ivy's shoulders. As they walked out of the restaurant, Brent said, "That guy is so nice, right?"

"Right," Alex and Ivy said in unison.

Alex couldn't get home to her empty apartment fast enough.

Chapter Six

On Monday, Alex was back at work and still fuming.

Even Jack steered cleared of her, when he heard her banging around in the back room, swearing about Gabe drinking all her creamer.

Ivy had called her Saturday, and Alex had spent an uncharacteristic hour getting out…feelings about Spencer. Which she guessed was a good thing. She felt marginally better. Now she was just swearing about Gabe drinking her creamer, not actually murdering him over it.

She considered that an improvement.

Alex wiped her forehead and tried to focus on the engine she was rebuilding. But her mind couldn't stop wandering to the conversation she'd had with Ivy. Her sister had said Spencer had come into Delilah's, buying jewelry for a friend, and then talked as if he couldn't imagine Tory could support a high-end consignment shop.

He was probably regretting the night they spent together already. Which made Alex clench her jaw until it cracked. Why did he have to come back? Because now there was conflict and exactly what Alex didn't want to deal with.

She needed to forget about it. What did it matter if he regretted it or if he didn't?

It *didn't* matter.

It *didn't matter.*

She tried to tell herself that, but Robby's words, said in his hate-filled voice, filtered into her brain, words said against her sweat-slick skin as he held her against the wall, his hand between her legs. *This is all you're good for, and you're just lucky I'll put up with your bullshit because I like how you moan for me.*

She squeezed her eyes shut and took a deep breath. On her to-do list was scheduling an extra therapy session this week. When Robby's words replayed in her head, she knew she needed to get them out or they'd consume her. She stomped into the back room, threw open the refrigerator door, and threw her bag onto the shelf. When she turned around, Brent was leaning casually along the wall.

She jumped and braced herself on the fridge. "Fuck, you scared the shit out of me, you asshole."

He grinned. "Sorry."

"No you're not."

"You're right, I'm not." He took a bite of his banana. "What's got you all angry?"

"Nothing." She walked over to the coffeemaker and poured some of the coffee into her favorite mug she kept on the counter.

"Nothing?"

"Don't you have my sister to bug now?"

"But you're more fun to irritate. Irritating her means I get laid less."

Alex groaned. "Please stop talking."

"No can do." He took another bite of banana and said with a full mouth, "Are you over your shit fit about the creamer? Because Gabe just pulled in and I know we're not worried too much about stains around here, but we draw the line at blood."

Alex pointed a finger at Brent. "Tell him to buy me creamer to replace what he used, okay? I can't talk to him about it or I might smack him."

"I will make sure he gets the message."

Alex huffed out of the room.

GABE SCRATCHED HIS head and watched Alex's fingers as she worked on a Honda's engine. He was doing a decent job today of not staring at her tits, which she considered a highlight. Oh, how low her expectations had fallen.

It was almost quitting time, which was great, seeing as she'd had about enough of babysitting Gabe. Not that he was a bad guy, but she'd always preferred to work alone. In silence. But Jack had asked her to let Gabe shadow her, and after all that Jack had done for her since she moved, she'd do just about anything he asked.

He watched them now, from the doorway to the office. An unlit cigarette dangled from his lips, his arms crossed over his wide chest.

"Boy!" his voice boomed across the garage.

Gabe's head shot up.

"You leer at her one more time and I'm going to stick your head in a vise, you get me?"

Gabe nodded vigorously. "Sorry, Jack."

The big man only grunted in response and then ducked inside the office.

Alex blushed, thinking while the guy's delivery could use some work, he meant well. He was kind of like the father she never had.

Gabe grinned at her sheepishly, blinked his long lashes over liquid brown eyes. "Sorry, A. You're hot."

She laughed. "Thanks, Gabe. I really work hard on this grease monkey look."

He looked relieved she hadn't slapped him. So she straightened up from her position over the hood of the car and cracked her back. "I think we're done for today, what do you say?"

Gabe nodded. "Yeah, I got tow truck duty tonight too, so I need to head home and grab something to eat before my shift starts."

"Tomorrow, we'll continue going over the engine," she said. "Sound good?"

"Yup. Uh, thanks a lot. For, ya know, helping me out."

"No problem."

She cleaned up the tools area, knowing Jack liked everything in its place. Brent liked to screw it all up just to rile up his dad, but Alex wasn't interested in pissing off the boss. Sometimes, she even got a smile out of him. Cal and Brent had already left for the day, so once Gabe pulled out of the parking lot, it was just her and Jack. He walked over to where she stood at the tool bench. "Go," he said.

She jerked her head up. "Why?"

"Because I said so."

"I told Cal I'd get some cleaning done." And this was her MO now, finding odd jobs to do around the garage to avoid going home.

Jack's gaze slid to the sky outside. It wasn't dark yet, and really, as much as she appreciated Jack's concern, she was a grown woman.

Jack opened his mouth, but Alex cut him off. "You go home. Or go spend time with Asher or something. I got this, okay?"

His teeth clacked shut and he frowned at her. She waited him out, until finally he grunted and strode away. "Fine, I'm going home then."

"Good," she called after him.

Jack had been gone ten minutes when a red car pulling into the parking lot caught her attention. She tightened her fingers on the hoses she was coiling and dropped them on the tool bench. She leaned back against it as the Mercedes bypassed the parking spaces and pulled right into the empty garage bay where she was standing.

She crossed her arms over her chest and waited, working hard to maintain an impassive expression. She hoped she succeeded because inside, her nerves were rioting.

Spencer stepped out of the car, mirrored sunglasses hiding his eyes, a green tie flapping in the breeze. He wore a fancy suit again, expensive watch peeking out from beneath the white cuffs of his shirt.

He didn't seem surprised when he spotted her this time, and walked toward her, stopping when he was about five feet away.

She spoke first. "You case the place until you could get me alone?"

His glasses hid his eyes and his voice was even when he spoke. "What if I told you I did?"

She shrugged, but inside her stomach rolled. "I'd say that's kind of pathetic."

He smiled then, all teeth. "Maybe."

"What do you want?"

"I wanted to talk to you."

"What about?"

He took off his glasses and tucked them in his shirt. "I felt there were some things that needed explaining."

Her lip curled. "There's nothing that needs explaining." That was exactly the last thing she wanted to hear from him. Because just by standing in front of her, he was making what she hoped to stay in the past surge to the present.

A muscle in his jaw jumped. "Well, humor my British side that hates conflict, okay?"

"So I have to endure this conversation just so you can ease your conscience over spending one night slumming it with some girl from a small town? No thanks." Why was her voice so bitter? Because no matter how surrounded she was by family and friends, Robby's voice would never leave her.

Spencer looked confused, and then his expression shifted to exasperation and then to anger. "You know, this tough-girl act is a little outdated."

"Well, you liked it for one night!" Her voice was rising. Was she yelling? She needed to control herself. It was a small town, but they could manage to avoid each other for however long he was in town. She turned away and began walking toward the office door. "Look, why don't you just leave, so we can both get out of each other's presence like we originally agreed on and—"

Hands grabbed her wrists from behind and she froze. Shut down.

She'd learned not to struggle. Although Robby never struck her, he used his weight to overpower her all the time and struggling only got her tangled further in his net of control.

So she didn't move, and she closed her eyes as a warm body plastered itself against her back. "Sprite," he said in that deep, accented voice.

"What?" she whispered.

He didn't say anything for a minute, and his hands on her wrists loosened, but he didn't let go. "Why are you so angry?"

Oh, she couldn't even count all the ways. "For starters. You're here. When I never thought you would be again."

Another long pause. "Is that what this is about? You're mad I came back? And that you thought I'd…what? Be embarrassed by you?" Alex swallowed and stared at the wall in front of her. Spencer kept talking. "Don't assume you know everything about me. I certainly wasn't *slumming it* when we spent the evening together."

His thumbs moved in a circular pattern on the inside of her wrists and she stifled a groan.

He must have heard it, because he pressed in closer, and now his lips were at her ear, his voice low. "I haven't been able to stop thinking about that night. You above me, your hair and those lips and that body…" His voice trailed off.

She couldn't stop herself from asking, "My lips?"

He let go of a wrist and brought his hand up to her face, tilting it to the side. Then he brushed a thumb over her mouth. "These red lips. With your hair and your eyes. Fucking gorgeous."

Robby had hated her makeup. Called her a whore.

Why couldn't she forget about him? Especially now, with Spencer's body against hers, his hand cupping her jaw.

She turned around slowly, letting him keep control of her wrist. She looked up into his eyes, his stubbled jaw. She licked her lips.

One minute, she was in the middle of the garage, the next she was against the wall, her legs around Spencer's waist, his hands cupping her ass as he devoured her mouth.

She ground into him, unable to help herself, not caring if it was slutty because Spencer liked her like this. He liked that she sought her own pleasure, so she moaned into his mouth and gripped his face, her fingers spearing into that gorgeous silver-streaked hair at his temples.

She hadn't dry humped since high school but her body was so lit up, she thought she might be able to come just from grinding herself against Spencer.

He pulled down the front of her tank top along with the cup of her bra, lifted a breast, and stuck the tip into his mouth. He sucked hard, using tongue and teeth, and she cried out, clenching her thighs tighter, gripping his hair so hard, she worried she caused pain.

But Spencer didn't appear to mind. He lapped at her breast like a starving man before pulling down the other side and leaning back slightly to stare at her.

She wondered what she looked like, smashed up against the wall of the garage, her breasts hanging out, her lipstick smeared all over her mouth.

Spencer's eyes were wild as he took her in. "I'm the luckiest man in the world to be here right now."

Her heart ached, because they would be only this, a screw in a bed, a fuck against a wall. Quick, dirty deeds that would never have a future. Oh well, she'd make the most of it.

She didn't want to face him again, not when they did this, so she pushed him away and he helped her drop her legs to the floor. She smacked the button to shut the garage door, then sauntered over to his Mercedes, taking her top and bra off along the way, leaving them on the floor of the garage in her wake. She toed off her boots and socks as Spencer stared after her, his hair rumpled, his mouth wet, the bulge in his pants obvious.

When she reached his car, she was naked, completely naked. Then she leaned over the trunk of the car, ass out, and looked at Spencer. "I always wanted to get fucked on a Mercedes."

THIS WAS A little unreal, and Spencer wasn't sure he wasn't dreaming. Because right now, his debauched sprite was leaning over the boot of his car, completely naked, asking him to…shag her. On his car.

He wanted to high-five his sixteen-year-old self, who had this exact fantasy.

When he began to walk in her direction, he tried to appear confident, like he meant to be here, like he deserved this. In reality, he wasn't sure he deserved this woman who was right now providing him wank fodder for the next ten years.

He stopped behind her, so the front of his pants brushed the perfect curve of her arse. He raised a hand and ran tentative fingers down the knobs of her spine, the dip of her lower back, and then over one round hip. She was curvy, with a large arse and thick thighs. Everything about how she looked and acted was his dream come true.

She watched him from over her shoulder, blue eyes full of heat.

"I wish I could describe how perfect you look right now," he said softly.

"You can show me by fucking me." She waggled her arse, so the hard ridge in his pants ran the length of her crease. He groaned as he unzipped his pants, pulled his cock out, and gave it a couple of strokes.

He reached down and cupped her, sliding a middle finger into her wetness.

"Fuck, this really turns you on, doesn't it?" He tapped her clit.

She jerked and threw her head back. "Obviously."

He fisted his cock again and was about to ram home when he remembered something important. Vitally important. "Uh, I have no rubber."

Alex's hips were moving, grinding onto his hand. "So?"

"What do you mean, so—?"

"I'm on the pill, Posh. Are you safe?"

"Yes, always—"

"So, just fuck me already."

He gripped her hip tighter. The last time he'd shagged without protection was…ten years ago, with his uni girlfriend.

But Alex was here, in front of him, bent over his car. So he trusted her and slid into her in one motion.

The feeling was…everything. All encompassing. All consuming. He was inside Alex and it was just them, nothing stopping them each from experiencing their union to its fullest.

Alex's head was tilted to the side, so he saw her eyes closed, red lips parted. He gripped her hip and began to thrust slowly, but Alex wasn't having that. Not his sprite. Her lips curled and her eyes opened to gaze at him halfway, and then *she* began to move.

Bracing her arms on his car, she rocked into him, controlling the speed and tempo and depth, and all he did was hold on, hold on tight as she rode him hard. He'd never been with a woman like this, the sexual aggressor, and he thought now he'd been missing out, because this was the biggest turn-on of his life.

With every slam of her arse against him, she grunted, the sounds turning high as she seemed to reach for her orgasm while his barreled down on him without conscious thought.

"Bloody hell," he muttered. "Can't hold on much longer, Alex." She was too hot, too tight, too everything for him to hold back while his body was screaming at him to finish.

"It's okay, I'm coming," she said breathlessly, and thank God because he was undone now, releasing into her body, unable to stop himself from holding her against him, shoving her fully onto the car and covering her body with his as they both came.

When they both lay limply on the car, he registered that her body shook below his. He tried to coordinate his limbs to get off her, for fear he hurt her, when he realized she was laughing.

Her breath misted on the red paint of his car, and a part of him hoped she left lipstick behind. She looked at him out of the side of her eye. "Well, hot damn, Posh. You do know how to get dirty, don't you?"

If only she knew. He pulled out of her with a groan, looking around him for something to clean them up. He found a roll of paper towels and did his best with himself before handing her a sheet. She smirked at him, did her business, then sauntered around the garage, picking up her fallen clothing and pulling it on her body piece by piece.

He cleared his throat, unsure what to do now, but acutely aware she was walking around with his release in her body.

And it was making him hot all over again.

"So," he said.

"So," she said back. "You get what you came for then?" Her voice sounded forced, as if she was trying to keep a light tone when neither of them felt anything but light.

"That's not…that wasn't the plan, Alex. And you know it."

She tilted her chin. "Well, that might not have been your plan, but fuck you if you think you can walk into my garage and dictate how everything will go between us."

She had a point. "I don't want you to think—"

"I wish you wouldn't try to tell me what to think," she said, her voice lowering. "I think that we have incredible chemistry and great sex. But I also think that's all this will ever be. And I think two times is about the limit, so we'll do our best to avoid running into each other while you're in town again. How does that sound?"

She'd summed it up, basically. He knew this should end before feelings got involved and everything about Alex went from easy to extremely fucking complicated. But the thought of avoiding her presence didn't sit well with him. He liked just…looking at her, which was maybe weird. But even being around her made him happy.

This was ridiculous. So he nodded. "Yes, that's…about right."

"Great."

He pulled out his keys and her gaze shot to them. He held up the keychain she gave him. "I, uh, have interestingly enough gotten some questions about this in New York."

She smiled at that. "Yeah?"

"Yeah. Wanted to know if you did good work. Offered deals on oil changes. Things like that."

She laughed. "Well, you know, I didn't give you that as publicity or anything. More as something to…"

"Remember you by," he said softly.

"Sure." Alex chewed her lip. "How long will you be in town, then?"

"Another week or two."

She nodded and ducked her head. "Will you be back after that?"

"Probably not."

She stared at her feet with her hands on her hips. "Right. Well, thanks for showing me the high life while you were in town, Posh." She lifted her head then, a smirk tugging at the corner of her lips.

He smiled, remembering her words in the hotel room. "I appreciate your hospitality."

She laughed, her blue eyes bright. "Don't tell too many people. We like our town without outsiders, ya know?"

"It's between you and me."

She was backing up now, and his instincts screamed at him to tug her back, align her petite body with this. But that would just delay the inevitable. He needed to get away from here. He had a life that wasn't in Tory, Maryland. A life that didn't involve Alex. And he needed to remember that if he was going to get out of this town with his heart intact.

And why all of a sudden did that life not seem as appealing as it used to?

He cleared his throat and took a step back, the distance between them growing. "Right, then, I'll be going. You take care, Sprite."

"You too, Posh."

She pressed the button to open the garage door, and then she was gone, closing the office door behind her. All he could do was get in his car, drive back to his hotel room, and do something, anything, to take his mind off Alex Dawn.

Chapter Seven

SPENCER LEANED AGAINST his car and crossed his arms over his chest. He gazed at the back of Payton and Sons Automotive and thanked God it was Sunday so no one could see him standing there as Penny and Nick evaluated the location for the umpteenth time that week.

Penny was frowning, which Spencer thought was a good sign, as Nick talked about where the grocery store would sit, where the parking lot would be located, how they could tear down Payton and Sons and place the gas pumps there.

Spencer resisted the urge to chain himself to the brick building to prevent an imaginary bulldozer from razing it.

Penny turned to look at Spencer, her finger tapping her lips. "What were your reasons for not recommending this location?"

"It's in the report," he answered gruffly.

Her lips twitched. "Humor me."

He huffed out a breath and straightened from the car. "Because as it stands now, it'd sit behind this garage. Taking over property isn't easy, so I don't see why we'd make it difficult and try to get this land from the Paytons. A hotel would be a nuisance to the community here rather than an aid."

"We have a lot of hotels that are in the business district," Nick said.

"Business district?" Spencer echoed. "There're a couple of stores on this main street but I think it's a big stretch to call it a business district."

"I still think this is our most visible location."

This would be the first Royalty Suites in Maryland, and although Tory was a small town, it was a main thoroughfare for travel from Baltimore to the busy northeast cities.

Spencer had to admit, he was starting to fall for Tory. When he'd visited a couple of weeks ago, he'd spent some time at local parks and restaurants. The town had its own vibe, which was peaceful and yet full of hope. There were a lot of entrepreneurs and small businesses—like Delilah's Drawers. Weeks ago, it had annoyed Spencer how much it reminded him of home. But when he'd been back in New York, he'd realized that wasn't home either. Once he set foot on Tory soil again, he'd enjoyed breathing this air into his lungs. What did all that even mean?

Penny was looking at the land, her hand shading her eyes from the glare of the morning sun. She was giving nothing away. "Okay, now let's head to the location Spencer recommends."

He sighed and got into the car, waiting for Penny and Nick to settle into the Mercedes with him.

This was going to be a long day.

SEVERAL HOURS LATER, Spencer turned his grocery cart around the corner of the aisle in Souter's Grocery and nearly crashed into a tiara-wearing little girl staring at the cookies on the end cap. "Oh, I'm sorry."

The girl looked at him with big blue eyes and Spencer recognized her right away as Violet. He looked around for her mother and father and—good Lord, her aunt.

Violet smiled. "Oh! You're the British man we met! Hello! Do you remember me?"

He didn't know how to talk to children. He was an only child and he wasn't sure he'd ever really been...a child. His father didn't believe in coddling. Spencer cleared his throat. " 'Course I remember you. And how are you?"

"I'm good. I just really want some cookies, but Brent said I can only have them if I also eat my vegetables."

Spencer nodded awkwardly. "Erm, that's a good deal, I think."

Violet sighed and stared longingly at the cookies.

A male voice called out, "Vi? Where'd you go, Princess?"

"I'm here!" Violet called out.

A second later, Brent rounded the aisle, spotted Violet, and then lifted his gaze to Spencer. "Oh, hey man. You following us around or something?"

Spencer jerked in alarm. "Oh, uh, not at all, I—"

Brent laughed. "I'm just kidding. Small town. How's it going?"

"It's, um, going."

Brent glanced at Spencer's cart full of snacks. "You stocking up?"

Spencer shrugged. "I'm a little tired of takeaway, although I don't have a kitchen so…trying to come up with some snacks and things I can put together in my hotel room."

"You should come to our cookout!" Violet piped up.

Brent's face brightened. "Hey, that's a good idea. We're having a big thing tonight with family and friends to celebrate…uh…nothing really. We just like to grill meat before the weather gets too cold. You should come by."

He'd tried for a long time to beat the British out of him, but the instinct to never turn down an invitation, to always accept and be polite, was something he'd never been able to cure. "Oh, I wouldn't want to impose…"

"You can bring your friends too. What were their names? Nick and Pam?"

"Uh, Penny."

"Right," Brent said. "So what do you say?"

"Please?" Violet batted her big blue eyes and Spencer floundered. He had no excuse. None. It was Sunday and he'd decided to stop at the grocery store after dropping Penny and Nick off at the hotel. Tonight he'd planned to…well, he wasn't sure, really. Watch TV in his big hotel bed and eat cheese and crackers.

"Well, I guess we could swing by for a bit—"

"Great!" Brent cheered loudly. "You want Cal's address? That's where the cookout is."

Oh, God. Cow. "Um, are you sure he won't mind—"

Brent waved a hand. "Nah, he won't care. Just pull up in the flashy Mercedes and we'll all know it's you."

"Yes, um, okay."

Brent stared at him expectantly. "You wanna take out your phone and get the address down?"

"Oh, yes." He pulled his phone out of his pocket and typed in the address as Brent gave it to him, still trying to think of a way to get out of this. "And it's not just family?"

"Nah, we'll have all kinds of riffraff there. Just swing by. There'll be food and beer, although I can't promise sophisticated conversation."

Spencer smiled at that. "Sophisticated conversation is overrated."

Brent grinned. "Now you're talking my language." He patted Violet on the shoulder. "All right, Princess. Let's get a move on. Your mom is going to think we got kidnapped."

Violet giggled and skipped ahead of Brent. "See you tonight, Mr. Spencer!"

ALEX HELD THE bowl of broccoli salad against her chest as she walked toward Cal's backyard. His house sat on secluded acreage that was perfect for Cal and perfect for backyard barbecues when they sometimes got a little rowdy. Sunday dinners at his place had become a tradition lately, and Alex couldn't say she didn't love it. For once, she felt a part of a family—albeit a flawed family with too much testosterone. But it felt like hers nonetheless, and Sunday dinners were a part of that.

She rounded the corner of the house and found Asher and Violet throwing a tennis ball with Honeybear. Jenna and Ivy were drinking beer on chaise lounges and Cal was manning the grill. Brent stood next to him, clearly directing him how to cook while Jack stood nearby, arms crossed over his chest, a scowl on his face as he occasionally barked orders at his two sons.

Max was there, the youngest Payton, with his fiancée, Lea. Alex had met him only once or twice since he was a teacher in Pennsylvania. He stood with his arm around Lea, watching Honeybear as she twisted in the air to catch the ball. Davis sat next to them in his wheelchair, the beer in his hand resting loosely on his thigh.

A warmth, an unfamiliar but comforting contentment, settled in Alex's gut. Yeah, *this* was home.

She set her broccoli salad on a foldout table near the house and walked toward Ivy and Jenna. They were laughing as Alex approached. Ivy looked up, blue eyes bright. "Hey, you."

"You guys started without me." Alex pointed toward the beers.

"It's five o'clock somewhere," Jenna said, sending the girls into another fit of giggles.

The sound of gravel pinging and loud music sounded from the front of the house. Alex cocked her head as an engine shut off. "Delilah must be here."

Soon enough, the tiny dynamo bounced around the corner of the house, wearing a large tunic, leggings, and purple platform sandals. "How do you even walk in those?" Alex asked as Delilah strode up to them. Alex noticed her eyes darting toward the man in the wheelchair.

She shoved her sunglasses on top of her head. "I walk better in these than in my bare feet," Delilah said. "So, what's to drink?"

"Cooler's over there." Jenna pointed. "Take your pick."

In the next half hour, Gabe showed up with his brother Julian, who immediately paired off with his boyfriend, Asher. A couple of other friends came by, and then Cal hollered that the burgers were ready. Alex sat down at a chair with a full plate on her lap and Delilah settled in beside her, oversize glasses covering her eyes from the setting sun. Alex could still feel Delilah's gaze on her. "Nice to see you dressed up for the occasion," Delilah said with a smirk.

Alex stuck a forkful of broccoli salad in her mouth. "My Sunday best."

Delilah grinned and crossed her legs, tilting her head back to take a huge gulp of beer. Alex owed a lot to the woman next to her. Delilah was a friend of a friend who'd told Alex about the opening at Payton and Sons. Delilah had also employed Ivy, so all around she was aces in Alex's book.

Plus, girls' night out was always interesting with Delilah present.

"So I heard your one-night stand is back in town." Delilah's glasses were on top of her head now and she eyed Alex.

So the downfall of Delilah was that she loved to gossip.

Alex sighed, pushing around her food, clamping her lips shut so she didn't correct Delilah that technically it was a two-night stand. Or, a one-night stand plus a fuck on a car.

Jesus.

Alex took a sip of her beer. "You and Ivy are old gossiping biddies."

"Look, this town never sees action, and the Kardashians are all getting knocked up now. I need entertainment."

"Del—"

"He's very attractive in this dark, frowning British way."

"He doesn't always frown," Alex muttered.

Delilah giggled. "I guess not."

"Oh, shut up."

"Please go on, tell me what he does with his mouth besides frowning."

"I hate you."

"You love me and you know it."

"Don't you have some man of your own to worry about?"

Delilah waggled her eyebrows. "Worrying about your men is much more fun. Less mess."

Alex sighed, unwilling to confess about the fuck against his car. "Look, he's only here in town to work with his friend and her husband—"

Delilah's eyes widened. "Oh, plot twist!"

"How is that a plot twist?"

"Because he's in a ménage relationship?"

Alex cackled. "I'm pretty sure he's not in a ménage."

Ivy looked concerned. "What if he is? What if that's, like, a weird New York businessman British thing?"

Delilah tapped her chin. "I think I read about this in a book or something."

"Oh, stop." Alex rolled her eyes. "No, you didn't."

"What'd you read about?" Jenna stopped in front of their chairs holding a beer bottle in her hand.

"Threesomes in New York," Delilah said, as if it was a perfectly normal thing to be discussing over a Sunday dinner.

"I feel like I read that too?" Jenna said, her voice rising into a question. "Who was it by?"

Alex was done. "You two are ridiculous."

Jenna pulled up a chair and sat next to them. "Why are we talking about ménages? Because Cal won't be into that, Delilah. I guess you could ask Brent and Ivy."

"How much have you had to drink?" Alex demanded.

Jenna stared at her beer. "Um, a bunch?"

"A bunch of beer?"

Jenna nodded, biting her lip, then dissolved into giggles.

Alex needed to drink more to deal with this. She was about to stand up and grab another bottle when the doorbell rang inside the house. She dropped the burger onto her plate and turned around to peer through the screen door into the house. "Who the hell are the newbies ringing the doorbell?" Alex asked Jenna.

Jenna frowned. "Huh, I don't know, actually. Maybe Cal invited someone."

Which made them both laugh. Because Cal didn't invite anyone.

Jenna went to stand up, but wobbled a little.

Alex rolled her eyes. "Sit down, lightweight. I'll get the door."

"I can get it!" Jenna protested.

Alex was already walking into the house. "Too slow!"

She wiped her hands on her jeans and straightened her old, faded Metallica T-shirt. She opened the door, and was about to explain that no one ever knocked on Sundays, but her voice died in her throat.

Spencer stood on the porch, his mouth tight, while Penny and Nick flanked him. Penny was craning her neck behind them to take in the front yard, while Nick looked unimpressed with Cal's house.

Spencer's mouth was tight, his shoulders tense. "Um, hello, Alex."

At the sound of Alex's name, Penny whipped her head forward. Her smile split her face. "Hello again, Alex."

Alex just stared, one hand on the door, the other hanging limply at her side. "What're you doing here?" Which was rude, yeah, but honestly, why the fuck were they there?

Penny lifted her eyebrows but Spencer's expression didn't change. He cleared his throat. "I ran into Brent at the grocery store, and he invited us."

The anger burned in her throat, and she had to count to ten so she didn't bark at them to leave. All she could think was that Spencer had invaded her sanctuary. Her private, Sunday, family-friendly sanctuary.

He couldn't have declined? Made up some excuse on why he couldn't come? She narrowed her eyes a little. "I'm surprised you have time for something like this, what with all the work you have to do while you're in town."

A muscle in Spencer's jaw ticked. "Seems we were able to spare a few hours."

Penny cleared her throat and held up a paper bag. "We brought dessert, some cupcakes from the bakery outside of town. I hope that's sufficient?"

Alex hesitated, but this woman didn't deserve her ire. She took the bag and nodded. "Yes, that's, uh, very nice of you. You can head down this hallway and out the back door. Everyone's in the backyard."

"Come on, Nick," Penny said, her gaze lingering on Spencer. "Nice to see you again, Alex." She set off down the hallway, her husband at her heels.

Spencer took a step inside after Penny and Alex shut the door behind him. His arm brushed hers, and he smelled the same as he had before.

He wore a pair of jeans and a button-down shirt with the sleeves rolled up, revealing his veined forearms. His clothes were casual, yet he still carried himself as Leslie Michael Spencer.

Everything Alex didn't want to be attracted to, but yet she inexplicably was.

He gazed around the living room. "This is a nice place. Peaceful."

"It is."

"Look, Alex—"

"Don't," she said sharply and his head shot up. "There's nothing to apologize for or explain. There's nothing…between us, right?" Her stomach rolled as she said the words. "What we did—twice—is all there's going to be, right? You'll be gone again soon, so let's just spare ourselves another repeat. It's what we both want." She forced herself to take a step back. "Food's out back. Burgers are done." And then she turned on her heel, willing her heart to stop beating out of her chest when she heard Spencer's footfalls following her.

Chapter Eight

NOTHING BETWEEN US.

Spencer had been telling himself those three words since he left Tory the first time but out loud, they sounded wrong and sour. Now, Alex sat on the other side of the backyard, picking at her plate, surrounded by her friends and family. Spencer wanted to go over there, pull her to her feet, and force her to admit she was wrong. That there was something between them.

She was under his skin with every look of those big blue eyes, every word that escaped those red lips.

He took a deep breath, knowing he needed to clear his head, to quit focusing on her and what they'd done. He'd been invited and he had damn well better act like he was grateful. The weather was lovely and the food had been delicious. The beer was cold. Laughter sounded from all corners of the backyard, and it was a little infectious.

Spencer turned to Penny, who was staring at him. Nick was off filling his plate for the second time.

"What?" Spencer asked.

"What's with you and that woman?" Penny's directness served her well in business, but it was irritating to Spencer on a friendship level.

"What do you mean?"

"Don't play dumb with me."

"I'm not playing dumb—"

"I've known you since you were a skinny, sneering teenage transplant from Manchester. So knock it off. Did you meet her when you were in town last?"

He didn't want to kiss and tell, but this was Penny. She knew everything about him. He walked to a rubbish bin and tossed his empty plate inside, then returned to Penny's side. "Yes, we spent…an evening together."

Penny's eyebrows rose into her hairline. Her mouth opened and closed like a fish.

"You're actually speechless for once?"

She smacked him. "Look, I…don't mean to judge, but that's usually not the type of woman you go for. And if I'm not mistaken, I'm pretty sure you're not her type either."

"Yes, well, that didn't stop us, apparently." *Twice.*

"And were there hard feelings when you left?"

He shook his head. "Because that's just it. I left. I never thought I'd be back, and she didn't either until she saw me at that restaurant."

"Ooooh."

"Yeah, Oh."

Penny looked at Alex, her head tilted. "She is very pretty. A little rough around the edges. Kind of reminds me of how you were when we met."

"I'm not that boy anymore."

Penny didn't respond and when he looked at her, she was chewing on her lip. "Right?"

When she looked at him, her eyes were soft. "I think...you have more in common with that boy than you think."

He swallowed. "Penny—"

"What're you guys talking about?" Nick asked as he approached them with a plate brimming with food. "Man, these people really know how to cook, right?"

"Yes, delicious," Spencer muttered. "Excuse me, I need to grab a beer."

As he walked away, Penny and Nick were guessing the ingredients of the broccoli salad and Spencer was happy for the reprieve from the conversation.

Along the outside of the house were several coolers. He lifted the lid on each one until he found beer bottles peeking out among crescent-shaped ice. He grabbed one, twisted the cap off, and stayed along the wall, wishing he could blend in.

Alex had finished her dinner now and was playing a game that Spencer had never seen before toward the edge of the backyard with Asher, another boy he was told was Asher's boyfriend, Julian, and Violet.

Two large, flat wooden boxes were connected with a chain. The boxes were rectangular in shape and only about five inches high. On the top surface of each box were three holes, about a foot apart. Alex stood on top of the end of one of the boxes, metal disks in her hands. She tossed one at the other box and whooped when a disk fell into the second hole.

He watched as she stuck her fists in the air and danced in her big boots, her dark ponytail bouncing.

His face hurt and when he touched his cheeks, he realized he was…grinning.

Good God.

"Mr. Spencer?"

He looked down to see Violet standing beside him, blue eyes gazing up into his face. "Yes?"

"Would you want to play washers with us?"

"Play…what?"

"Washers. That's what we're throwing. Big metal washers."

He didn't understand what she was saying at all. "Washers."

She giggled. "You say the word funny."

He smiled. "I do?"

"Yeah. Waaaashas," she said, trying in vain to imitate his accent. It was cute the way she screwed up her face.

"Are you teasing me?" he asked.

She shook her head, smiling. "So, you wanna play?"

"Well, I—"

She took his hand and pulled him toward the game, and he thought to himself that he really needed to work on better hiding places. Or looking inconspicuous.

When they stood next to the box, Alex looked up at them, the smile still on her face, but it dropped off quickly when she…well, when she looked at him. His chest tightened.

She hopped down off the box. "What's up, Vi?"

"I want Mr. Spencer to play with us. Is that okay?"

"Yeah, I'll just bow out—"

"No, I want him to be on our team. That's okay with you, right, Asher?"

The teenager nodded. " 'Course, Violet."

He could pretty much see the words *damn kid* in Alex's expression. She blew out a breath. "All right, then, let's teach Posh how to play."

FRANKLY, HE WAS awful at the game. Turned out the holes were labeled. The farthest one earned three points, then two, then the closest earned one.

Spencer had…zero points.

Violet thought it was hilarious to watch him throw. She said his forehead wrinkled and his lips got white. Yeah, well, he was trying bloody hard to get this fucking metal disk in a hole. If he wasn't in mixed company, he would have made a crude joke.

Another reason for his serious lack of game skills was Alex. She was the worst distraction. Whenever it was his turn, she stood close enough that he could smell her, with her arms crossed over her chest, an amused expression on her face. It was irritating.

"Are you quite pleased at how bad I am at this game?" he asked her.

Her expression didn't change. "Quite pleased."

"I find your smug expression distracting."

Alex laughed, and he enjoyed that, watching her eyes light up. "Well, I find your ugly throwing distracting."

"Hey now, I'm working on my form."

Violet giggled and Alex ruffled her niece's hair.

Then she took pity on him. She stood on the ground next to the box he was on. "Now, I can't help you with your pitiful hand-eye coordination—"

Spencer growled.

"But I can help you with technique. So, okay. Stand with one foot in front of the other."

He mimicked her stance with his right foot forward.

She nodded in approval and he felt something warm unfurl in his gut. What the hell?

"Okay," she said. "Now throw underhand. You're whipping it overhand like a kid who's throwing a tantrum."

"The insults are not necessary."

"So take your right arm, keeping your eye on the hole in the box, and throw."

He took a deep breath, licked his lips, and threw.

The washer bounced off the front corner and landed in the grass.

They both stared at it.

Alex started to laugh, and Spencer tried to scowl, but he could feel his lips twitching. "I think my poor marks are because of my teacher."

She was bent over, hands on her knees, shaking her head as she tried to catch her breath. "You are so awful at this game."

"I don't think that needed to be said, as we're all thinking it."

"Oh, poor Posh," she said, straightening.

"I think it might be the beer too."

"How many have you had?"

"Erm." He stared at the bottle. "Half of that one."

Alex licked her lips as her voice pitched lower. "I recall your tolerance being a little better than that."

She motioned for him to get off the box. He stepped down as she took his place and shot him a look over her shoulder. "Watch how the master does it."

On her first throw, she scored three points. Spencer knew he was supposed to cheer for her—he was on her team, after all—but instead he glared. "Show-off."

"Oh, you're just jealous a girl is beating you," Alex said, sticking out her tongue.

He wanted to kiss her.

Her guard had dropped slowly as the game went on. By the time it was over and Alex and Violet were declared the winners—Spencer too, although he hadn't contributed a thing—Alex's face was flushed, her smile warm and open. Spencer knew she was in her element here. This was where she felt comfortable.

These were her family and friends, and he'd threatened that a little with his presence.

But he wouldn't have changed it. Not when he got to see Alex dance with her sister, singing Bob Seger at the top of her lungs. Not when he got to see her wrestle with Honeybear on the ground.

Not when he got to see her play fighting with Brent, throwing soft punches at each other until Violet joined in, tackling Brent to the ground as he howled dramatically that he was being ganged up on.

Alex on a normal day was radiant, but here, surrounded by people who loved her and whom she loved back, well, she was breathtaking.

Yes, Spencer was in town for only an indefinite period, but he didn't want to spend the whole time fighting his attraction to her.

Of course, Alex had to agree to that. To want to see him knowing all along there would be an end date. So maybe they could spend the time he was in town casually. Together. In bed. Against the boot of his car.

Maybe a shower.

He glanced up in time to see Alex walk into the house, shutting the screen door behind her. He glanced around the yard. Everyone was winding down a little now. The sun was almost set. Penny and Nick were cuddling on a chaise.

So Spencer took a deep breath and followed Alex inside.

ALEX WET A tissue and wiped below her eyes. After all the laughing and running around she'd done, her eyeliner and mascara weren't holding up as well as they normally did.

She fixed her hair, eyeing herself in the bathroom mirror.

She looked…happy. In a way she wasn't sure she'd been happy in a long time. Sunday dinners were always a highlight of her week, but this one was even better.

She didn't want to think that the reason was the posh Brit who couldn't throw a damn washer to save his life.

Dropping her head between her shoulders, she chuckled, remembering his frustration and cursing under his breath.

Turned out Posh was kinda fun. Who knew?

She finished up in the bathroom and when she opened the door, the very man she couldn't stop thinking about was leaning on the wall in the hallway, arms crossed over his chest, feet crossed at the ankles.

He looked up and met her gaze. "Hey, Sprite."

She motioned behind her. "Uh, bathroom's open."

"I didn't come in here for the restroom."

She blinked. "Oh."

He turned until he faced her, with his one shoulder braced against the wall. "I came in here to talk to you."

"Oh." When did she lose the ability to talk in sentences?

He ran a finger through his hair and glanced around. "Is there somewhere we can talk? Or…"

Alex blinked. "What's wrong with here?"

Spencer's fingers tapped a nervous rhythm on his leg. "Maybe somewhere private?"

Alex hesitated.

He blew out a breath. "Look, I'm not trying to…I don't want to…attack you in your boss's house. I'd just like to talk to you is all. Without being interrupted. Is that all right?"

She appreciated the explanation. "Um, sure, we can just…" She waved a hand toward the front door. "Maybe just sit on the porch? No one will come out front to bother us."

He nodded and placed a warm hand on her lower back, which he kept there until they stood leaning on the railing of the front porch. He rubbed his thumb in a circle and then dropped it at his side. Alex bit her lip to keep from asking him to keep touching her.

This was all a little too close. A little too comfortable. Alex knew enough about herself to know that when she fell for someone, she fell deep, with all she had.

The last person she'd fallen for had been Robby, and look where that got her.

She couldn't do this again. She just couldn't, especially with a man like Posh, so unlike her in every way and from New York, for God's sake.

Spencer cleared his throat and looked down at his hands where they gripped the railing. "Look, I...don't have anything rehearsed, but I know there're some things I want to say. Will you let me?"

Alex nodded.

He turned toward her, with one hand braced on the railing, and raised a tentative hand. He brushed back some strands of hair that had escaped her ponytail and ran his knuckles over her cheek. She stared at him, willing herself not to flinch at the touch.

His fingers skimmed her shoulder, down her arm, until he gripped her hand and held it. She stared at their intertwined fingers—her rough, tanned ones next to his long pale ones.

"I'd like to take you out on a proper date."

Alex's gaze jerked to his. "A date?"

"A date."

"B-but why?"

"Because I like you." His blue eyes were scanning her face, his lips parted as he seemed to carefully plot out his words. "Because I want to get to know you better."

"I—"

"You like casual, right?" he asked softly.

She couldn't look at him anymore. She turned her head and examined the cars parked without rhyme or reason in Cal's front yard. "Yes, yes I do."

He squeezed her hand, but she wasn't ready to look at him yet. "And have you always been that way?"

His voice was still calm, soothing, and she wished he wasn't so perceptive. Damn, smarty-pants Posh. She shook her head and dropped her eyes to the garden below, which was in serious need of weeding.

He tugged on her hand, so she finally looked up at him, those beautiful high cheekbones, the full mouth that she knew intimately could kiss very, very well.

"So this can be casual, right? While I'm in town?" he asked. "It can't be more…because I'll be leaving. But while I'm here, why deny this…spark between us?" He stepped closer and raised their clasped hands to her chest. "You feel it too, right?"

She could do nothing but nod mutely, because her whole body was a spark right now. The heat of Spencer, the smell of his cologne, the rush of his breath along her flushed cheeks.

She remembered his voice. *Tell me what you like.*

This could work. They could burn bright until the spark died and then Spencer would return to New York and she'd go back to her life.

She smiled a little, altering her voice into a tease. "Want to rough it a little while you're in town, then? Before you go back to dating women who know which fork to use for their sherbet?"

Spencer laughed. "You don't use forks for sherbet."

"Whatever," she muttered.

He cupped her cheek and swiped a thumb over her cheekbone. "Maybe I've always liked it a bit rough, hmm?"

She lifted onto her toes and kissed him, not caring about their differences right now or where they'd be next month—or anything.

Because Spencer was here now, and he knew how to touch her and talk to her. He tasted like beer, and she gripped his shoulders, trying to get closer, so much closer.

Spencer groaned and gripped the back of her thighs, hauling her up his body. She wrapped her legs around his waist as he set her down on the edge of the railing. He ground his hips into her, and she made a pleading sound in her throat as he began to lick along her jaw and down her neck.

"Bloody hell," he panted against her skin. "We need to meet in public so we stop trying to rip each other's clothes off."

"What if being in public doesn't stop us?" she asked, clutching his shoulders tightly and rolling her hips against his hardness between her legs. She reached down and stroked him through his pants, grinning as he moaned heavily and bit down on her shoulder.

"You drive me mad," he said, cupping a breast through her thin shirt.

"Feeling is mutual," she said, squeezing the hard ridge tighter.

He lifted his head, his mouth wet, his eyes heavy-lidded. "So you'll let me take you out?"

"I'll let you take me out. If you promise to take me to bed afterward."

He laughed, although the sound was a little strangled since she was still teasing him through his pants. She wondered if they could get away with a quick hand job.

"I don't know. Taking you to bed wasn't part of the original deal."

"Sorry," she said, then licked a wet strip up the side of his neck. "That's my stipulation."

There was a cracking sound, and Alex froze. Her gaze met Spencer's, who stared back at her with his brow furrowed.

"What was that?" he muttered.

"I don't—" The railing shifted under her weight, and she had a moment of recognition before she was falling backward, Spencer coming with her, since she was still clinging to him like a spider monkey.

There was a moment of freefall before she crashed hard on a bush, the cracking of twigs and ripping of leaves echoing around her. Spencer landed on top of her and she cried out as the railing dug into her lower back.

He swore under his breath and tried to untangle their limbs, but everything was twisted among pieces of railing and a bush and clothing, and once Alex realized exactly what had happened, she began to laugh. Hard.

She threw back her head and roared until tears streamed down her face.

Spencer gripped her face, running his hands down her body, testing to make sure her limbs were all in working order while she lost her mind. "Are you okay?" He gripped her face, and she blinked at a bleeding cut on one of his sharp cheekbones. "Alex? Answer me, dammit. Are you crying or laughing or what is this noise you're making?"

Which made her laugh harder, until her stomach cramped and she couldn't breathe. He must have figured out she wasn't dying because he rolled off her, muttering curses and blaming faulty American hardware.

She lifted a hand to his face and swiped at the cut, sobering. "Posh, you're bloody bleeding."

He frowned and looked at her finger, which was now stained with his blood. "I'm what? Oh, hell." He waved a hand, dismissing his injury. "You okay?"

She nodded, then winced as her back protested. "I'm okay. A little sore maybe from hitting the railing."

He stood up, his nice clothes covered in leaves. "Let's get you up."

"What the hell is going on?"

Alex looked up to see Cal stomping toward them with Brent on his heels. Following them were Jenna, Delilah, and Ivy. Violet was on Asher's shoulders, while Davis rolled along beside them. And they were all looking at Alex and Spencer with a mix of reactions, ranging from pissed off, to amused, to confused.

Cal was glaring. "What the hell did you two do to my porch?"

Alex groaned and placed her hands over her eyes, waiting for her sluggish brain to catch up to the situation. It's not that she necessarily needed to keep Spencer a secret, but she certainly didn't want to confess to everyone here that they'd been making out like teenagers and broken the railing. That would lead to more questions and some raised eyebrows and a few dirty jokes from Brent.

She wasn't in the mood and could really use some Advil.

Spencer scratched the back of his head, glancing at the remains of the porch railing, then down at the debris on the ground. "We…I…I, uh—"

Alex rolled onto her hands and knees and rose to her feet with Spencer's help. "Spencer was standing at the railing and I came out to heckle him about how much he sucks at washers. I think we were both leaning on it too hard and it…uh…broke."

"What do you mean, you were leaning on it too hard? I lean on the damn thing every day."

"I guess it just got weak over time?" Alex offered.

Brent stood with his arms across his chest, head cocked. "I think we need a reenactment. Why don't you show us exactly what happened?"

Alex glared at him. "I'm not reenacting it, you dumbass."

"Aunt Alex swore!" Violet crooned.

Alex pointed to Cal. "He swore first!"

"But your word was badder," Violet said.

"Worse," Asher corrected.

Alex heaved a sigh.

Cal's eyes were narrowed as he gazed between Alex and Spencer. "That's the story you're going with?"

"There is no other story," Alex said.

"She's right," Spencer added. "That's, uh, the story, all right. That's all there is to it."

Alex turned to him with big eyes so he'd stop talking. He got the message and clamped his lips shut.

Penny and Nick rounded the corner of the house next, and she stopped suddenly when she saw the mess, so that Nick ran into her back. "What happened?"

"The railing broke and two grown-ups are swearing," Violet said.

Penny nodded, as if that was all the explanation she needed. Her gaze went to Spencer. "Oh, you're bleeding, Spence."

He lifted a hand to his face. "Oh, it's just a scratch."

"Yeah," Alex said. "You need to weed, Cal. Just saying. If I get poison ivy on my ass, I'm putting laxatives in your coffee."

"What are laxatives?" Violet asked.

Penny was walking toward Spencer. "You sure it's just a scratch? Maybe you need stitches."

"I don't need stitches," he growled, maybe a little harsher than necessary, because Penny looked stunned.

"Okay, no need to snap at me."

The man wanted to get out of the situation. That was clear. Alex knew that feeling. "Okay, so is everyone done gawking now?"

Spencer cleared his throat. "Cal, I'll pay to replace what I broke."

Cal's eyes flashed a little. "I can afford to fix my own porch."

Jenna laid a hand on his arm and whispered something in his ear. A muscle in Cal's jaw jumped, but then he nodded shortly. "Okay, well, uh, if you're offering, then I guess that'd be nice." His face was twisted up painfully.

Spencer stuck his hands in his pockets. "I'd love to take care of it for you. It was my fault, after all."

That wasn't entirely true, but Alex didn't speak up for fear of blowing their already flimsy cover.

Cal and Brent began to pick up the pieces of the shattered railing out of the garden. Nick and Spencer tried to help, but the Paytons waved them off.

It took a half hour for the yard to be cleaned up and the broken section of the porch to be roped off. Alex stood in the bathroom, checking out the scrapes on her arms. When Spencer left, she'd merely lifted her arm in a wave. No one needed to know their business. Not when she barely knew what was going on.

And this new tentative relationship with Spencer felt private. Between them. Her family was nosy enough, she didn't need them prying and asking questions and spreading gossip around town about Alex and her Brit.

The door to the bathroom swung open suddenly and Alex only had time to say, "Hey," before a mouth crashed down on hers and she was wrapped in strong arms surrounded by the smell of Spencer.

He pulled back and gripped her face, a grin splitting his. "I...forgot to do that before I left."

She laughed. "I'm glad I didn't miss out then, because that was good."

He stuck his hand in her back pocket and pulled out her cell phone. He tapped away at it, then a chime came from one of his pockets. He handed her phone back to her. "I needed your number."

She stared dumbly at her phone. "Oh. Oh yeah."

He kissed her forehead. "I told them I left my phone here so we had to come back. I have to go."

"Okay."

He cupped her face. "Until our date, Sprite."

"Until then, Posh," she said.

He smiled and then was gone.

Chapter Nine

ALEX HAD CHANGED lipstick three times.

Because she'd bought three new lipsticks to add to her already ridiculous collection in anticipation of this date.

She'd also bought four dresses, two pairs of shoes, and three bracelets. She'd also endured some snootiness at the lingerie store when she'd stomped in there smelling like car oil after work to purchase a new bra-and-panty set.

She was wearing her new underwear and nothing else, because she hadn't decided what to wear among her four new dresses and the rest of the stuff in her closet. Rubbing off her third lipstick application, she glared at herself in the mirror.

A hand on her shoulder made her jump, and Alex turned to see Ivy in the doorway. She'd told Ivy about the date, and she knew her sister enough to know Ivy had made some excuse to come over when Alex had to get ready. She'd been there for the past hour puttering around while Alex fretted.

When she'd shown up, Alex was annoyed.

Now, she was grateful.

Alex blew out a breath, fluttering the loose hair around her face. "Can I just wear this?"

Ivy's gaze slid down Alex's near-naked body. "Um, your Brit probably wouldn't mind actually, but the public might."

Alex bent to apply the glue to her fake eyelashes. "He's not my Brit," she muttered.

"Well—"

"It's really not a big deal. I don't know why we're even doing this"—she fluttered a hand and blew on the glue stripe on the eyelashes—"this date thing."

"Because he wants to get to know you?"

"Dumb." Alex blinked and then placed the eyelashes on her lid, pressing so the glue would adhere. Then she leaned back to check out her appearance in the mirror. "I always feel very *Clockwork Orange* with one fake eyelash on."

Ivy laughed. "Well, that's a great movie to think about to get you in the mood for a date."

"I heard the book was better." Alex ran the glue over her second eyelash.

"Never read it."

"I prefer your romances."

Ivy waited until Alex had pressed the eyelashes to her lid before hugging her from behind. "I want you to prefer your own romance."

Alex snorted. "That shit doesn't exist in real life." Their eyes met in the mirror, and Alex shrugged. "Well, I guess it did for you. It won't for me, though. Which is fine. I don't need it." She slid out of Ivy's embrace and tossed her makeup in her bin, blinking quickly because that dumb burning in her eyes let her know tears could fall if she wasn't careful.

"Alex—" Ivy began, but Alex shook her head and brushed past her, walking toward her bedroom. On her bed were no fewer than ten outfits.

Alex hated them all on sight. "This is ridiculous," she muttered as Ivy came into the room behind her.

"Alex—" her sister began again.

"Just tell me what to wear. I can't decide."

"Alex." Ivy turned her so they faced each other. "Come on, talk to me."

"I am talking."

"What was that in the bathroom?"

"Me putting on my makeup?"

Ivy was losing patience. "Look, if I believed for one second that you meant what you said, that you don't want romance, I'd leave you alone. But I don't believe you. Not at all. Because you love to love, Alex. And you love to be loved. And you deserve it. You deserve it all."

Shit, the burning in her eyes was starting again. Alex didn't have another pair of fake eyelashes, so she was going to be pissed if her sister made her ruin them. She lifted her chin. "You love me. Violet loves me."

"Everyone loves you," Ivy shot back. "That's not the point."

Alex looked away, her voice dropping with her bravado. "Can we please not talk about this right now?"

"I hate him," Ivy said viciously, and now Alex's nose started to tingle. "I hate him so much and if he was here right now, I think I'd castrate him."

That made Alex smile. Because although Robby was a big man, hell hath no fury like a pissed-off Dawn. She met her sister's gaze. "I love you."

"I love you too. Now promise me you'll take this seriously, that you'll have a good time."

"I will."

"And that you…let yourself be open to more."

Alex shook her head. "I can't do that. He doesn't live here, Ivy. This isn't…this isn't what this is. We both know, and we're both okay with that. Someday, Ivy, someday maybe I'll find someone." She swallowed the lump in her throat. "But it won't be this man." Even as she said the words, she could hear Spencer's voice in her ear, his hands on her skin. She could feel his eyes on her body, his surly tone in her ear when she teased him about washers.

"Okay, you go ahead and believe that while smiling that dopey grin while you're thinking about him." Ivy crossed her arms over her chest.

Alex immediately slackened her face muscles. "I did not have a dopey grin!"

"You totally did."

"I have never done anything that could be described as dopey in my life, and that includes grinning," Alex huffed.

A laugh burst out of Ivy's lips and then they were both doubled over bracing themselves on the bed and sufficiently wrinkling several of Alex's outfits. When they composed themselves, Alex gestured to the bed. "Seriously, will you please just tell me what to wear?"

Ivy glanced at the bed and shook her head. "None of those."

"What? I don't have—"

"I work at a damn consignment store that has tons of high-ticket dresses, you dumbass." She led Alex out of the bathroom. "Please step into my—um, your—living room to select your clothing for the evening."

While Alex had been applying her makeup, Ivy must have brought in clothes, because they were draped all over her living room, hanging from the trim on the doorways, off doorknobs—dresses and skirts and tops in fabrics and styles Alex had never worn in her life.

She stood in her living room in her underwear, turning as she took in all that Ivy had brought. "Wow."

"By the way, I'm liking the, uh…" Ivy gestured toward Alex's black lace set.

"Yeah? I like it too."

"But you still have to wear clothes."

"Unfortunately."

It took a good hour, but they settled on the simplest dress Ivy had brought. It was a dark purple—aubergine, Ivy had said—and it fit Alex perfectly. The top was tight and low cut, showing a substantial amount of cleavage, and the way it flared out from her hips down to her midthighs made her waist look tiny.

They tied a thin black belt around her waist, and Ivy pulled a pair of black peep-toe heels from one of the new pairs Alex had bought.

Alex turned slowly, eyeing herself in the full-length mirror that Ivy had dragged out into the living room. "Wow, I look…"

"Beautiful," Ivy whispered.

Alex bit her lip. "But it's so different from me."

"You said you wanted different, right?" Ivy frowned.

"Yes, I know that's what I said, but…"

"Do you want to try on something else?"

Alex shook her head and took a deep breath. It was okay. What was wrong with dressing a little differently? She was still Alex.

As Ivy gathered the clothes she'd brought to take back with her, Alex fiddled with the hem of her dress, wondering if she actually knew who the real Alex was anymore.

She wanted to rip off her clothes and put on her jeans and a stained T-shirt and boots. But Spencer had asked for a date, and surely he'd take her out somewhere ultra fancy and *posh*, and hell if she was going to embarrass him.

By the time Ivy left, after ensuring a phone call from Alex after the date, Alex had beat herself up so completely, she wondered if the bruises were visible on the outside.

She'd never cared before how she dressed for a date. She was who she was and screw any man who didn't like it. So why was she trying so hard to impress this one? And why the hell did that mean dressing like some other woman?

Someone like Penny.

But then the doorbell rang and she didn't have time to change. She pulled out her lucky lipstick, the one she wore every day, and slicked it on her lips. At least when she looked in the mirror, she'd recognize her face.

And then she walked to the door, wobbling a little on the heels and cursing herself for not practicing walking in these damn things.

Because the last thing she needed was to fall flat on her face on this date.

Then she took a deep breath, placed her hand on the doorknob, and turned it.

AT FIRST, SPENCER thought he had the wrong apartment.

The woman in front of him was a vision in high heels and purple.

But then those blue eyes blinked at him, the ones he couldn't get out of his head. And those full red lips parted, the ones he couldn't forget kissing.

The woman in front of him was Alex but…not. She was in a dress that accentuated every single curve—and she had a lot—and her heels made her legs look longer than normal.

He wanted to say fuck the date, grab her and wrap those legs around his waist, feel those heels digging into his ass—

"Spencer?"

He snapped out of it, realizing he hadn't said a word to her as she stood in front of him, her hands fidgeting with the fabric of her dress. He cleared his throat. "Alex, you look…gorgeous."

She shook her head and looked away, and without thought, he reached out and grabbed her hand, tugging it so she took a step toward him. Her breasts brushed the front of his shirt as she blinked up at him.

He cupped her neck. "Absolutely gorgeous."

Her cheeks reddened and she licked her lips. "You don't look so bad yourself."

Compared with her, he was way underdressed. He glanced down at his jeans and plain button-down shirt. "Um, maybe I should change…"

She rolled her eyes. "No, I just"—more fidgeting—"don't dress up much so I thought, why not?"

"Erm, yes," he stammered. "Well, you should dress up more, because it suits you." Her eyes widened and he held out his hands. "I mean, no, that came out wrong. You don't have to dress up. Or dress, um, any differently than you want to. You look gorgeous in your jeans and shirts too."

Alex's face was tight. "Well, thank you."

This date was going to hell already. "Uh, well, how about we get going?"

She nodded and grabbed a purse, then shut the door behind her.

They stood awkwardly outside her door and he wondered what he should do. Hug her? Kiss her? But this was a date and he was trying to be a gentleman.

So instead he placed a hand on her shoulder and led her to his car.

The same car they'd screwed on.

Bloody hell.

He went to open the door for her, but she pulled on the handle before he could get there, so he stopped short and watched her fold herself into the car. Then he sat in the driver's side and turned the ignition. "So, I had to ask around for a place to take you. I thought...I thought of some place I thought you'd like. So, um, I hope you do."

She was watching him, her hands gripping her thighs. "Okay."

The car ride was silent except for the radio. There was no playful conversation or smiles or lustful looks. Hell, Spencer didn't remember how to make small talk anymore. He knew how to talk business and he knew how to fuck, and right now neither was appropriate.

"How's work?" he asked, the two words sounding dumb even to him.

"Uh, good," Alex said, her gaze on her lap. "I'm training a new guy and he's...yeah it's good."

Silence again.

And Spencer was relieved because the empty words were worse than the silence.

When they pulled into Bomer's Burgers half an hour later, Alex sucked in a breath, staring at the neon sign.

Spencer had spent way too much time on his laptop looking for a place to take Alex. He hadn't wanted to take her to Bellini's, because he'd wanted to take her someplace new. "Have you been here before?" he asked as he shut off his car.

She shook her head but didn't look at him.

"Okay, so they have a beer sampler. I thought you might like that. And this appetizer apparently is very popular. A fried onion thing that supposedly looks like a flower? Very American, I'd say. And their burgers are supposed to be quite delicious. And I…" His voice trailed off as Alex's face tightened by the minute.

He'd thought this place was perfect. He wanted Alex to be somewhere she was comfortable and so he'd stayed away from uptight, posh places. He thought a pub with beers and burgers would be ideal for Alex.

Although he hadn't anticipated showing up at her house and her wearing that dress either.

He…might have miscalculated.

But there was nothing for it now. So he got out of the car, and when he walked to her side, she'd already stepped out and was smoothing her dress over her thighs. When she looked up, her eyes seemed a little wet. "Alex?"

She blew out a breath and shook her head, tossing her hair over her shoulder. "Yes?"

"Are you okay?"

"Fine. Why?"

He didn't know. He didn't know at all.

She began to walk toward the front door, and he followed, wishing they were back in Cal's yard playing washers, because then Alex had been happy. Now? Not so much. He didn't know how to fix that, to put a smile on her face. How had this gone so wrong in such a short time?

This is why he didn't date. Because apparently he was awful at it.

Bomer's was a large brick building with a massive red neon sign. Spencer mused, as Alex pushed open the door in front of him, that this restaurant could probably be seen from space.

There were several couples sitting on benches along the wall near the hostess station. Spencer walked up to the desk and smiled politely at the pretty teenager. "Uh, hello. I have a reservation for two. Spencer."

"It'll be fifteen minutes," the girl said, smacking her gum.

"I'm sorry?" Spencer asked. "But I have a reservation."

"Yeah, I know. Sorry. Little bit of a wait."

He turned to Alex, who stared at him with a blank look on her face. "Um, they said it'll just be a minute."

"Fifteen," she said.

"Well, yes, fifteen."

Her jaw clenched and then she turned around, sitting down at an empty space on the bench. Spencer ducked his head and took a seat beside her.

The couples talked around them, some holding hands. Alex sat stiffly, flexing her feet in her heels, drumming her fingers where they gripped the pleather seat.

"I heard they have great burgers," Spencer said.

Alex shifted her eyes in his direction, then resumed staring into space in front of her.

"Are you…did I do something wrong?" He didn't want to ask, but so far, this date was torture.

Alex shook her head and looked down at the floor. "No," she whispered.

"You sure?"

"Yep." She popped the *p*, and he leaned back, crossing his arms over his chest and hoping like hell they were seated soon.

A rumbling sound came from outside and necks craned toward the clouds beginning to roll in. Spencer glanced at the weather app on his phone. "Looks like it's going to storm."

A small smile crossed Alex's face. "I love storms."

"Where I'm from, it rained more than stormed," he said.

She turned to him, light in her eyes for the first time since he'd picked her up. "Really? Summer storms are the best. When it's so humid all day, you can't even bear to be outside, but then right around dinnertime, the storm comes in and the sky opens up and it pours." Her gaze returned to the window. "Fall storms are great too. Looks like it's gonna be a good one."

Five minutes later, the hostess called his name. She led them to a booth in the corner and Alex slid in one side as Spencer took his seat across from her.

The menus were almost as large as the table, laminated until shiny and smelling faintly of grease.

The pictures showed juicy burgers and massive drinks and gooey desserts. Spencer scanned the menu for something that wasn't going to give him an instant heart attack.

When the waitress came, Alex ordered a shot and a beer. Spencer stared at her, but she didn't meet his gaze. He ordered a pint.

When the drinks came, Alex downed the shot and then gulped half of her beer.

"Better?" Spencer asked.

Alex shifted in her seat and tugged at something in her dress. She took a deep breath and exhaled with her mouth shaped in an O. Finally, she met his eyes. "Why'd you bring me here?"

Spencer took a swallow of his beer and set it down on the table gently. "What do you mean?"

She gestured around them. "Why here? Why not somewhere else?"

Irritation crept up his spine. "What do you mean? Where'd you want to go? Someplace with a Michelin star?"

She stared at him, eyes wide, nostrils flared. Through gritted teeth, she asked, "What's a Michelin star?"

"It's a..." He waved his hand. "A culinary award. Given to top restaurants."

"And what? That would be ridiculous to take *me* to a place like that?"

"Well, yes!" Spencer said, knowing his voice was rising but unable to stop it. Why was she being so difficult? "I mean, you're *you*!"

Alex jolted back into her seat as if she'd been slapped, a flush of red creeping over her chest, up her neck, and into her face.

Spencer replayed the conversation, what he said. "Wait, I didn't mean—"

Alex swallowed thickly. "I think that's exactly what you meant." She threw her napkin on the table, slid out of the booth, and walked out.

"Bloody hell," Spencer muttered, throwing cash on the table to cover their drinks and following her through the restaurant. By the time she burst out the front door in a flash of purple, Spencer at her heels, the sky had unleashed hell.

Fat raindrops fell on Spencer's head, immediately soaking his hair and shirt. "Alex, what the hell?" he yelled, trying to cover his head, but giving up when his arms were no match for the torrential downpour. Alex was stomping ahead of him toward the car, wobbly on her heels, and he was worried she'd twist an ankle. "Will you slow the hell down and tell me what the fuck is wrong?"

She whirled around, fists clenched at her sides, long hair dripping, dress plastered to her body like a second skin. She hopped on one foot as she pulled off a shoe and hurled it at him. He dodged that one, but the other one hit him in the thigh when she threw it with a frustrated growl. "What the fuck, woman?"

"I can't believe..." She growled again. "I can't believe I did *this*." She gestured to her body. "I spent an hour and a half getting ready. Do you even *know* the last time I spent an hour and a half getting ready for anything?"

Spencer stood, staring at her as she hollered at him in the rain. He shook his head.

"Never!" she yelled. "I've never spent that much time putting on makeup and doing my hair and picking out a stupid fucking dress!" She reached up and cupped her breasts, shifted the dress over them, and tugged on the fabric. "Ugh. I hate this dress. I hate those fucking shoes that hurt my feet. And I hate, *I hate*, that I took all this time trying to impress you. To show you that I can be a fucking lady, worthy of...I don't know...being on your arm. And instead, you bring me here. Because that's all I'm worth, right? A beer and a burger?" She snorted. "The thing is, you're not wrong. That is all I'm worth. Those burgers looked goddamn delicious. I'm so fucking angry at myself that I expected something different. That, for once in my life I expected something more."

She shook her head, her shoulders slumping, as she seemed to run out of steam. She looked so tiny without her heels, shaking in the rain as it continued to pour buckets on their heads.

He'd done that. Him. He'd taken the light of his sprite's eyes. In an attempt to make her feel comfortable, he'd done the exact opposite.

He ran his hand over his hair and looked up at the sky. "I'm an arsehole."

"No—"

"Yes. Yes, I am, Alex. Fuck, I'm so sorry, I…"

She was watching him, her top teeth sawing into her bottom lip. He held up his keys and gestured to his car. "How about we get out of this rain and talk?"

Alex looked down at herself and wiggled her feet in the puddle she stood in. "But we're wet—"

"I don't care," he said. "I don't care one bit. I want to talk to you. Will you let me explain? Please?"

She took a deep breath. "Okay."

Spencer let out a breath. "Great." He took her hand and led her to his car.

Chapter Ten

ALEX CURLED HER prune-y toes into the carpeted floor of Spencer's Mercedes, wrapped her arms around herself, and shivered.

Spencer reached into the backseat and tugged some kind of jacket around her shoulders. She gripped it and looked up at him through strands of wet hair. "Thanks."

He smiled uneasily, and she wondered what the hell he was thinking. Because that back there...that had been a little crazy. Surely her mascara was tracking down her face in little black rivers. Her hair that she'd spent time curling was now a wet mop on top of her head.

But most of all, she'd thrown her shoes and yelled at him in the rain. Like a crazy person.

The giggle bubbled up her throat uninvited and she tried to stuff it down. But that only made it worse, so she curled in on herself and let out the laughter.

When she was able to regain her breath, she leaned back in the seat and looked over at Spencer. He'd turned on the car and was blasting the heat, but he made no move to drive.

He ran his hands over the bottom of the steering wheel, brow furrowed.

She wiped her face and under her eyes, trying in vain to get rid of the raccoon look she knew she was sporting. A quick glance in the side mirror told her that yep, she looked like a train wreck.

Which was how she felt.

Her muscles ached and her head pounded, but here, in this car, with the white noise of the hot air blasting from the vents, she stared out the windshield, feeling protected since the world outside was a blur.

She hadn't felt safe in…a long time. And maybe it was the breakdown she just had in the rain or the steady presence of Spencer at her side, but she was too tired to replace the armor that had melted off her body in the parking lot.

"I've only lived here for about a year," she began. "Before that, I lived in Indiana with my boyfriend." She licked her lips, preparing for the name to drop off her tongue like acid. "Robby." She stared straight ahead, but she felt Spencer's gaze on her skin. She didn't talk about Robby. Not even to Ivy. "I loved him. Or, I loved him in what I thought at the time was love. And I thought he loved me back. Things were great, until…until I realized they weren't good. They were horrible, actually. He…" Her voice trailed off.

Spencer took her hand. "Alex—"

"He didn't, ya know, hit me or anything. I mean, sometimes I thought he might, but he didn't. His words were slaps and punches and stabs to the heart enough without the actual...physical pain." She took a deep breath. "I hadn't realized how much damage he'd done until Ivy moved in. And then it was like, I finally saw our relationship from her eyes and it was horrible. I finally realized that it wasn't okay for my boyfriend to call me a whore and tell me that he was the only one who'd put up with me. That he kept me around because he liked how I blew him." Her voice shook, and she wasn't sure anymore of the source of wetness on her cheeks. "So we moved. One day while he was at work. It'd been years by then, and Ivy had Violet. Violet...heard the things he said and is still sort of scared of men. I blame myself for that."

She lifted her head then, to see if Spencer's lip was curled, to see if he was looking at her like Robby had for all those years, like she was weak.

But Spencer looked...angry. His jaw was clenched, lips thinned, eyes hard. She registered pain in her head and winced, noticing Spencer's knuckles were white where he held her hand. He let out a ragged breath and let go of her hand, then stared out the windshield, gripping the steering wheel.

"So that's why I kinda lost it. Out there," Alex said. "It wasn't about you, really, or this date. It's about me and my fucked-up head. And my baggage. I know that's not what this is. That you just wanted something fun while you're here in town and now I made it...not that at all. I'm sorry, I—"

"Don't apologize." Spencer's voice was whip-sharp, but he didn't turn to look at her. "Don't apologize for an asshole who needed to beat down a woman to feel like a man."

She curled her lips between her teeth and bit down.

Spencer turned then, his blue eyes icy. "I'm…not always so good at saying what I feel. But right now, I'm angry. Really fucking angry. Because Alex, you…are vibrant. And confident. And so beautiful, it hurts to look at you sometimes. I think about you in Cal's backyard, playing with your friends and family, smiling and laughing, and to think that a man wanted to take that spark from you…" He exhaled loudly. "It makes me fucking crazy. If that arsehole was in front of me right now, I might commit vehicular homicide."

He sounded like Ivy, but Alex's mouth wasn't working—to talk or smile. Because Spencer wasn't done talking and every word was pumping fresh, hot blood into her limbs.

He ran a finger down the side of her face, his voice softening. "He was threatened by you. Because you loved and were loved and he wanted some of that for himself. He was jealous of you. Wanted your strength and your confidence and your talent and he tried to suck it right out of you for himself."

She closed her eyes. "He succeeded."

"Ah, Sprite." She lifted her lids to meet his gaze. "No, no he didn't. Because I saw it in you when we first met."

"You did?"

"I did. It's why I wanted you so badly. Not so I could have it for myself, but because I wanted so badly to bask in the afterglow for a little while."

He turned in his seat to face her fully. His hair was sticking up where he ran his hands through it. She touched the top of one spike and smiled. He blew out an exasperated breath and patted it down.

"But I—"

"I brought you here because I thought it was what you wanted. I…thought you'd be more comfortable at a place that wasn't posh and stuffy." He reached out and took her hand. "I didn't stop to think how that would look to you, that I thought this was all you were—a beer-and-burger joint. I'm not good at this. At reading people. And especially at reading women. My mum died when I was a kid and I was raised by my dad. But those are all excuses, really." He stared at the windshield as the rain drummed on the car. "I miscalculated this. It's why I haven't dated in…who knows how long."

She wanted to cry. How big of an asshole was she? What had she expected, a five-course dinner at a country club? He'd tried to do what he thought she'd like. "Well, shit, when you put it that way, I just sound like a big brat."

He tugged on her hand so she'd look at him. "No, no you don't. Tonight you…" His gaze trailed down her body and then back up. "You look beautiful."

"Looked," she smirked.

"You still look beautiful, just a little drowned."

She shook her head, her voice dropping, because this was a confession she hadn't wanted to make. "I wanted to look good enough for you. So you weren't embarrassed to be seen with some roughneck girl."

She hadn't known Spencer could move that fast, but with a cry of alarm, she was tugged out of her seat and splayed across his lap, her knees on each side of his hips. Spencer's hands were on her face, pushing back her wet hair, and he was swallowing convulsively, his lips thinned. "Oh, Sprite. Oh no," he muttered.

She gripped his wrists. "What?"

He huffed out a sad laugh. "You don't even know."

"I don't even know what?" She wasn't cold anymore, even though the jacket had slipped from her shoulders. The warm air blowing through the vents heated her back, and Spencer's body was like a furnace. He surrounded her with his big arms and shoulders. A drop of water ran down his temple and she caught it with the tip of her finger.

Spencer's chest expanded against hers, then contracted. "I grew up in Stockport. Do you know where that is?"

"No."

"It's a small town outside of Manchester, which is north of London."

"Okay."

He paused a moment, his eyes going distant before focusing back on her. "My father is a mechanic. He owns his own repair shop. He does all right, but we were poor. Always poor."

She sucked in a breath. "Wait, what?"

He nodded. "Yes, I grew up working on cars with my dad."

She was about to ask why he hadn't told her, but then stopped herself. Because that wasn't what they'd been. It wasn't what they were, to talk about themselves. So she realized the shift now, from what they had to what they were building. This was something, this closed-off man admitting his roots. And it was something for her to admit what Robby had done to her. "Okay."

He soldiered on. "But I didn't want to work on cars. I never did. I don't even really like cars." She gasped in mock outrage, and that made him smile. "My dad and I never got along. He thought I was embarrassed of him, and as a punk teenager, I was. I didn't want anything to do with him or his shop or my fucking low-class town. I wanted money and success. So as soon as I could, I left. Went to school in New York and got a job and that's that."

She ran a hand over his shoulder. "And you have that, right? The success, I mean. And the money."

He didn't answer her for a minute, and his hands settled on her hips. "Sure, sure, I have that."

She frowned then. "So why…why me? Why this? I'm basically everything you left, right?"

He licked his lips, his eyes on his hands where they gripped her hips. "I don't know. At first, I only saw a female mechanic. A sexy one, but just a female mechanic nonetheless. But since I've been back, I've seen *you*. And your family and your town, and it's not about what you do and what you are, but *who* you are." He looked up then. "I can't seem to stay away from who you are, Alex." His hands cupped her neck, his thumbs brushing under her jaw. "So he didn't take that away. He dulled it, maybe, but it's coming back, that light you have. I hope you believe it."

She wasn't sure. "Maybe I'm starting to."

His lips parted. "What do you want to do?"

"What do you mean?"

"Right now, what do you want to do?"

She blinked, and answered without thinking too hard about it. "I'd like to kiss you."

He nodded. "Then go ahead."

She ran her fingers around his mouth, feeling the ridges on his lips. "Then what?"

He blinked lazily, his tongue snaking out to wet the tip of her thumb. "I think you know what you want. And I want you to be free to ask for it. To take it." He huffed out a breath. "I'm sitting here, soaking wet, with the hottest girl I've ever met on my lap, and I'm telling you that you have all the power here. All of it. You might have felt powerless with him, but he didn't take your power from you. It's not mine to give back, either, because you've had it all along. It's still yours."

Her face was dry, her eyes clear. There were no tears now, not while this man in front of her, a man she never in a million years thought she'd connect with, was speaking directly from his heart, in that deep, accented voice. "You're amazing."

He laughed softly. "I'm really not. I think you're rubbing off on me."

"I'm not that amazing."

His hands settled on her shoulders and squeezed. "That's the one time I'll tell you that you are so, so very wrong, Sprite."

She pushed forward, her chest smashing into his. He was passive beneath her in his actions, letting her lick his lips and run her fingers through his damp hair. But his eyes burned whenever their gazes met. She parted her lips and his opened with hers. She licked inside his mouth, deepening the kiss, and he moaned, the sound rumbling from his chest, vibrating against her already hard nipples.

She ground down onto him, feeling the hard ridge in his pants that let her know he wanted her as badly as she wanted him.

But he made no move to direct their actions. His hands rested on her hips, his fingers digging into her skin, but not trying to take charge.

She let go of his lips reluctantly and rained kisses over his stubbled jaw and down his neck. She wanted his shirt off. She wanted her dress down. She wanted skin and saliva and something inside her where she ached so badly.

"Spencer," she whispered at the base of his throat. "I need you."

"Fuck." His hips were moving now, and he made a frustrated sound in his throat, like he couldn't stop them from thrusting up into her. His head lifted, and then he froze.

She did too, her teeth latched onto his collarbone. She pulled off. "What?"

"Uh…"

"Spencer?"

"Alex, the, uh, rain stopped."

"Okay."

"So we're more visible through the windows."

"Uh…"

"And, erm, there's a small human looking at us right now."

Alex slowly turned her head and there, right beside the driver's side window, was a little kid eating an ice-cream cone, staring at them with a cocked head. "Oh my God."

"Yeah, that was my thought as well."

"We should probably…" She gestured toward the passenger seat.

Spencer nodded, the muscles in his neck straining. He had to be in pain. She was in pain. "Yes, that would probably be good."

She slithered back over to her seat as the kid began to wave at them. Spencer lifted his hand and smiled tightly. They put on their seat belts in silence and Spencer put the car in Reverse, pulling out of the parking lot as the parent of the child collected him and directed him toward their van. Alex tried not to burst out laughing as she stared out the window as they drove to her apartment.

Chapter Eleven

THEY WERE A mile away from the restaurant before Spencer could find humor in the situation. After the tension of their conversation, and the kiss that had blown his mind, he needed to release some steam. He started to laugh and Alex joined in with him. "So, that was bloody awkward."

"I was about to take off my dress."

Spencer nearly swerved off the road. "In the car?"

"You said a bunch of amazing things that made me want to get naked, okay? Quit being nice and stuff and I'll keep my clothes on."

Oh, well, that wouldn't do. "Alex, you are the hottest woman to ever wear coveralls and hold a tire iron."

Her eyes shifted to the side, and she hesitated for a moment. Spencer held his breath, then she pulled down the straps of her dress so they hung loosely on her arms. "Yes?"

This was incredibly unsafe, but at that moment, Spencer didn't give a rat's arse. "Your breasts are a work of art."

She laughed and shimmied the top of her dress down to her waist, revealing a black lace bra.

"Oh, Christ," he muttered.

"You like it?"

"Don't ask questions you know the answer to."

She hummed under her breath, entirely too pleased with herself, and stretched her arms over her head, glancing at him from under her lashes. "Tell me more, Posh."

He swallowed. "Being inside you was the closest I'm sure I'll ever get to heaven, especially since I'll probably crash this car in the next five minutes and kill us both."

She lost the sex-kitten look as she doubled over and cackled. "Oh, shit, Posh, that was a good one."

"Yeah? What do I get for it?"

In a flash, she took her dress off. She now sat in the passenger seat, on his black leather seats, in a set of black lace lingerie that made his mouth water. "Sprite, you're killing me."

"Guess we're both going to hell then." Her fingers ran along the tops of her breasts, along skin that had pebbled into goose bumps from her wet dress, then her hand slid down her torso, over her hips, and then along the crease of her thighs. "God, I need you so badly, Spencer."

He gripped the steering wheel harder and worked on breathing properly. "Sprite—"

"When we get to my apartment," she said, those fingers now slipping under the top of her panties, causing Spencer to think he was going to hyperventilate, "I'm going to put on your jacket. And you're going to follow me into my apartment knowing that I'm only wearing this under it." Yep, he was going to go into anaphylactic shock. "And then once we're inside, you're going to sit on the chair in the living room. And I'm going to dance for you. I'm going to enjoy it. And so are you. And then I'm going to get naked. And then I'm going to take off your clothes, straddle you, and ride your cock until we both come." She moaned as her fingers moved under that thin fabric. "Because we both deserve it. What do you think?"

He wasn't really thinking anything at all. "I, uh, I think you're right."

She smiled wickedly. "Of course I am."

Spencer drove the rest of the way to her apartment pressing the heel of his palm against his erection.

When he parked the car, Alex pulled his jacket around her shoulders, balled up her dress in her hand, and winked at him.

Winked.

He didn't find it amusing how badly he wanted her, how he was falling so hard for her after their shared confessions. This was so much, too much, this craving he had for the crazy sprite.

But he didn't care, not at all, not while she was walking ahead of him, barefoot, her heels dangling from one hand, his jacket barely covering the bottom of her ass. Night had fallen, plunging the parking lot into mostly shadows. That was good, because he didn't want anyone else to see her like this.

Only him.

What a mind fuck.

When she opened her front door, she pointed to the chair in her living room and he sank down on it, gripping the plush armrests, digging his fingers into the fabric.

Alex's hair was half-dry now, and she'd wiped her face on the way home, so she looked fresh, like she'd just stepped out of the shower. He liked that, as if the rain washed away her needless attempt to impress him.

Of course, she pulled out her red lipstick and smoothed it over her lips. He understood that was for her, the lipstick, and that made him smile. However, the smile quickly fell from his face when she dropped his jacket to the floor. Because he sort of lost control of all motor function.

All that skin, all that pale skin right there for him to touch.

But Alex had plans. She turned on the stereo and a beat echoed from a set of speakers near the TV.

She began to dance.

Her movements were small at first, just a slight roll of her hips, her fingers threaded through her hair on each side of her head.

He'd been to strip clubs. He'd danced with women, but he'd never seen anything like Alex right now. Eyes closed, head back, and as she turned her dark hair brushed the top of her ass, which was bared to his gaze in her thong underwear.

She reached around to her back with one hand, and unclipped her bra. It fell to the floor at her feet. She shot him a look over her shoulder, a smile on her face, and it was all heat and lust, and it sliced into him like a lightning strike.

"Alex."

She faced him, her arms crossed over her chest, hiding her breasts. "What?"

He wanted to tell her to hop on his lap and make them both happy, but this was her show. And he wasn't sure he wanted it to end anyway. "You're gorgeous."

She smiled bigger then, which he hadn't thought possible, then dropped to the floor in a crouch. Her hair covered half of her face as she crawled toward him, the muscles in her shoulders rolling, her hips swaying, like a panther. She licked her lips. "Take your shirt off, Posh."

It was a struggle because his limbs weren't working very well, but he managed somehow to get his shirt off himself.

When she reached his feet, she took off his shoes and socks, then slid her hands up his calves and thighs. She undid his belt, tugged down his zipper, and then pulled out his cock. He sucked in a breath as she stroked him with a strong, sure grip. Her tongue flicked out, and she lapped at his tip. He jerked and then cursed himself to stay put.

She smiled, then took him in her mouth.

His head bounced on the chair as he threw it back, unable to stop the loud moan from escaping. Her mouth was perfect, her rhythm flawless. Her hands dug into his thighs as she bobbed her head in his lap. He didn't touch her hair, not wanting to guide her, because she didn't need it anyway.

As suddenly as she started, she stopped, stood up, and dropped her last remaining piece of clothing to the floor.

He wanted to stop time for a minute, take a picture, and store it away so he'd never forget the moment of Alex standing in front of him, hair wild, red lips smeared, grinning like the devil herself.

"You're not real," he muttered. "Right? This is a dream and we're actually still standing in that parking lot in the rain."

She straddled his thighs, grabbed his cock, and sank down on it. "Does this feel like a dream to you?"

No, no it didn't, because that tight heat was real, spreading throughout his body, until he swore he was burning from the inside out.

She ground into him, rolling her hips as he latched onto a perfect nipple and sucked. She moaned, spearing her fingers in his hair, and began to work her hips harder, bouncing on his lap now. He let her nipple slip from his mouth and stared down where they connected, where he watched his hard cock slip in and out of her body.

She was beautiful everywhere, all curves and arse and breasts, like her body was made to be cherished.

"Tell me what you want," he said.

And she moaned, her eyes flickering open. "T-touch me."

He reached down and found the hard bud of her clit with his thumb. He rolled it as he thrust his hips up to meet her. She was panting hard now, those gorgeous breasts bouncing, brushing his chest and neck. "So close," she whispered. "So close."

He didn't even think of himself in that moment, or his need to come, because this was all about her, about that flush that was covering her whole body, the way her eyes were hazy, the way she bit her red lips as she worked herself harder on his cock. He reached up and flicked a nipple, then gripped the back of her neck. "Wish you could see yourself right now, how fucking beautiful you look when you're in control. When you have the power."

She cried out and slammed her lips onto his as her body froze and convulsed. Her inner walls squeezed his cock as she whimpered into his mouth, her hips snapping against him. He gripped her back, holding on, so she knew he had her. That he was there. And he'd be there when it was over.

Her hips worked slowly as she panted against the skin of his neck. Her fingers twirled in his hair as her back heaved. "I just…need to catch my breath," she said, as she tightened around his cock inside her.

"Can I move us to the bed?" he asked.

She nodded.

He picked her up and wrapped her limp legs around him as she clung to his neck. When they reach the bed, he laid her down, then climbed on top of her. She encircled him in her arms and guided him back into her body. "I want to feel you."

He began with slow, gentle thrusts because he knew she'd be sensitive, and the whole time she stroked his hair, his back, grabbed his arse and squeezed. When he came, it wasn't explosive. It was an orgasm that rolled throughout his entire body, into each finger, and to the tip of every hair on his head. He gasped against her chest as he swore it went on forever, him pulsing into her body.

When he was done, he rolled to her side, pulling her against him, her hair spread across his chest. He sighed, a sigh that he felt down into the marrow of his bones. He wanted to sink down into the mattress, fuse themselves to the bed so he never had to get out and deal with anything or anyone but this woman in his arms.

ALEX COULDN'T MOVE her limbs. All she could do was lay limply on Spencer and wish she never had to get up.

Okay, well, she could move a finger. One finger. A finger that was currently tracing the tattoo on his left pectoral. It was a fox, and not a particularly well-done fox. It was a little basic, the shading simplistic, the head in profile.

But it was over his heart. It had meant something to him, at least at one time.

"Why the fox?" she asked, tracing the outline of an ear.

His brow furrowed in confusion, then his face cleared as he glanced down at his chest. "Oh." He blew out a breath and ran his hand through his hair. "That damn fox."

"You don't like it?"

"I don't…no. Not really, to be honest. I don't like it."

She rested her chin on her fist propped on his chest. "That sounds like a story."

"My brain hurts."

"You didn't use your brain for what we just did. Now tell me the story, dammit."

He rolled his eyes, but his lips quirked into a small smile. "I got it when I was sixteen. I was still in that stage where I wanted to impress my father. This fox is the symbol of his repair shop. It's Red Fox Auto Repair. Because…I don't know. He likes foxes, I guess. And Manchester United." She raised an eyebrow and he laughed. "So anyway, I went and got this tattoo to impress my dad. Lied about my age and the whole bit and finally found a tattooist to do it. Surprisingly," he said drily, "he wasn't the best. Anyway, my father thought it was dumb. So that was that. I just have this fox on my chest now for no reason. I could get it lasered off, I guess, but I'm not a huge fan of pain. Or lasers."

She touched its snout. "It's kind of cute."

"Foxes aren't bloody cute. They're cunning."

"It's really not that bad."

"It's not that it's a fox, it's that…for years, it reminded me of where I was from. And what I wanted to get away from. So I hated it. Kind of awkward in college when I would mess around with a girl and I refused to take my shirt off."

"Well, that's a shame, since you look pretty hot with your shirt off."

He smiled and ran a hand through her hair. "You're just being nice."

She shook her head. "You should know by now, I don't do much just to be nice."

"You offered me a ride that first day we met."

He had a point but… "Who said I didn't have ulterior motives to that?"

"Oh? I looked easy, then?"

She laughed and scooted up his body to press a kiss to his lips. "I don't know that anything about this is easy."

He sobered at that, his fingers teasing the strands at her temple. "No, no, I don't think there is."

"So does your dad still live in Britain? Do you get to see him often?"

His eyes went a little distant, like this wasn't something he wanted to talk about. "He does. He lives in the same house I grew up in, and works at the same garage he did when I was a kid." Spencer continued to play with her hair. "I do not get to see him often, no. After I graduated, I would go back a couple of times a year but it seemed like…the more I visited, the less close we became. Which is so backward, but it's the truth. He acted like he didn't want me there, like it wasn't my home anymore. And so I stopped visiting."

Alex rarely saw her mom anymore, so she knew what it was like to lose touch with a parent. "I'm sorry."

He sighed. "It is what it is. How about we not talk about this?"

She nuzzled his jaw. "Will you stay tonight?"

"What? And miss out on my instant coffee in my hotel room?"

"I thought you Brits drank tea."

"I'm a transplant."

Something rumbled, and Spencer's eyes widened. "Um…"

"Was that your stomach?"

"Er—"

Alex sat up, bracing her arms on his chest. "Oh my God, we never did eat dinner, did we?"

Spencer shook his head.

Alex jumped out of bed and threw on a T-shirt and a pair of panties. "I can order a pizza. How does that sound?"

"You don't have to do that, I'll—"

"Oh, quit being all polite Posh on me. You're hungry, and I want some damn pepperoni."

He laughed. "Okay, then."

Alex ordered pizza and forty minutes later, they sat in her kitchen as she systematically picked the pepperonis off her pizza, let her head fall back, and then dropped them into her mouth from greasy fingers. She caught Spencer watching her. "What?"

"I've never seen anyone eat pizza that way."

"What way?"

"Like you could give a wank how you look."

She dropped another pepperoni in her mouth and moaned. "I don't. I take my pizza eating seriously. I have a system."

"I see that."

"Pepperoni comes off first, then I eat the crust, then I eat the cheesy-saucy bit."

"That's arse backwards, you know."

"In case you haven't noticed, I like to be difficult."

He grinned at that. "Yes, well, call me a masochist, but that's what I like so much about you."

That warmed her belly more than the pizza, which was a hard thing to do. She ducked her head and began to tear off the crust.

"So," he said. "I know you said you've been here a year, but it seems the Paytons are basically an extension of your family."

She swallowed her bite of crust. "Yeah. They...really are. I had some issues last year and they rallied behind me like no one ever had in my life. For so long, it was just Ivy and me, so to have this…support system around me was incredible. I'd do anything for them."

He spun his glass of water on the table. "What kind of issues?"

Alex bit her lip, not wanting to rehash, but she'd told him everything already, so one more thing didn't seem to matter. "I heard…uh…that Robby was looking for me. Asking around my old job. Wanting to know where I moved, where I was working. I kind of lost it. Looking back, I'm not sure I was entirely rational, but it didn't matter. I was terrified. I wanted to move to Florida or Siberia or anywhere that was as far away from him as possible."

Alex hadn't realized she was strangling her napkin with a white-knuckled grip until Spencer reached over and covered her hand with his. She took a deep breath and relaxed her muscles.

"So when I threatened to leave, they basically had an intervention with me. Sat me down and told me that they'd help me. And I think the clincher was Jack. Have you met Jack?"

"He was at the barbecue, yes? Although I didn't speak to him."

"So, he's like, the big kahuna. The boss. The dad. He told me if he ever had a daughter, he thought she'd be like me, and then he asked me to stay." Her eyes watered, remembering gruff, gravel-voiced Jack telling her he'd make sure Robby never breathed her air again. "So yeah. I owe them so much. This is my home, my family. And since I know what it's like not to have that, I guess I value them all the more."

Spencer wasn't looking at her anymore. His gaze was out the back window of her apartment. He licked his lips and then stared down at his empty plate. "I, uh, know that feeling too. Not to have that."

"I'm sorry," was all she could think to say.

"Yeah," he said softly. "Sometimes, I'm sorry about it too." A brief, tense smile flashed over his face. "Not sure I've ever admitted that, though."

Alex blew out a breath. "Look at us, sharing a heart-to-heart. Never thought I'd be doing this with you when we first met, huh?"

Spencer chuckled. "No, no, I didn't either."

She tore off another piece of crust and shoved it in her mouth. She'd avoided thinking about this, had pretended it wasn't looming, and now that she'd bared her heart to this guy, she couldn't pretend anymore. "How long do you think you'll be in town?"

He flinched, like the question hurt.

He cleared this throat. "I, uh, don't know. I already recommended where to build the hotel, and now it's all just a formality to get the final approval."

"Where did you recommend?"

He paused a minute, and something flashed over his face so quick, then it was gone. He met her gaze. "That area of land by MacMillan Investments."

Alex nodded. She knew the place. Easy to get to and right near the highway. "That sounds perfect."

"Yes, I think so."

"And then you'll...go home?" Her voice cracked at the end. Shit.

A muscle jumped in his jaw. "Yes, then I'll go home to New York. I'm up for a promotion, actually."

She couldn't look at him anymore, so she looked down at her pizza. "Wow, that's...that's great. I really hope you get it."

"Me too," he whispered, his voice edged with something that sounded a little like regret.

Communicating and talking about this shit was her least favorite thing to do, but after today, after the date from hell and her outburst in the rain and the sex that was the best she'd ever had, they really needed to set some ground rules. "So, this lasts until you leave, right? We can handle that." Even as she said it, she was only about 25 percent certain they could.

"We can handle it." His voice was deeper than normal. "As long as you're okay with it. But I'd like to see you more, while I'm still here."

Alex nodded, part of her grateful for that deadline that would prevent this from becoming too serious, too much. *But wasn't it becoming that already?* "Yes, of course. We can do that. We enjoy each other's company and the sex is kinda good. I guess." She grinned at him.

He barked out a laugh, the sound echoing off the walls of her kitchen, and Alex's shoulders shook while she tried to hold in a giggle. "Bloody liar," he said, smiling.

She launched herself at him, and then the pizza was forgotten, and so was his return to New York, as they lost themselves in each other again.

He'd leave. Of course he would. But for now, he was here, and she was going to enjoy it.

Chapter Twelve

ALEX LEANED BACK in the chair behind the counter of Delilah's and dropped some peanuts into her mouth. She rattled the plastic bag and dug around for some whole ones.

"Hey, you could always help me, you know," Ivy said as she hung up some dresses on the sales rack.

Alex held up her greasy, salt-covered hands. "I don't think Delilah wants me touching the merchandise."

"You do that on purpose, eat messy stuff when you visit me at work so you don't have to help," Ivy said with a scowl.

Alex grinned, then turned her attention to the door as the bell rung, signaling someone had stepped inside.

Alex saw the blonde hair first, and her body stiffened. She knew that her reaction to Penny was irrational. Spencer had assured her Penny was very much only a friend and very much married to another man. But this was a person who knew Spencer a hell of a lot better than Alex did, and Penny's presence made her a little uneasy. She wondered what Penny thought of her.

The woman glanced around the shop, running her hand over a couple of tops on a rack, before approaching the front counter where Alex sat.

"Hello," Penny said, her smile warm.

Alex really needed to get over this feeling of inadequacy. "Hey, can I help you with something?"

"Alex, you don't even work here," Ivy said as she slipped a dress on a hanger. "Give me a holler if you need help."

Penny's smile never wavered. "Sure. Spencer told me this was a lovely place."

Alex nodded. "It really is. Delilah is good at what she does."

Penny hummed under her breath as she eyed some earrings. "I hear you're good at what you do too."

Alex raised her eyebrows. "Oh?"

"Aren't you training a new hire?"

Spencer must have told her. What else did he tell her about Alex? "Uh, yeah I am." Alex cleared her throat, unsure what else to say. She darted a glance at Ivy to bail her out, but Ivy seemed to be enjoying this, if the smirk on her face was any indication.

Perfume hit Alex's nose as Penny leaned close. "I want to thank you for the invitation to your Sunday dinner the other night. And for making Spencer smile."

"Smile?"

Penny's gaze was steady. "I've known him for a long time. I don't think he would have attempted that game—what did you call it, washers?—for just anyone. He likes to look in control at all times." She paused. "I like who he is when he's around you. And most important of all, he likes who he is when he's around you."

Alex admitted she'd judged Penny when she first met her, with her perfect clothes and hair and flawless skin. But Penny was anything if superficial. She was direct, and kind, and ambitious, as Spencer had told Alex.

Spencer wasn't surrounded by brothers like the Paytons were. He didn't have a large crew of guy friends who would voice their approval of Alex to him. All he had was...Penny. And she mattered, Alex realized. She mattered a lot and so did her opinion.

So instead of a snarky comeback, a sarcastic, "Thank you for your opinion," Alex thought the best thing to do was act like a grown-up and give Penny the respect she deserved, as an honored friend of Spencer's. "Thank you. I like who I am around him too."

Penny smiled, then took a couple of bangles off the shelf beside her. "I think I'm going to get these for my daughter. She loves jewelry."

As Ivy made her way to the counter, Alex fingered one of the bracelets. "Yeah, my niece is really into jewelry right now too. And dressing up. She keeps trying to steal my lipstick." She glared at Ivy without heat.

Her sister rolled her eyes. "Oh, don't act like you're annoyed. You'd do anything for her."

Penny was watching them closely. "Have you both been raising her?"

It was a direct question and if anyone else asked it, Alex might have told the person to shove it, but something about Penny made Alex want to be honest. "We have been, yeah. Her dad didn't want to be involved, and I...well, I got out of a bad relationship, and being a good example for Violet is one of the reasons I had the courage to get out."

Okay, so that was really honest, and Ivy was staring at her, hands poised above the cash register.

Alex bit her lip and went to duck her eyes when Penny reached across the counter and squeezed her wrist. "I did the same thing. I was married to a man whom I left because I didn't want my children around the toxicity. And I know it's hard, but it's a good thing too. Forces you to learn to love yourself." She smiled then and leaned back. "And that's more important than the love of anyone else." Then she turned to Ivy, as if she hadn't just rocked Alex's world. "Do you take MasterCard?"

CENTRAL PARK IN New York City was lovely but it was still Central Park. There were still tourists and people and the sounds of the city all around.

There was still the knowledge that right outside the park was the hustle and bustle of New Yorkers, the honks of the taxicabs, the smell of trash and food trucks and too many bodies.

Here, in Tory Park, Spencer didn't feel anything but peace. Even as he listened closely, inhaled deeply, all he heard were the sounds of families in the park, all he smelled was fresh air. He let his head fall back and he closed his eyes, the fall air warming his face. He probably needed a jacket, but he didn't care because the cool breeze felt good on his face, on his skin, the sun burning brightly behind his closed lids.

He inhaled the scene of the nearby lake, the newly cut grass.

He knew that outside this park was a small town, full of Alex and the Paytons and that was it. He'd been so ingrained in New York City life for so long, that he'd forgotten how others lived. He felt refreshed down to his bones.

The only thing preventing him from fully relaxing was the replay of the conversation he'd had with Penny and Nick that morning. They were leaving in a couple of days, having wrapped up the last of their studies. Penny still hadn't mentioned which site her father was leaning toward, but Spencer had confidence.

He was the best, after all.

The sound of footsteps reached his ears and he looked up. Alex stood before him, sunglasses over her eyes, sipping some drink through a straw. Her eyebrows lifted behind her shades. "You're early."

He glanced at his watch. "I've been here an hour."

She shifted her glasses to the top of her head so he could finally see her blue eyes. "Good God, why?"

He shrugged. "It's beautiful outside."

Alex didn't look impressed. "You're probably sitting in so much duck crap right now."

He laughed at that. "You really know how to make the moment."

She grinned. "My specialty."

He wiped his hands together and stood up beside her. They were at the park to attend a cookout for MacMillan

Investments employees. He had been invited, which he still found strange, but Jenna had told him he'd better be there.

Small-town hospitality. Nothing better.

Apparently the MacMillan parties ended up being attended by most of the town now that Jenna had taken the helm of publicity to improve the image of the company.

Spencer wasn't complaining. It gave him another excuse to spend time with Alex.

It was Sunday and once they walked around the pond to the area where people were gathered, he noticed that a lot were wearing their Sunday best.

Alex, however, was in her standard uniform of jeans and a T-shirt.

He liked that, that she didn't give a shite, that she remained herself no matter what.

If she had been a woman who wore dresses all the time, that would have been lovely too. But she wasn't, and he appreciated her lack of fucks.

He reached out and squeezed her hand, then let go. She smiled up at him.

Penny and Nick had been invited too, but they declined. Which was fine with Spencer. He didn't want questions about Alex. He and Alex had talked and planned to keep their rekindled relationship between them. Neither wanted to deal with the rumors and the questions, and since this would end eventually anyway, they decided to keep what they had in a small, insular vacuum between themselves. Ivy knew and that was enough for both of them.

It would be hard not to grab her and kiss Alex in public, but he could manage.

Although, with this family, Spencer wondered if any secret ever really stayed a secret.

He vowed to be good to Alex though, to follow her lead. This was her town, her life, and after what she'd been through, the last thing he wanted to do was cause her problems.

And he was really, really hoping karma came around and totally demolished Robby. Like, drawn, quartered, and beheaded. Maybe castrated too.

The man had to be insecure down to his bones. There was no other explanation why someone could look at Alex and treat her as anything but a queen.

"You know," he said, as they approached the large group of people standing around picnic tables and under pavilions, "we'll have to redo that date sometime. One where we don't fuck up royally."

Alex smiled and kicked a clump of grass. "I don't know, I thought naked pizza was kind of fun."

"We weren't naked."

"We were shortly after ingestion of said pizza."

He thought about that. "Okay, that's true."

A blur of purple rushed toward them, and then Alex was scooping up Violet into her arms.

"Where'd you go, Alex?" Violet asked.

"I had to go get Mr. UK over here. He seemed to be lost."

Violet stared at him with big eyes. "You know, you can get directions on your phone."

He poked Alex with his elbow and then smiled at the little girl. "I know, but luckily your aunt here found me before I had to resort to that."

Violet gripped Alex's face to make her aunt look at her. "They. Have. Hot dogs," she said with wonder in her voice.

"Yes, I'm sure they do," Alex said with a laugh.

Brent approached them, one arm slung around Ivy's shoulders, the other extended to Spencer, who shook it. "How's it going, man?"

"Going nicely, thanks," Spencer answered. "The party looks well attended."

"Yeah, Jenna puts on a good show." Brent leaned in. "But no beer. Apparently Jenna thinks that's tacky at a company party. I disagree with that wholeheartedly and tried to tell her, but Cal threatened to smack me so I let it go. I'll work on it for next time, though."

Spencer nodded gravely, because Brent appeared to take his lack of beer seriously. "Okay, then."

"You'll back me up, right?"

"Of course."

Brent nodded. "Good man."

Alex was watching them with amusement and when Brent turned around, Spencer rolled his eyes. She giggled.

ALEX SAT BY herself at a picnic table that had long been abandoned.

She watched Violet and Spencer throw a ball to Honeybear, who was delighted by the attention. They were all stuffed from paper plates heaped with hot dogs and potato salad and some caramel brownies that Asher had made.

Alex didn't want to get up, and she certainly didn't want to run around. A nap would have been great.

She smiled as Honeybear nearly knocked Spencer over in her excitement while Violet squealed with delight.

He's leaving, she kept repeating in her head. That was a good thing, right?

The bench under her moved and she looked up to see Cal taking a seat beside her. He clasped his hands on the table and watched the scene in front of them with narrowed slate eyes.

He didn't talk, so she didn't either. That's what she liked about Cal. He was good with silence.

"So you and the Brit, huh?" he said after a while.

That's what she didn't like about Cal. When he did speak, it usually meant the other person was put on the spot.

"There's no me and the Brit," she said.

Cal's face didn't change. "I know my porch railing didn't break itself."

"Hey—"

"Quit being cagey, Alex."

She scowled at him.

He didn't look deterred.

"Look, I wasn't on the clock when we hooked up the day he came into town, okay?"

Cal raised his eyebrows. "You think I give a shit about that? You work your ass off, so if you did take a break to…get off, you won't hear me complaining."

Alex gasped out a laugh. "I can't believe you just said that."

Cal grinned.

"Look, he's not in town for long, but we like each other, so we're hanging out until he leaves, all right? I hadn't planned on telling the whole goddamn family, but you all are such nosy fuckers."

Cal sighed and watched Jenna as she talked to a couple of lingering employees. "Yeah, we all kinda are. But I wouldn't have it any other way. Means we all care and shit."

Alex picked at a loose nail at the edge of the table. "Yeah, I know."

"Look, I…just want you to watch yourself, okay? I think you're a tough woman, but you still have a soft heart. And I worry you're gonna get really attached to this guy and then it's gonna be real bad when he leaves."

Alex turned to him. "Are you for real lecturing me on what it's like to get attached to a man? Like I don't have experience with that shit?"

Cal had the decency to blush and duck his head. "Yeah, guess I should keep my mouth shut."

"No, I get that you're just trying to watch out for me, but telling me not to get my heart involved is something I already know. And you know what? It's my decision to give a little bit of my heart to Spencer because it's been a long damn time since anyone made me feel like he does."

Cal nodded. "You're right. Can I ask you one thing, though?"

She rolled her eyes. "What?"

"That coworker of his—Nick?"

"Yeah?"

Cal squinted his eyes, watching Honeybear bark for the ball. "I dunno, there's just something about him I don't like. He's squirrelly. Spencer say anything about him?"

She shook her head. "No, he hasn't."

Cal grunted and scratched the graying hair behind his ear. "Maybe it's all in my head, then."

"Want me to ask Spencer?"

Cal shook his head. "Nah, forget I said anything."

"Okay." But Alex was frowning now, thinking back to her conversation with Penny. While Alex didn't want any woman in a bad relationship, it had comforted her a little that someone as poised and beautiful and successful as Penny had found herself in a similar situation as Alex. And got out.

She hoped for Penny's sake that her second marriage was better than her first. But something told her Penny would be okay if it wasn't. Alex was gaining confidence that she'd get there too. Because Spencer *was* leaving. And she had to remember that.

Jenna walked over and sat down across from them, blowing her hair out of her eyes and collapsing her head onto her folded hands on top of the table.

Cal smiled and reached out, massaging her scalp. Her groan was muffled. "You did good, Sunshine," he said.

"I know, but these things always wear me out." She lifted her head and rubbed her eyes. "Ready to head out? I hired a crew to clean this time. Best decision ever."

Cal stood up and helped Jenna to her feet. "Yeah, let's head out." He looked back at Alex. "You all right?"

"Just peachy, Cal." She stood up too. "And, uh, thanks for the chat."

He winked at her, then walked toward the parking lot with his arm around Jenna's shoulders.

When Alex looked out across the park, she saw Brent and Ivy had now joined Violet and Spencer. They all sat on the grass, Honeybear panting on the ground.

Alex walked over and came to a stop in front of them. Four heads looked up at her. "The dog tire you out?" she asked.

"I'm not tired," Violet said.

"I am bloody wiped," Spencer said.

Alex plopped down beside him and nudged his shoulder with hers. "Aw, got bested by a little girl and a dog, huh?"

"I'm man enough to say yes, that was indeed what happened."

But despite his words, Spencer was smiling, his eyes were bright, and he seemed to nearly vibrate with…happiness.

Maybe they could…

No. She shut herself down before she could start on the maybes and the what-ifs. That way led to madness and heartbreak.

"Come on, Princess," Brent said, hauling the little girl to her feet and helping Ivy to hers. "Time to go home. You can play with Honeybear more there."

Violet launched herself into Spencer's arms, surprising the man, who hesitated before wrapping his arms around the little girl's back. "Thanks, Mr. Spencer."

"Uh, it was my pleasure." He patted her back awkwardly and looked askance at Alex, who hid a laugh.

Then Violet was off, skipping ahead of Brent and her mom, Honeybear tagging along at her heels.

"You riding with us?" Ivy called over her shoulder to Alex.

Alex shook her head. "I'll get Spencer to give me a ride."

"Who said I'll give you a ride?" Spencer protested.

Alex ignored him and continued to talk to her sister. "Have a good night."

"You too," Ivy said, then grabbed Brent's hand to follow her daughter and dog.

Alex turned to Spencer. "No ride, huh?"

"So presumptuous," Spencer huffed.

She nuzzled closer to his side. "Oh my, that was a big word."

"Yeah? Do you like that? I have more where that came from."

"Do tell."

"Obfuscate. Mendacious."

She moaned. "That's hot."

"Ostentatious. Peccadillo."

"Oh please, take me now," she wailed.

Spencer squeezed her waist. "Can you wait until we get to my car? She told me she's been feeling lonely without a naked Alex."

She threw back her head and laughed, warmed by the easy conversation, the comfort of sitting with a man she trusted. "Well, we can't have that, can we?"

"No, indeed." They rose to their feet and Spencer tucked her arm into his. "Your red chariot awaits."

Alex couldn't stop laughing all the way to his car.

Chapter Thirteen

ALEX LEANED BACK in his arms where they sat against the trunk of a tree, staring at the moonlight glittering off the water.

They were at River's Edge, a park in Tory that Alex promised him was peaceful and beautiful. She hadn't been wrong. After the party, they'd parked and walked back to the river as the sun dipped below the horizon. Luckily they'd brought flashlights to guide them back, although Spencer was still a little concerned about breaking an ankle. Alex had laughed at him.

They'd been watching the water for the past twenty minutes in silence.

Spencer had forgotten how much he loved the absence of spoken words. Because they weren't needed here, not with the sound of the rushing water, of the breeze blowing through the trees, birds chattering, and Alex's breath, softly wafting over the arms he had wrapped around her.

She ran her fingers slowly up and down his thigh, the heat of her hand entering the denim of his jeans to warm his skin.

He didn't want to get up. Ever. Maybe they'd stay like this, and two thousand years from now, someone would find their skeletons, still locked in an embrace.

Okay, that was bloody morbid.

He nuzzled his face into her hair and closed his eyes. She shifted where she sat between his legs, rubbing against him, which woke up certain parts of his anatomy. Well, one certain part.

He made a sound and she paused, then wiggled her ass again, this time on purpose. "Alex," he warned.

"What?" Her voice was mock innocence.

"I think you can feel *what*."

She made a humming sound in her throat, then turned her head and opened her mouth on his neck. He moaned and tilted his head so she had better access.

He was a thirty-five-year-old man, and he was making out under the stars like Alex was his first girlfriend.

And maybe she was. Other women had been nice and lovely and some very hot but none of them had been Alex. None of them stirred his blood and spoke to his soul and got him like Alex had. Maybe he'd been looking in the wrong places all along. The high-society women from good families weren't enough like him, didn't know the struggle of growing up like he had.

Alex knew, and being with her was like returning to his roots—roots he'd tossed aside carelessly when he was younger and a little less wise.

She was squirming between his legs, snuggling her ass back against his erection. He reached down and cupped her through her jeans. She stilled immediately and made a small whimper in her throat. He smiled against the back of her hair. And then with one hand, flicked open the button of her jeans and pulled down her zipper.

Alex was panting now, her chest heaving. But she wasn't protesting or moving, not when he ran his fingers along the elastic band of her panties, not when he slipped beneath them and ran a single finger along her wet, aroused flesh.

"Spencer," she whispered, moving her hips and clutching his knees raised on each side of her. He gritted his teeth because what he wanted to do was pull down his own pants and fuck her until she couldn't speak, but this was too much fun—Alex in front of him, at his mercy, about ten seconds away from begging.

"What do you want, Alex?" he asked.

Her head fell back and her lips moved but no sound came out as he pressed two fingers against her clit.

She sucked in a breath. "Please."

It wasn't that he was turned on by hearing her beg. He was turned on when she told him what she wanted, when she was honest about what gave her pleasure. "Please what?"

"I want your fingers."

He heaved in a breath as his cock twitched. "Where, Sprite? Where do you want them?"

She licked her lips, her eyes half-closed. "Inside me."

"You want me to fuck you with my fingers? You want to ride my hand?"

"Jesus Christ, Spencer, just get me off," she said with a strangled gasp.

He bent down and latched his mouth onto her earlobe as he plunged two fingers inside her wet heat.

She cried out and rolled her hips, gripping his knees harder now, digging her fingernails into his jeans. "Oh, God," she muttered. "Oh, fuck."

He went slowly at first, pulling out to run his fingers all around her entrance. Then he was back inside her, his thumb at her clit, working her, turning her into a moaning mess between his legs.

She rolled her head back and forth on his shoulder, all inhibitions lost now as she thrust her hips and sought the orgasm he could feel beginning in her quivering body.

She was beautiful like this, her red lips parted, her cheeks flushed, hair askew. Her breasts shook through her thin T-shirt, and he reached up with his free hand to flick a nipple through the fabric. That forced a scream from her lips and then she was coming, her inner muscles squeezing his fingers. Her hand gripped his wrist, keeping his hand where it was, against her, inside her, and he didn't want to be anywhere else.

When the tremors in her body lessened, she heaved in gulping breaths and, with a shaky hand, brushed the hair off her face. "Holy shit, Posh."

His fingers were still inside her and neither of them seemed to want that to change. Her hips were still moving, slightly, jerking. He ran his tongue down her neck and gently nipped her shoulder. "You don't even know what you do to me, Alex."

She huffed out a laugh. "I think I do. Because you do the same to me."

He pulled his hand away slowly, taking care that she was sensitive, and she shuddered a little as he zipped up her jeans.

He was still hard, beyond hard, but he wasn't in a hurry to do anything about it. Basking in Alex's afterglow was good enough.

Except Alex had other ideas.

She turned around, shifted him so that he lay on the ground flat on his back, then she began to kiss and lick his jaw and his neck.

"Alex." He sighed, running a hand through his hair. "I—"

"Shhhh," she murmured, her tongue dipping below his shirt to taste his collarbone. "Let me."

So he stopped talking as she rucked up his shirt and licked his abs and navel. He was silent while she undid his pants and tugged them down until his hard cock slapped against his belly.

But he wasn't silent when she took his cock in her fist and then took him in her mouth.

"Oh, fuck," he said, his eyes rolling back in his head as she licked and sucked his shaft. She moaned and the vibration went down to his balls. Which she didn't neglect, not at all. She let go of his cock and rolled his balls in her palm, lapping at the sensitive skin. No other woman had done that to him, and he realized he'd really been missing out.

Alex pulled back and blew on the head of his wet cock. He jerked at the sensation and she grinned before taking him back to her throat.

Her hair was down now, falling out of her ponytail long ago, so he gathered it up and held it loosely in a fist at the back of her head. He didn't pull or push, but he wanted a view of those gorgeous eyes watching him, those full red lips wrapped around him.

He wanted to remember this moment back when he was in his sterile apartment all alone in the city. He'd remember this moment. Under the stars. With Alex Dawn.

And that's what put him over the edge. Alex didn't pull back, swallowing everything he had until he was a wrung-out mess lying on dried leaves and twigs.

He was now about 50 percent sure he was never getting up and they'd find his skeleton and remnants of his belt, proving he'd wasted away here with his pants down.

But Alex—God, she was perfect—saved him from that fate as she pulled his pants back to rights then crawled up his body and lay on his chest.

He closed his eyes and ran his fingers up and down her back. He was so tired. Of everything. The rush and the next big thing and always, always searching for what made him happy.

This moment. This moment made him happy. For once in his life, he wasn't glancing at his watch, at his calendar, looking to see what was next, always what was next.

Because he didn't want what was next.

He wanted now. With Alex.

But it wasn't going to last forever. Eventually he noticed a stick digging into his ribs and with a grumble he righted them so he was leaning against the tree trunk again, Alex between his legs.

He pressed a kiss to her temple and she sighed.

"I leave this week," he said, breaking the spell. He hated to do it but it had to be done. She needed a warning.

Her body stiffened slightly and then relaxed. "Okay."

He didn't know what to say now. "Should we call? Or—"

"Let's not do that," she said softly.

He nodded, unable to speak around this odd lump in his throat. How this little sprite of a woman—the last kind of woman he ever thought he'd fall for—had gotten under his skin, he didn't know. It was going to hurt to leave; he knew that now more than anything. "I'll have to break this cone of silence and tell you that I will miss you. So very much, Sprite. I can't explain to you, despite everything, just how much joy you've given me."

Her body tensed again. Then she slipped out of his arms, and he made a grab for her, but she wasn't leaving him. She turned around in her spot between his legs and faced him on her knees. Her eyes were a little wet, glittering in the light of the stars above. "I'm only going to say this once. Here. While I feel warm and safe and somewhat protected in the dark. But Posh, I . . ." She leaned closer, so he could smell her hair, so he could see every freckle on her pale skin. "I promised myself I wouldn't get my heart involved with another man. That I was done. Bachelor-ette for life. And as much as I don't want to admit this—Out loud, to myself, to you—my heart got involved with you. And it'll suck when you leave, but at least I know there are men like you. Who could care about someone like me."

"I care more than you know, Alex." He brushed her hair off her face as she blinked rapidly. "I—"

She kissed him. Which was probably a good thing, because he was about to say words that he couldn't take back. Words that would stick with them, that would change this even more than how it had already changed tonight.

So it was better this way. He said the words with his lips and his tongue and his roaming hands. They made out like teenagers, knowing it wouldn't go further than kisses and some mild groping. They didn't need more, not after what they'd done and the words they'd said. The words they hadn't said.

THEY WALKED BACK to his car holding hands, and as Spencer drove her to her apartment, Alex stared out the window. "So, what's next for you. I mean, in New York?"

"Well, as long as everything goes well here, I should get my promotion."

"What would the promotion mean?"

"Well, it'd be more responsibility."

"Would you still travel a lot?"

"I'd still travel, but not as much. I used to be a hotel manager. That's what I did right out of college for Royalty

Suites. And I liked it, but I was plucked out of that by my boss now—Penny's dad—and I've been doing this ever since."

"So you want this promotion?"

"I…" Did he? "It's the next step in my career. It's more money." That he didn't need. "A more important title."

Alex was staring blankly at him. "But is it what you want?"

"I…"

"Yes or no, Posh. I don't need a fucking thesis on it."

He looked at her sharply. "That was a little uncalled for, wasn't it?"

She gritted her teeth and looked away. "Sorry."

"I wish things were different—"

"No. I don't. This is good. We'll leave each other before it turns sour, because long distance will never work." She turned to him. "I'd love to have one relationship in my life that I didn't have to steal out of in the middle of the night, okay?"

What the hell was that prickle in his eyes? Shit. He swallowed, but his throat felt tight, his mouth dry. "Yeah, Sprite."

While looking out the window, she said quietly, "Good luck." But he wasn't sure how much she meant it.

He wasn't sure so much anymore either.

Chapter Fourteen

SPENCER STARED AT his hotel room phone, biting his lip and jiggling his leg. He'd last spoken to his dad almost a year ago at Christmas.

And even then the conversation had been short and filled with awkward silences.

He didn't know what it was, that today he wanted to hear his father's voice. Rubbing his chest where the fox tattoo lay beneath his shirt, he remembered as a kid when he'd wanted to do nothing but impress his father. He'd learned his father wasn't someone who was impressed easily, not even by his only kid.

Spencer didn't know if he was a painful reminder of the wife his father lost or what, but he'd never been what his father wanted. At least, that's how he'd been made to feel.

So he'd run away. From everything that had been home to him, and hadn't he really been running ever since? He'd never found home again.

And it wasn't until last night, sitting under the stars with Alex in his arms, that he had felt like putting down roots. Settling.

He wasn't sure what that would mean. He was here on an ever-renewing work visa so he had to keep working. He couldn't up and quit and wander around aimlessly in the United States.

Blowing out a breath, he picked up his phone and dialed the number to his father's shop. It would be in the afternoon there, probably around one of his father's dozen smoke breaks.

After a series of clicks, there was finally ringing and Spencer tapped his fingers on the ink blotter of the hotel desk.

"Red Fox Auto," a gruff voice answered, followed by a loud exhale.

Yep, smoking. "How many fags has it been already today, Pop?"

There was a pause. "Get off my arse."

Spencer smiled.

"How are you?" his father asked.

"All right. Working. Uh, in a town in Maryland."

"Where's that?"

"East Coast."

His dad grunted. He'd never been to the United States and said he never had the desire to. And Spencer hadn't been back for a couple of years. He wondered what his father looked like now. If his hair was completely white now. If it was thinning. If that spare tire around his gut had grown. He sighed. "Did you care that I didn't stay?"

"What are you on about?"

"Did you care that I left? Or did you want me to stay and work at the garage?" He'd always thought his father didn't care either way.

Another pause, this one longer, punctuated by a series of harsh coughs that made Spencer cringe. " 'Course I cared."

"Yeah?"

"Always thought you'd be working beside me, but didn't want you to do it because you felt like you had to. You were…eh…smarter." He drew out the word, with a little bitterness. "Like your mum. Always thought you'd leave and be happier that way."

"Do you ever…wish you had left?"

"No." The answer came quick and sharp. "I'm lucky. Knew where I belonged right away, and that's here. Sometimes it takes people their whole lives to figure out where the hell they belong."

"But you don't think I belonged there?"

"Not when you were eighteen. Now? Maybe. I don't think you belong in that fancy city of yours, though, either." There was a banging sound and his father cursed at someone before speaking to Spencer again. "You think you figured out where you belong yet?"

"I don't know."

"This have to do with a woman?"

Spencer hesitated. "It might."

His dad grunted. "That'll do it. Bring her 'round sometime. Gotta run." And then he hung up.

Spencer stared at the phone, then began to laugh. There really was no one like his father. He'd spent a lot of energy when he was younger hating him, but that had been the result of a lot of miscommunication and teenage angst.

He stared at the phone in its cradle, thinking he was glad as hell he called. And he was still laughing when there was a knock at the door of his room.

He opened it and Penny walked past him into the room, wrinkling her nose at the clothes he'd left on the floor. He rolled his eyes, picked them up, and threw them into a chair. "Better?"

"I thought you liked tidy."

"It's a hotel room, and we're checking out soon, right?"

She fiddled with a half-full soda bottle on the desk. "Yes, we are."

"Why are you acting odd? Is there something wrong?"

Penny sat down on the end of his bed and Spencer frowned, taking a seat in the desk chair. Her shoulders were tense, which was really the only indication she was nervous. Penny tended to face things head-on. She met his gaze. "The team back in New York liked Nick's proposal."

Spencer stared at her, frozen.

"It's a good location, within walking distance of a convenience store. It's visible and the lot is cheaper."

Spencer finally got his jaw to unhinge. "Wait, what are you talking about? My report was perfect. I scoured this town—"

"Nick mentioned that your report may have been colored by your…personal life."

Spencer rose so fast that the chair slammed into the desk and Penny jolted. Through gritted teeth, he said, "Tell me he didn't say that."

She swallowed, her complexion a little white. Spencer knew he was towering over her, his body radiating fury, but he couldn't seem to calm himself.

"I didn't know he was going to do it," she said. "And for the record, I disagree with him, but this isn't a dictatorship and—"

He ran a hand through his hair and strode to the window, staring out at the pool below, his mind on overdrive as he tried to sort through the issue while also working to control his temper.

When Penny spoke again, her voice was softer. "The decision isn't final, but we will be moving forward with inquiries to buy the Payton land. If those are…unsuccessful, then we will resort to the location you recommended."

He closed his eyes and banged his forehead on the window. He knew how persuasive his company's lawyers could be. They weren't crooked, but they sure struck a shrewd deal.

He thought about the first time he saw Alex, when she stood in front of the garage, tire iron in her hand, blue eyes bright.

It'd been him who had brought Royalty to this town, who'd told his company to build here. He'd brought this down upon the head of Alex and the only family she'd ever known. He knew for a fact that his relationship with her hadn't clouded his judgment, but fucking Nick would use anything he could to get his way. "Shit," Spencer whispered.

A hand landed on his shoulder and he shrugged it off. A heavy sigh came from behind him, but he ignored her, because his chest hurt and all he wanted to do was get in his car and drive far, far away. For a second he thought about leaving without telling Alex, but that would be the coward's way out. He had to do something, even if it cost him everything.

Maybe he could go down to Payton and Sons. Warn Alex. But that seemed ill-advised. What, would she forgive him just because he gave her a heads-up? No, no way. She'd still blame him. She'd still hate him. She'd asked for them to part ways with happy memories, and now they'd be tinged with betrayal.

"Shit," he said again.

"Look, that shop is old anyway. They'd get money to rebuild and—"

He whirled around and pinned her with a glare. "You don't know these people."

"Oh and you do?" she said through narrowed eyes. "You know all about them after sleeping with Alex for a couple of weeks?"

He pointed a finger at her. "That was a little low."

Color stained her cheeks. "Sorry, I shouldn't have said that. I like Alex too, but this is business."

He shook his head. She didn't understand. "I know these people, and they don't care about a fancy garage or anything like that. That shop has been there for forty years, and it's going to take an act of God for the patriarch of that family to give it up. And I don't want him to be pressured and hassled. I want to leave here with them happy and healthy, knowing that a hotel will be built on land that won't affect them, and that hotel will create much-needed jobs for this town. That's what they want. And that's what I want."

"We don't always get what we want, Spence," Penny said softly.

"What does that mean?"

She lifted her chin higher. "There's no deeper meaning. It's a fact of life."

Spencer was done keeping his mouth shut about her husband. "Well, Nick's not getting this, Penny. He's not. It's like he's spent his whole marriage to you proving he is a better husband to you than I would have been. When's that going to stop? When's he going to realize we're not in competition?"

She pressed her lips together and kept silent.

Spencer wondered why Penny found herself in these relationships with men who couldn't hold a candle to her. "Penny, I know you love Nick. And I know I'm sticking my nose somewhere that it doesn't belong, but can you honestly say your marriage is okay? That Nick is the one for you?"

Her top teeth peeked out to nibble on her bottom lip. "When we first met, I thought he was just competitive, but…"

"But what?"

"But now I'm starting to think he's insecure." She shook her head. "I don't know. I can't make any decisions right now."

Spencer sighed, thinking the similarities between Penny and Alex were more than he had previously thought. Both were strong women who couldn't seem to find a man who appreciated that. Except him, maybe. His heart ached. "I'm sorry to bring it up."

"No, it's okay," she said softly. "You've always been honest with me. I wouldn't want you to change now."

Spencer glanced at the door. "Where's Nick now?"

"He said he was going to the park to go running."

Spencer glanced outside. It was drizzling. "In this weather?"

Uncertainty crossed Penny's face.

Spencer's gut rolled. "Penny?"

"That's what he said." Her voice shook a little now.

And that was all he needed. He grabbed his coat and was out the door, Penny at his heels. He'd be damned if Nick got to the Paytons first.

Chapter Fifteen

ALEX WIPED HER forehead, leaned her elbows on the front of the car, and glanced at the clock on the wall of the garage. It was about half an hour from her lunch break, but her stomach was already growling.

She was starting to get a little *hangry*, evidenced by her complete irritation at Gabe. Which wasn't fair. He was trying to focus, but the guy had a worse attention span than Violet.

Brent was in his bay, muttering to himself as he replaced a rusted muffler. Jack was in the office eating already and Cal was replacing a serpentine belt.

She was doing an inspection, which wasn't necessarily hard, but there were steps to follow that Gabe needed to be aware of. Which he wouldn't be, because right now he was sneaking food to Honeybear, who sat at his feet.

"Brent, I thought I told you not to bring Honeybear to work anymore," Alex huffed.

He looked up from his task. "Huh? She never bothers anyone."

"It's not her, it's *him*." She pointed at Gabe. "He can't handle having a dog here."

"Hey!" Gabe protested. "I can handle it!"

Alex raised her eyebrows at him.

He scrunched his lips to the side and in a small voice said, "Okay, maybe not."

She rolled her eyes. "Ignore the dog so we can get this over with so I can eat, okay? I'm starving."

"Oh, man!" Gabe's eyes light up. "Let's get burritos. I can take the order and pick it up."

"Gabe," Brent said sharply. "We're not paying you to take burrito orders. We're paying you to learn car shit."

"I *am* learning car shit."

"Then quit talking about burritos!"

"Will you all shut up?" Cal growled.

That did the trick. Alex and Gabe dutifully ducked their heads. Out of the corner of her eye, she saw Brent mimicking Cal and tossing him the finger behind his back. She hid her smile.

Ten minutes later, a car pulled into the parking lot and a man got out. He wore slacks and a button-down shirt with a hooded jacket to protect himself from the rain. Alex squinted at him, because he looked familiar. As he drew closer to the office, she recognized Nick, Spencer's coworker. She couldn't remember the guy's last name, but he was the one Cal had warned her about.

She glanced at Cal, who was watching the guy with a steel-eyed glare.

The man ignored them, expensive shades firmly over his eyes. He walked into the office, and even Honeybear was on high alert, her ears swiveling, her body tense.

Cal swallowed and carefully put away his tools, then walked into the office.

She heard Jack's gravelly voice as the door shut behind Cal.

Brent had stopped his work too, and stood with his hands on his hips, staring at the door, a frown on his face. Brent rarely had a frown on his face, and unease crawled down Alex's spine.

Did this have something to do with her? And Spencer? Maybe his relationship with her was against the rules of his job. But surely, he would have told her that, right?

"Brent," she said, but he shook his head and made his way toward the office.

"Cal doesn't like that guy," he said. "And he's a good judge of character. I'm going in there to see what's going on."

She dropped her tools, told Gabe to go ahead and get burritos, and then followed Brent into the office.

As soon as he opened the door, Jack's booming voice hit them like a wall. "I can't believe you're standing here in front of me spouting that bullshit. You think I'm dumb?"

Alex peeked from behind Brent to see Nick standing with his hands on his hips in the middle of the office, Jack in front of him with his arms crossed over his chest. Cal stood behind the counter, his gaze darting between the two of them, lips thinned into a white line.

Something brushed her hand, and she looked down to see Honeybear, who'd slipped into the office behind her.

She dug her fingers into the dog's fur, to ground herself, because the air was thick with tension and anger and a whole lot of distaste.

"I think," Nick said, "you won't know a good opportunity when you see it, so I wanted to make sure you listen to the whole offer."

"What's going on?" Brent asked, widening his stance.

Jack jerked his chin toward Nick. "This asshole wants to buy our land."

"Our land?"

"Yeah, this land. Right here. Where I've worked and sweated and bled for forty years. He thinks we want something fancy, isn't that right?"

Alex was having trouble keeping up. Buy their land?

"Buy our land for what?" Brent asked.

Nick's gaze shifted to him. "For a Royalty Suites. The lot behind this shop is perfect, but we'd also like this land too."

Alex sucked in a breath. Spencer had told her they were building out by MacMillan Investments. Not here. Had he been lying? She couldn't move or speak, stung by betrayal so sharp, she wondered why she wasn't bleeding. She reached in front of her, gripping Brent's belt, needing as many anchor points as she could get. Because, she wasn't alone, thank God. Nick was facing off against three Paytons. He didn't know them. He didn't know that he'd have better luck ripping down this building with his bare hands than trying to convince a Payton to do something he didn't want to do.

Brent leaned back a little into her touch, like he knew she needed it, and honed in on the enemy. "You...broke bread with us and now you want to buy our land out from under us? Seriously? That doesn't take balls, man. That takes no brain."

Nick wasn't backing down. "You haven't heard the offer yet," he insisted. "Royalty Suites lawyers will be in touch soon."

Alex's mind spun. Why was Nick here and not Spencer? Why hadn't Spencer given her a heads-up?

"Fuck your lawyer," Jack growled. "I ain't moving my shop until I'm dead. And if my boys move it when I'm dead, I'm coming back from the grave to haunt their asses."

"Which means we sure as hell aren't moving because he's bad enough when he's alive," Brent muttered.

Alex managed a small smile. Nick wasn't smiling, and now his gaze shifted to Alex. She dropped her hand from Brent's jeans and tilted her chin up. Nick's eyes narrowed. "Finally realizing you were just something to pass the time, huh? Like Spencer would ever have real feelings for someone like you."

A lot of things happened at once then. Honeybear growled. Alex and Brent surged forward. Cal hollered, but Jack beat them all. In seconds, he had Nick sandwiched between the wall and his big chest. He didn't put his hands on him, but it was clear he wanted to, because his fingers were curled into tight fists at his sides.

For the first time, Nick looked a little alarmed. "You touch me, and I'll press charges," he said, but his trembling voice gave him away.

Jack smiled, an eerie smile that was all teeth. "You think I give a fuck? You think I don't know the captain of the local police? You think any of them are gonna give a shit if some stuck-up New Yorker gets a black eye?"

"They probably wouldn't mind a bloody nose either," Brent said.

"I'm sure they'd even look past a broken arm," Cal said nonchalantly.

Alex was vibrating. The only thing holding her back from not running to Nick and swinging her fists was Honeybear at her side and Brent's hand clamped on her arm.

Nick looked less certain now, although he clung to his bravado like it was a life preserver, tilting his chin up and refusing to look away from Jack's glare.

The fury inside Alex was building now, and her hackles were raised. This was her family, this was her livelihood, and while they couldn't take this land without Jack's consent, this was still a threat. Spencer's company wanted the very soil she stood on and he'd neglected to tell her that while they made love under the stars.

Fuck him. And fuck Nick. And fuck all hotels. Fuck the whole goddamn city of New York. She blinked rapidly as the pain swelled in her chest.

This was just like Robby all over again. A man reeling her in and then changing who he was. At least Robby had done it to her face. Spencer had done it behind her back. He'd pretended to be the white knight. A savior. When all along, he'd known that everything she held dear was under attack.

Her teeth pulled back into a snarl and, while she wasn't a violent person, she envisioned her fist slamming into Nick's face.

She opened her mouth to defend herself, her honor, but screeching tires outside the shop drew their attention.

SPENCER SAW NICK'S car in the parking lot of Payton and Sons and wanted to throw up.

"What's Nick doing here?" Penny muttered, her brow furrowed.

He loved Penny but he hated this about her, how she seemed to not see what kind of person Nick was. She loved him unconditionally, and Spencer often wondered what their relationship was like behind closed doors.

He couldn't think about that now, not while he squinted through the drizzle into the dirty windows to the office. He saw several people in there, so he jumped out of the car and jogged to the front door, Penny at his heels.

When he opened the door, he stepped inside and stopped abruptly.

Jack had Nick pressed against the wall. Cal was standing behind the counter, shoulders tensed, and Alex and Brent were in front of the other office door that led into the garage, Honeybear at Alex's side.

They all were looking at him, and they all looked downright pissed off.

Nick had already brought the tornado, and now he was going to have to clean up the mess. He held his hands up, palms out. "Look—"

"Fuck you." Brent pointed a finger at him. "And I'd say fuck you to Nick's wife too, but I was told not to swear at women. But you all came to this town and acted like our friends and then did all this shit behind our backs. And frankly, we don't like you very much."

"Good speech, Brent," Cal said.

Brent rolled his shoulders. "Thanks."

Spencer looked at Alex pleadingly, but her face was blank. His heart ached and he took a step forward, but Jack turned away from Nick, effectively freezing Spencer where he stood. Spencer licked his lips and tried again, knowing he needed to speak to Alex privately soon, but right now he wanted to defuse the situation. "I'm not sure what Nick told you, but whatever he said was out of line. This is completely against our policy to—"

"Fuck your policy," Jack said.

Spencer took a deep breath to calm his own anger. The Paytons clearly used *fuck* a lot when they were angry. He didn't blame them.

He looked to Alex again, hoping maybe she'd speak up, maybe she'd call off the three guard dogs and the real actual canine at her feet, but again, he was met with a blank look. Alex had checked out. *Shit.*

Spencer changed tactics and looked at Nick. "I can't believe you did this."

"You're the one who didn't tell your girlfriend we've been looking at this land for months," he said.

"Nick!" Penny spat.

"Correction," Spencer said. "*You* were looking at this location. I crossed it off my list and recommended the one I told Alex about." He turned to her again. "Remember I told you that, Alex? The land over by MacMillan Investments."

She didn't move or acknowledge that he spoke to her.

He sighed and rubbed his forehead, then looked at Cal, thinking he was the one who was the most reasonable out of the three men. "I'm sorry. I didn't know Royalty was going to seriously consider this location. And Nick had no right coming down here to talk to you about it instead of waiting on the proper channels."

Cal seemed to think on that. Then he leaned on the counter. "Apology not accepted. Now I'd like the three of you to leave before I call the police. As of now, you're trespassing."

Spencer could absolutely not get arrested. Not as a British citizen in the United States on a work visa. He swallowed and nodded. "Okay, I—I *am* sorry. For what it's worth."

Cal met his gaze steadily. "It ain't worth shit."

Spencer ducked his head, listening as Penny left, Nick's arm brushing his as he walked past him. It took all his strength not to reach out and strangle the guy.

"Please, can I just speak to Alex?" Spencer asked.

Brent turned his head to her. She looked up at him, shook her head once, and with the action, Spencer's heart cracked.

Brent shrugged. "Her choice and she said no. Time for you to leave."

"Alex," Spencer whispered, hoping to appeal to her, but she'd turned her head, purposefully staring away from him. He wanted to see her eyes again, the bright blue shining with happiness, not unshed tears of anger.

"You got ten seconds to get out the door," Jack said, taking another step toward Spencer.

He backed up, his hand on the door behind him. "Alex, I can explain. You know where to find me if you want to hear it—Room 333." And then he was out the door, because Jack was coming for him and he knew his time was up.

Out in the parking lot, Penny and Nick were facing off. Spencer had never seen her this furious. And Nick looked more scared now in a fight with his wife than he had back there with six feet four inches of pissed-off mechanic.

"This is so out of line, Nick, I don't even know where to start," Penny was saying.

Spencer wanted words with Nick too. But they needed to get off the property. And he needed time alone to deal with what he'd just lost. "Guys, we need to get in the cars and leave."

They ignored him. "We have proper steps for a reason," Penny said. "They might have been persuaded to sell, but now they'll just dig their heels in on principle. I cannot believe you!"

Nick's nostrils flared. "They'll see the money and roll over. They always do."

Spencer shook his head. Not these people.

"I'll have to tell my father you did this, you realize that, right?"

"He doesn't need—"

"Yes, he does need to know. You accused Spencer of taking this entire project personally, but what the hell was that back there? You've been taking this whole thing personally—this competition between the two of you—and you forgot to remember these are real people's lives we're affecting."

"I didn't forget that," Nick said.

"You did," Penny shot back. "You did. And I don't know if I can deal with this."

Nick took a step forward with his hand out. "What does that mean?"

She wrenched open the door to Spencer's car. "I think you know." She turned to Spencer. "Let's go." Then she sat inside and slammed the door behind her.

Spencer wasted no time rounding the car and getting into the driver's seat. When they pulled out of the parking lot, Nick was still standing in the same spot, staring after their car.

"I hope they do call the police on him. I hope he gets arrested." Penny was mumbling beside him, staring out the window, lost in her anger.

Spencer didn't respond. He didn't have the energy. And that told him something, that he couldn't give a shit anymore about the job. He knew Nick would never get the promotion now, not once Penny told her father what he'd done. But Spencer didn't care. Not one bit. For the first time in a long while, his thoughts weren't about his job. They were about the little mechanic in Tory who'd stolen his heart. Who'd shown him there was more to life than money and a successful career.

And he'd repaid her by betraying her with the very thing he was supposed to love—his job.

He'd give it all up if he thought it would get her back, but that was wishful thinking. She wasn't a pawn to be moved around in a game.

She was Alex—smart and fun and scarred.

And he'd reopened those wounds, hadn't he?

He slammed his hand down on the steering wheel, startling Penny. But she didn't say anything, just offered a comforting hand on his arm.

But he didn't want her arm, or her sad, reassuring smile.

He wanted Alex. And he was pretty sure she was lost to him forever.

Chapter Sixteen

You know where to find me.

Like that was going to happen. Like Alex was going to approach him on his turf, his hotel room.

The only thing that made her feel slightly better was that this time, she wasn't running. No way. This time, her broken heart made her even more determined to stay. Now he was running, back to where he came from with his tail between his legs. Back home where he probably had some posh apartment. And a house cleaner. And a chef.

She had maintained a cool facade at the shop but in her apartment later that night, she felt anything but cool. Her whole body hurt from tensing it all day, listening for the rumble of Spencer's Mercedes, thinking he would come back to finish what he started. To beg her again for her attention.

Fuck that.

He'd looked crushed. Heartbroken. But maybe he was a good actor. She didn't think he'd gotten close to her because he had ulterior motives for the shop's land. That was ridiculous. But it dug under her skin that he hadn't told her or warned her or done something. If she meant to him what he said she did, why hadn't he come clean?

Maybe she'd only been something to pass the time. Maybe he didn't care that much and he only felt guilty for hurting her, not sorry for losing her.

She asked him for one thing, for this relationship to end peacefully, and that'd been shot to shit with one visit from that Nick asshole.

The doorbell rang and Alex froze. It was either Spencer or Ivy. She sat on her bed quietly, wondering what she should do. Then her phone beeped a text message.

Answer your door, jerk.

Alex smiled. It was Ivy. She ran to her door and flung it open and then she had an armload of her sister, the first person to ever be there for her.

Ivy rubbed her back. "Brent told me what happened."

"I don't really want to talk about it."

Ivy pulled back. "Are you sure?"

"Look, it's not a big deal."

Ivy didn't look convinced.

Alex picked at her fingernails. "I'd really rather talk about something else."

"Okay."

"Ivy?"

"Yeah?"

Alex touched her hair where it lay in front of her shoulder. "Thanks for knowing I needed you here."

Ivy rolled her eyes, but her cheeks pinked, like she was pleased. "Duh, you're my sister. We have that mental link or whatever. So I brought those mini doughnuts you like and some wine. Wanna get drunk?"

Alex smiled. "Best idea ever."

BY THE TIME Alex rolled out of bed the next morning, she had a hangover and she was still thinking about Spencer.

Brent had shown up to take Ivy home last night, while she giggled and told him she liked his face and his butt as he dragged *her* intoxicated butt out the door.

Designated drivers were great.

Alex, however, was alone, and now that the wine was no longer making her happy, she was right back to being miserable.

Even Robby hadn't had this effect on her. When she left him, she'd been plagued with fear and regret for staying with him for as long as she did. She'd never been filled with longing. She'd never missed him. At least, not the way he'd been in the end. She'd missed having someone, but that certainly wasn't Robby.

Now, she didn't just miss having someone, she missed having a very certain someone. She missed Spencer. His voice and that accent. The sound of his car. The way he touched her, the way she could touch him. The whole package. She missed him.

That asshole.

By the time she managed some coffee and some food, she'd made up her mind to go to his hotel room. Because that wasn't his turf. It was her turf. This whole damn town was her turf. She needed answers and she needed closure and until she got it, she wasn't sure she could move on.

She pulled on a pair of jeans and a T-shirt, then tugged a hoodie over top. She wanted to be comfortable, dammit. But, of course, she smeared her trusty red lipstick on her lips and lined her eyes with eyeliner and applied mascara.

When she looked in control—even though she felt nothing like it inside—she got in her truck and made her way to the Tory Inn.

When she pulled into the parking lot, she silently conceded that the town could use another hotel. There were a couple of cracks along the foundation. One window was boarded up. Okay, so it was worse than Alex had thought. She had a little chuckle thinking about Penny staying here, then hopped down out of her truck.

She didn't bother stopping at the front desk. She remembered Spencer's room number—333. She rode the elevator by herself, which had no tinny Muzak.

The lights in the hallway were dim, the carpet a little stained and ripped in places. When she reached the door of Spencer's room, she noticed the second three was a little crooked. She focused on that, took a deep breath, and knocked.

Nothing.

No sound at all.

Not running water, not footsteps, not the TV. She knew, because she pressed her ear to the door.

Her stomach rolled uneasily. Had he left? Like an idiot, she hadn't even looked around for his car in the parking lot. Her palms began to sweat, and her knees shook. No, no. This wasn't supposed to happen. This was supposed to be her big grand *fuck you*. Where she'd look composed and kinda pretty and she'd tell him off. And now—

"Alex?"

Her name didn't come from in front of her, where she still stared at the closed door. It came from her side. She turned slowly to see Spencer standing in the hallway, jacket on, holding his bags, key card in his hand.

They stared at each other for a moment. He blinked rapidly at her, like he wasn't sure he was seeing things right. "I, um, was about to leave actually, then realized I left my phone charging in the room." He held up his key card. "Want to, um, come in?"

She nodded, wishing he didn't look so damn good in his suit and coat, so posh with his dark hair slicked back, his jaw stubbled.

A silver watch peaked out from beneath his shirt.

The hot British fucker.

Spencer took a step toward her and she stepped back, well away so he had room to unlock the door. He frowned a little at the distance between them, but she didn't apologize. That distance was his fault. Not hers.

But yet as he opened the door and motioned for her to go in ahead of him, she wasn't so sure she had the upper hand.

Although she didn't think he did either.

It was like they were always destined to be completely lost around one another. Since this would be the last time she ever saw him, she didn't dwell on it, and walked into his hotel room.

HE NEVER LEFT his possessions behind. He traveled so much that he had a system to prevent things like this from happening. But as he heard Alex's breathing near him, he was so grateful for whatever made him leave his phone charging on a small table by the window.

The funny thing was, she was the reason he left his phone. He'd been so preoccupied with his thoughts, with everything that had happened the day before, that his entire system had been off.

He'd cursed it when he realized in the elevator that he'd left it. And now he was praising it.

He dropped his bags on the bed and turned around as he took his jacket off and threw it on top of his bag.

Alex stood near the door and watched him steadily, her hands shoved into the front pocket of her sweatshirt, her hood pulled up over her head. It shaded her eyes, made the blue irises sharper, the red of her lips brighter.

She looked beautiful, even just standing there in her boots, jeans, and sweatshirt.

But damn, she was here. She was *actually* here, and she wasn't screaming at him or throwing things or clawing his eyes out, so he figured even if she heard him out and then turned and walked out of his life, at least they had closure.

Which still made his chest ache.

He took a deep breath and said the only thing that mattered. "I'm sorry."

She stared at him, and didn't move or say a word. So he figured that was his cue to keep talking. Which he did, haltingly. "Yes, the Payton land was on my list, but I immediately discounted it. I didn't recommend it at all and, in fact, it was the last on my list. I hadn't known but my boss pitted Nick and me against each other for a promotion, and Tory was the competition site. Nick was in favor of the Payton location and said so, but I was…confident that I'd win. Overconfident. I'm good at my job, Alex. That's why I have the money I do. That's why I have no life but this job. So I didn't tell you because I didn't think it was important. I didn't think my boss would agree with Nick in any way and…" He blew out a breath and hiked his hands on his hips. "I was wrong. I was wrong, and Nick is an asshole, and I'm sorry for that. I'm so, so sorry."

She blinked at him. "So you knew."

"I did know. And looking back, I should have told you. I didn't because of my ego, and that's a mistake I'll have to live with."

She looked away before meeting his gaze again. "Okay."

"That's all you have to say?"

She looked like she wanted to say more as she bit her lip. He wanted to touch her, one last time. Run his fingers through her hair, over the soft skin of her cheek. "This was ending anyway. So now it ends."

The finality of her statement cut him like a saber slash across the chest. "But you didn't want it to end this way, and I didn't either."

She came alive then, as color rose to her cheeks and her hands dropped to her sides and gripped her thighs. "Of course I didn't want it to end this way. For once I wanted to be right about a man, to know for myself that my internal meter for finding men wasn't stuck on *asshole*. I know it was selfish to want this. But I gave everything once to a man who didn't deserve it. I was so close to doing it all again, but with a man who does deserve it. Or so I thought. Was I wrong?"

He should end it now, as a gift to her. Tell her that he didn't deserve it. And maybe he didn't. He wasn't the best man. But he knew a couple of things for certain and she should know those things. And even though he would be laying it all out there, baring his heart, he didn't want her to think she chose the wrong man. Again.

So he stepped closer, close enough that she had to lift her chin to meet his eyes. His sprite didn't take a step back, though, no way. Her eyes, while wet, were blazing, and her jaw was set. He admired her even more for that.

"I don't know if I deserved it. All I know is that you deserve a man who loves and respects you, and that was me. That *is* me, Alex. Every part of me loves every part of you. And even though this won't work, even though I know we don't have a future, I can't leave with you thinking you gave your heart to someone who didn't cherish it. I'll remember all my life that *I* was worthy enough to have a few weeks of your time."

She was cracking, he could see it by the wobble in her lower lip, by the drop of moisture threatening to spill over her bottom lashes. But then she dropped her gaze, sniffed, and wiped her sleeve across her nose.

He stepped back, giving her space, even though every part of him wanted to pull her into his arms. She wouldn't want that, though. Every line of her tense body screamed, *Don't touch.*

It hurt him to listen.

When she looked up, there were a couple of tear tracks on her cheeks and her nose was red. Her lip still trembled but she pieced herself together before his eyes. "Thank you," she said. "Thank you for this ending. This one here, with those words you just said. It's a good ending. A good ending to the best couple of weeks I've ever had."

And then, with jerky steps, she stood in front of him, and he bent down. Her lips grazed his cheek and then she was at the door, opening it up, before looking back at him over her shoulder. "Have a safe trip back to New York, and have a happy life, Spencer. You gave me mine back."

And then she was gone.

Chapter Seventeen

ALEX SQUINTED UP at the sun as she stood leaning
against the wall of the back of Payton and Sons Automotive, knee bent, one booted foot resting on the brick. She
tapped the bottle of cold soda against her jean-clad leg.

She'd seen a robin the other day, the first indication
that spring was well on its way. She was glad for that.
It'd been a hard winter with lots of snow. The shop had
been filled with cars that wouldn't start, alignments that
had been wrecked by snow banks, and lots of grumpy
customers.

The good thing about that was Gabe had the chance
to learn. A lot. And he was coming along well. Once he
focused, he really focused. It just took him a long time to
get there.

Jack said he was proud of her patience with Gabe and
that was why he'd asked her to teach him, because Brent
or Cal probably would have killed Gabe. She'd smiled at

that, happy she had a skill the others didn't, happy that she was wanted.

She leaned her head back against the wall and closed her eyes, enjoying the warmth on her face.

It'd been six months since Spencer had left. He hadn't contacted her, and she wondered every day how he was doing. She didn't want to wonder, but she couldn't stop herself.

They had heard from his company's lawyers. The negotiations—well, the lawyers called them that, but Jack called it harassment, because there was no negotiation on his end—were officially over a couple of weeks ago, when Jack said for the last time he wasn't selling. Construction apparently would start on a Royalty Suites near MacMillan Investments later that spring.

Even after she'd heard what Spencer had to say that afternoon in the hotel room, she'd clung stubbornly to her anger for months, comfortable seeing Spencer as the enemy rather than admitting how much she'd missed him.

When she'd left Robby, the bad times felt magnified, so all she could do was remember all the ways he hurt her. In fact, it was to the point she couldn't remember how she fell in love, just that she did, and he used that to hurt her.

But with Spencer, she hadn't been able to hold on to her anger for long. And she had definitely been furious. She'd felt betrayed and maybe a little like she'd been played for a fool.

As time passed, though, all she could do was remember all the good times they had, the way he smiled at her, talked to her, that night they held each other at River's Edge.

Her mind built up the good times so big that she knew nothing else would ever compare. Which should have told her something. About how what they had was real. Ill-fated, but real.

She thought about what Penny had said, that being on your own gave you time to learn to love yourself again. And that was what Alex had been focusing on. Now that her last relationship didn't make her nauseous, now that she wasn't haunted by it, her head was clearer. She remembered all her strengths—her job, her honesty, her loyalty. She spent time with her family, and she enjoyed the time she was alone. She'd even tried to learn how to cook. She hadn't been very successful at it, but she'd had fun failing.

She thanked Spencer often—in her head—for kick-starting her on the path she'd needed to love herself again.

She unscrewed the cap of her soda and tilted her head back, letting the sweet liquid fizz down her throat.

The sound of loud exhaust drew close and she wiped the back of her hand across her mouth, then tossed the empty bottle in a trash can. She wiped her hands to go back inside the shop when the exhaust grew closer.

She stopped and cocked her head, because there was something about that exhaust that was familiar.

Too familiar.

She waited for the dread to hit and it did, but at least she was prepared, and what surprised her was that the dread faded as quickly as it came, as a kind of serenity washed over her.

Serenity.

Ivy would laugh if Alex ever called herself serene, but that's exactly what she felt like, even as she saw the familiar head of her ex-boyfriend through the window of his Camaro. She had wondered when he'd find her. She'd been in the newspaper because of the battle over the land. There had been a shot of her standing outside the shop with Jack, right on the front page, her name in the caption. Robby wasn't a genius but he could use Google. She figured he might search her name and show up here.

She'd been right.

She walked around the corner of the building and watched him pull into the parking lot. It was another couple of minutes before he got out.

He looked about the same. Sandy-blond hair. Green eyes. A face that she'd once thought was so handsome but now filled her with…well, nothing really.

As he spotted her standing there, leaning against the wall with her arms crossed over her chest, his steps faltered a little and that was all she needed for her confidence to soar.

It'd been almost two years since she'd seen him.

He doesn't have power over me anymore.

That was why she couldn't be angry with Spencer anymore. It was because of him she'd found her power again. Her knowledge that she could be loved. Her knowledge that she loved herself.

And that was why, when Robby stood in front of her, his eyes narrowed as his gaze swept her body, she held her ground.

She knew Jack, Cal, Brent, and Gabe were inside the shop, but she didn't need them. In fact, she didn't want them. She could handle Robby herself.

"Hey, sweetheart, long time no see." Robby smiled. The charming smile stirred some memories back to when they first got together. What that smile didn't stir was affection.

"I'm not your sweetheart anymore," she said. "And it's been a long time on purpose. In fact, I think it's a little too soon to see you again."

Irritation flickered in his eyes before he smoothed it over. "You don't mean that."

"I do, Robby. I do very much. This is my place of business, and you aren't welcome."

He gazed up at the brick building with an expression of distaste. "Could use some new gutters."

"Thanks for your observation."

"Don't you think it's time to come home?"

She laughed at that, a loud outburst that made Robby jolt in surprise. "I am home. This shop is my home, and so is this town."

His jaw clenched and the familiar flush of his skin signaled his anger was rising. She didn't care this time. She wouldn't be scared. He leaned in and jabbed a finger at her chest. "Your home is with me."

A voice boomed from the back of the building. "Alex? Where'd you go? There's a cookie here that's labeled but my name is spelled wrong. Brent is spelled B-R-E-N-T, not A-L-E-X."

Alex rolled her eyes. "Don't touch my cookie."

"Ah, don't be like that," his voice came in answer. "Hey, where the hell are you?"

Robby's head whipped to the side as footsteps came around the corner. Brent stopped abruptly, holding a cookie that he'd already eaten half of. He stared at Robby, then Alex, then back to Robby. All traces of charming Brent were gone as soon as he took in their body language. "What's going on?"

"Who are you?" Robby asked. He looked at Alex. "Who's that guy?"

"I'm her coworker, and what I'd like to know is why you're standing that close to her, because she doesn't seem to like it, if you can't tell by how far she's craning her neck back to get away from you. Wanna step back, bro?"

Alex cleared her throat, figuring she should get this over with before he called the rest of the Payton cavalry. "This is Robby."

Brent's eyes widened immediately, then his silver eyes flashed. "Are you fucking kidding me? And you're here? At her work? That's not smart."

Robby hadn't ever been smart. And why she hadn't seen that from the beginning was her fault. Because even as another deep voice sounded, now from the front of the shop, Robby didn't back down. "This is between her and me. You're not needed here."

"I'm not needed here? Really?" Brent leaned against the wall beside Alex and took another bite of her cookie. "Huh. I dunno. I think I'm serving a real purpose. Go on, explain why you're here."

"Where the fuck did Alex go?" Jack's voice sounded closer now.

"Brent disappeared too." Oh great, Cal was with him.

Gravel crunched as the two rounded the corner and stopped dead at the sight of Robby. Cal's eyes took in the scene quickly, assessing, but Jack honed in on Robby immediately. "Step away from Alex."

Robby's green gaze lasered into Alex and his lip curled into a sneer. "I can see why they hired you now."

She didn't even answer him, because really, she didn't care what he thought. He could think she slept with every customer, for all she cared. It didn't matter anymore. He didn't matter. So she waved a hand and grabbed Brent's cookie, taking a bite. "Go on, Robby. Tell me more about my life."

She said his name on purpose, and she got the reaction she wanted when Cal surged forward at the sound of it and Jack cracked his knuckles.

Robby did one smart thing and stepped back, glancing around uneasily. But he wasn't done trying to convince her. "You didn't really mean to leave, right? We just needed a break. Come back, Alex. You know no one will love you like I did."

She swallowed her cookie and wiped the crumbs from her lip. "You're right, Robby, no one will. Because your love was fucked up, and it fucked me up for a long time. I'm now…finally…unfucked up. And I plan to stay that way. So good-bye. Good day. If I ever see you again, it'll be too soon."

She grabbed Brent's arm, wanting to make a graceful exit—a flouncing off—and he aided her, shooting a glare over his shoulder at Robby and then walking around the back of the building. As they turned the corner, she heard Jack say, "Alex told you the situation. Now you need to leave."

She didn't hear any more, because she didn't want to. She led Brent into the back room, where he watched her warily, probably thinking she was going to collapse or burst into tears.

But instead she threw her hands in the air, gave a loud whoop, and then shuffled her feet to imaginary celebration music in her head.

Brent laughed and began to clap as she danced, which was exactly what they were doing when Jack and Cal walked into the room, stopping dead at the sight.

Alex stopped dancing and smiled at them. "I did it. I fucking did it. I wasn't even scared, I was just annoyed. That asshole doesn't get to tell me what to do anymore."

Jack didn't seem as excited as she was. "How did he even know you were here?"

She shrugged. "Probably when I was in the newspaper."

His eyes narrowed. "Damn journalists."

"No, it's okay," Alex said. "Really, it's okay. It felt amazing to tell him to go to hell, to show him he didn't have control over me."

Brent threw an arm around her shoulders. "You really held your own. I'm proud of you."

She poked him in the ribs. "I'm proud of me too."

When Brent let her go, Cal was in front of her, and he pulled her into an awkward hug that she returned with vigor. He grunted when she squeezed. "I'm proud of you too."

Jack seemed reluctant to celebrate, his gaze darting to the door as if Robby was going to burst in any minute. Finally he sighed. "I don't like people threatening me or my business or my family."

Jack always chose his words carefully, so she didn't miss what he said. For the first time in a long time, the back of her eyes prickled. "Aw, Jack." She stepped forward and wrapped her arms around him but he stayed stiff, and huffed a little. She smiled against his chest.

When she let him go, his face was flushed. And then he clapped his hands and barked, "Back to work!"

He walked out and she grinned at his back. Yeah, everything was pretty good.

Now, if only she could forget about the British man who had thawed her heart. If only.

SPENCER FLIPPED UP the collar of his thin trench against the spring breeze and enjoyed the warmth of the sun on his face as he walked on the sidewalk of the meatpacking district in New York on his way to meet his boss.

The winter had lasted forever. And winter in New York sucked. Snow made everyone grumpy, and it seemed to turn gray as soon as it hit the ground. He'd found himself wondering what Tory looked like in the winter. He'd snuck peeks at their local newspaper online and smiled when he saw photos of local kids having a snowball fight, sled tracks on the hill in the background.

But it was spring now. And he'd avoided his boss long enough, as the negotiations for the Payton land finally ground to a halt.

Spencer was the victor, he guessed. Penny filed for divorce, and Nick resigned. Penny had showed up at his house and drank herself in a stupor. The only time he'd ever seen her drunk. She said she knew Nick had changed, that he wasn't whom she originally married, but she thought if she loved as hard and pure as she could for both of them, it would last.

Unfortunately, that hadn't been the case.

When she passed out, Spencer tucked her under a blanket on his couch, and they never spoke of it. The next time he saw her at work, she was poised as usual and said she was planning to be on her own for a while. She already had a weekend spa retreat planned with girlfriends and another vacation to the beach scheduled with her children. If Spencer was honest, he hadn't seen Penny this happy in a while. He was proud of her for standing on her own two feet. And he hoped Alex was doing the same thing, back in Tory.

Spencer pushed open the door to the Standard Hotel and went up the elevator to the patio overlooking the Hudson River.

Richard Moore sat at a table by himself, chin propped on his fingers, eyes gazing out at the water.

Spencer nodded to the waiter, who filled his water glass as he took a seat opposite his boss.

"Hello, Richard." Spencer shrugged out of his jacket and placed it on the back of his chair.

"Spencer." He pointed to a menu on the side of the table. Spencer held up a hand, indicating he wasn't hungry.

Richard's eyes narrowed slightly, then he nodded.

The waiter came over to take Spencer's order. "Just an iced tea, please."

"Unsweetened okay?"

"Yes."

Spencer focused back on Richard, who was watching him closely. Spencer cleared his throat. "Sorry to hear about Penny's marriage."

Richard's face didn't move. "Me too."

The waiter returned quickly and Spencer sipped his tea and waited.

The other man drummed his fingers on the table. "So I'm sure you've been waiting for months, but I'd like to officially offer you the promotion as the head of the new development team."

Spencer cracked a piece of ice between his molars. He knew this had been coming, and he'd thought long and hard about his answer. He'd practiced in front of the mirror, in the shower, in the car, how he would answer. Each time, he said something different. Each time, he decided something different.

Sitting here now, in what was quintessentially New York, the job he'd always wanted on the table in front of him on a silver platter, he couldn't imagine taking it.

He couldn't imagine staying here, working a job he no longer had the passion for. That wasn't fair to Richard, or his coworkers. And most of all, it wasn't fair to himself.

He cleared his throat. "I appreciate the offer of the promotion, but I'm going to have to decline."

Richard's face finally moved. His jaw worked and his eyebrows lifted slightly. "Excuse me?"

"I'm sorry, but I've decided I don't have the drive I used to for that job, and I don't think it's fair to anyone for me to take it."

Richard blinked at him, then his face changed, completely softening as he leaned forward and lowered his voice. "Spencer, is everything all right? Penny said some things happened on your last trip."

Things happened. That was a very simplistic way of saying it. "Yes, I'm okay. I'm scared to death, but I'm okay."

"So you're leaving Royalty Suites?" Richard asked. "I'd hate to lose you completely. I'll give you some time off, but is there another position I can offer you?"

Spencer smiled and shifted his gaze to the sun reflected off the water. He sighed and said, "Well, actually, there is..."

Chapter Eighteen

ALEX STEPPED OUT of her shower, wrapped one white towel around her body, and twisted another in her wet hair. She wiped the condensation off the mirror and squinted at her reflection. She needed her eyebrows waxed. And she should be wearing more moisturizer. She grabbed her lotion and smoothed it over her face, arms, chest, and legs.

As she finished up, her doorbell rang. She ran into her bedroom, glancing at the clock and frowning. Ivy was coming over to drop off a shirt she'd borrowed on her way out on a date with Brent, but she wasn't supposed to be here for another hour or two.

Alex didn't bother getting dressed as she padded to the front door in her bare feet and swung it open, saying, "Hey, you're early."

The last word was a whisper. Because it wasn't Ivy standing in front of her door. It was Spencer. Leslie Michael Spencer.

He wore a Henley with the sleeves rolled up to his elbows and a pair of dark jeans. He pushed his sunglasses up into his dark hair and dropped a bag he held at his side on the floor. "Um, I'm late actually. About six months too late." She clutched the towel knotted at her chest, realizing now she stood in front of him practically naked. He wasn't looking anywhere but her eyes, though. He held her gaze firmly, if a little hesitantly. "Hello, Alex."

Her mouth dropped open, and every word she tried to say dried up in her throat. He looked better than ever. More relaxed. Maybe a little more salt and pepper around his ears, but incredibly handsome nonetheless.

She'd convinced herself for months she was over him, but that clearly was a lie, because as he stood in front of her, all she wanted to do was fall into his arms.

His expression faltered a little. "May I…come inside?"

She nodded and stepped back, still clutching her towel, as he picked up his bag, walked through the door, and shut it behind him. He placed his bag on the floor at his feet.

They stood in her foyer staring at each other, and she scrunched her toes against the floor.

He licked his lips. "Please say something so I can gauge whether you are horrified to see me or not."

One word finally came out. "No."

"No what?"

"No, I'm not horrified."

"Can you give me a word in place of *horrified* then?"

He was here. In front of her. "Happy."

Spencer visibly softened. "Oh. Oh thank God." He gestured toward her living room. "Could we talk?"

Again with her muteness, because all she could do was nod, then turn around and take a seat on her couch. Spencer sat beside her, leaving a foot distance between them. He gripped the ends of the couch, then fidgeted his hands along the hem of his shirt, then dropped them back to his side.

"I had...things to say and now I'm not sure any of them will make sense and I..." He turned to her. "Frankly, all I want to do is look at you. All I've wanted to do for six months is look at you. I had to settle for a keychain."

She ducked her head and twisted the end of the towel on her legs.

"I'm sorry, do you want to go get dressed? I can wait."

She did, actually, because sitting here in her towel was making her body think weird things, and she needed at least some pants.

So she stood and held up a finger for one minute and ran to her bedroom. She quickly tugged on a pair of underwear and yoga pants, then threw on a tank top with a built-in bra. She twisted her hair up onto her head in a damp knot and then returned to the living room, where Spencer sat staring at the blank TV.

"Do you want some water? Something to eat?"

He startled. "Uh, actually, water would be nice. Thanks."

She grabbed two bottles from the fridge and handed one to him, then sat on the edge of the couch facing him, sitting cross-legged.

He took a drink with his eyes on her. "It's great to see you."

"You too."

"Are you still angry with me?"

The question was blunt, but she understood he wanted to know where he stood. She shook her head. "No."

"Because the hotel is being built elsewhere?"

She shook her head again. "No, I got over being mad at you long before that."

He cocked his head. "Really?"

"I…realized what you gave me in the fall was more important than what happened at the end. I tried to stay angry. I tried so hard. But I couldn't, not when I remembered everything that had been good about us."

"There's a lot of good about us, Sprite."

She didn't miss the tense change in his sentence. "I guess so, Posh." She squinted at him. "What are you doing here? I thought we agreed this…would end. Long distance wouldn't work with us."

"What if…" He licked his lips. "What if we didn't have to do long distance?"

"I'm not moving to fucking New York."

"I would never ask that of you. But what if I lived here?"

She stared at him. "What?"

"What if I changed jobs?"

"Changed jobs?"

He shifted closer to her now, and a warm hand settled on her knee, lightly. "I have the opportunity to take the job as the manager of the Royalty Suites in Tory when it opens. I'd live here." She opened her mouth to protest, to tell him that was a little presumptuous after they'd spent only a couple of weeks together, but he cut her off. "I didn't want to take the job without asking you first. What we had was…intense, and something we knew all along had an end date. I want to open it back up, and I didn't want to do that without your consent." He moved closer now, so that his thigh rested against her legs. "It's not just about you either, Alex. I'm tired of New York. Of the empty apartment, of the pace. I thought that's what I needed to be happy, to climb the infinite corporate ladder. But I fell in love with this town. The past six months I've missed it. The parks. Playing washers in backyards. Lying under the stars at River's Edge. And most of all, I missed you."

She leaned forward. "Let me get this straight. You're telling me you want to move here, work at the new hotel, and continue seeing me."

His lips twitched. "Maybe a little more than seeing you. I want to be with you."

"With me."

"Yes."

"You…could have your pick of women in New York—"

"I don't know about 'have my pick'—"

"And you want me. I'm what you want."

The muscles in his jaw bunched. "Yes, and don't insult the woman I love."

She laughed, a giddy feeling spreading through her limbs. "I'm not saying I'm not worth it. Because you showed me I am. I just want to make sure you know what you're getting into. I'm temperamental. I spend a lot of money on lipstick, and I smell like grease a lot."

"All things I've always wanted in a woman."

She shoved his shoulder. "You can't be serious about this. You want to move? Here?"

He nodded. "I'm dead serious. If you'll have me. If you want a posh British boyfriend."

She ducked her head and ran her fingers over his hand on her thigh. "What would your dad think of that?"

He gripped her chin and forced her to meet his gaze. "I haven't visited in a long time. I've called and we have awkward conversations, but that's it. With everything that I'd done, I didn't have anything to show for it. Anything to prove the man that I'd become, that I left everything behind for. But you…I think that if I showed up with you by my side, I'd have something for him to be proud of. That someone like you gives a fuck about someone like me."

"Ah, Spencer, you're making me cry." The tears were almost instant, spilling down over her bottom lashes as she pressed her lips to his. His hand slid along her cheek, to the back of her neck, as he reached his other arm around her back and hauled her across the couch into his lap. She straddled him and clutched his face as he deepened the kiss, his tongue tangling with hers, licking the back of her teeth, like he never wanted to separate.

She hadn't been with anyone since he'd gone, hadn't even wanted to, hadn't thought about it, her libido seeming to have fled when he did. But now it was back with a vengeance, lit up by the feel of him hard between her legs. She wanted skin. So much skin. She rucked up his shirt and slid her hands along his abs, up to his chest, and he helped her by taking off the garment and tossing it to the side. She ran her fingers over his tattoo, his nipples, as he moaned into her mouth and thrust his hips up as she ground down.

"I didn't imagine coming here and shagging you within minutes," he said breathlessly against her neck as she sucked on his earlobe.

She huffed. "Well, then you have a shitty imagination."

He laughed and grabbed her arms, pressing her into the couch on her back while he stretched out between her spread legs. She held her hands up as he pulled her tank top over her head and then cupped her breasts, sucking a nipple into his hot mouth. She arched her back, carving her fingers through his hair as he lapped and nibbled.

She loved his weight on top of her, his erection pressing against her, his mouth as he covered her torso in kisses. "I love you, Leslie."

He froze, his mouth hovering over her belly button. "What?"

She looked down at him, grinning. "I love you."

He scooted up her body so they were face-to-face. "You're not supposed to say it for the first time during sex."

"Oh." She widened her eyes in mock innocence. "Is that what we're doing?"

"Don't be cheeky."

"Well, then let's get this show on the road so I can say it again afterward." She kissed his forehead. "And later over dinner." Kisses to both of his eyes. "And then again before we fall asleep." A kiss to his nose. "And then start all over again the next day." She kissed him on the mouth.

When he pulled back, he shook his head. "Who knew my sprite was a romantic?"

"Your cock. In me. Now."

"Ah, there's my dirty girl."

"Damn right."

He didn't waste time after that, shoving her pants down her legs, doing the same to his, and then he was between her thighs, the head of his cock at her entrance, and entering her as he kissed her deeply. She wrapped her arms and legs around him, shoved her face in his neck, and moaned with each of his thrusts.

This was all she needed. Her town. Her shop. And Spencer in her arms.

She'd waited a long time to feel wanted. Loved. And she'd never thought it would come from the United Kingdom.

When she came, she bit down on his shoulder as he gasped into her neck, and they stayed locked together on the couch, hot and sweaty and absolutely so fucking happy.

SPENCER DIDN'T WANT to move. He was still inside Alex, as she clung to him like a monkey. The couch was soft and after the traveling he had done, all he wanted to do was sink down farther and fall asleep. He closed his eyes, thinking he should roll off Alex, allow her to breathe, but he was so tired. And she was so warm...

There was a knock at the door, and he jolted, tumbling off Alex and onto the floor with a thud. Alex was scrambling too, saying, "Shit, shit, shit," as she searched the floor for her clothes.

"Who is that?" Spencer hissed.

"My sister!" Alex hissed back and Spencer groaned. Ivy had tolerated him for a while when he'd been in town, but he never did seem to get on her good side.

"Yo, open the door!" said a male voice.

Alex sighed loudly. "Great, Brent is here too."

Oh, and wasn't that bloody lovely. Spencer tugged on his pants too. But the room smelled like sex and he straightened the couch cushions as best he could while Alex ran to the bathroom, then to her front door.

Her hair was falling out of her knot, hanging in damp tendrils around her face. There was a hickey on her neck, and this might be comical if he wasn't trying to impress her family into accepting him back into the fold. He stood awkwardly, rubbing the back of his head and wincing. "This is a cock-up now, isn't it?"

Alex blew out a breath, grinned, then flung the door open.

Ivy stood with her fist up, about to knock again, with Brent behind her. Thankfully, no small children were present because that would have made things even more awkward. But Ivy was staring at her sister like she had two heads, and Brent had already spotted Spencer. He didn't seem too happy either. "What the fuck are you doing here?"

Ivy's gaze shifted to him and she gasped. "Holy shit, the Brit is back."

Well, that was one way to put it. "Um, hello, Ivy. Hello, Brent."

Ivy shoved a shirt into Alex's arms as she walked past her sister into the apartment, never taking her gaze off Spencer.

She stopped in front of him and crossed her arms over her chest. He gazed down at the small woman and waited for her razor-sharp tongue to cut into him. He didn't even care. He was too blissed out, too happy to care, because Alex was smiling at him from behind Ivy, clearly amused at the situation. Even Brent's glare wasn't dulling his buzz.

"Alex has been doing fantastic since you've been gone, just so you know," Ivy was saying. "I don't really appreciate you coming back to drudge up old feelings again then…flit back to New York whenever you feel like it."

"I take offense to the fact that you think I flit," he said.

"Oh, shut up," Ivy growled.

He wanted to smile but didn't want to antagonize her. Frankly, he was glad Alex had family who loved her, who had her back.

Brent stepped forward. "Yeah, Alex even told off ol' Robby when he showed up out of the blue. Just about the best thing I've ever seen."

Spencer jerked his head to Alex at that. "What?"

She sawed her bottom lip and looked at him with her big blue eyes. "Uh, because of the whole land thing, Payton Auto was in the newspaper. My name was in it, so he found me."

"Motherfucker—"

"But it's okay." Alex nudged her sister out of the way so she could stand in front of Spencer, one hand on his chest. "It was good, actually. I finally got the closure I never had. I found out I was a lot stronger than I thought. He doesn't have power over me anymore, and it was amazing to look into his eyes when he realized it too."

Spencer gripped her bicep and squeezed. "That makes me so happy for you."

She beamed at him. "You helped me get there, don't you know that?"

"Me?"

"Yes, you. You showed me...I could be loved by a good man. And that I deserved it. I told you that you gave me my life back, and I meant it."

"We did that for each other then," he said softly.

She puckered her mouth, and he leaned down to press a kiss to her for-once naked lips.

A throat cleared, but he didn't pull out of the kiss until he was good and ready. When he looked up, Brent and Ivy were watching them, his arm over her shoulders. They both looked puzzled.

Alex turned to face them and Spencer wrapped his arms around her, pressing his front to her back.

"So here's the deal," she said. "Spencer is taking a new job as the manager of the new hotel. So he'll be living here in Tory. And we're together. Again."

Ivy's mouth dropped open.

"And don't tell me it's too fast," Alex said. "Because you and Brent got together in record time too. But Spencer and I want to make this work. He's changing jobs for me. For me." She jabbed her finger into her chest as her voice cracked on the last word. "The only other people who have done anything like that for me are you guys. So Spencer and I deserve this chance to be happy."

Ivy's eyes were wet as she blinked rapidly. "Of course you deserve it. You deserve it so much, and I can't handle all these emotions right now." She flapped her hands in front of her eyes and widened them.

Brent didn't even try to act macho, which Spencer appreciated. He wrapped Ivy in a hug, shuffled them forward until he could pull Alex into his arms, then jerked his chin at Spencer since his arms were full of crying Dawn women. "Come here and get in on this hug, English."

Spencer wondered if he'd ever get used to the open affection, but he figured he'd better start practicing.

So he held out his arms and enclosed them around the sniffling group and laid his cheek on top of Alex's head.

Yeah, he was home. Interestingly enough, it was the last place he ever thought he'd be.

IT WAS ANOTHER half hour before the sisters were done chatting and Brent was able to hustle Ivy out the door, telling her he was sure Spencer and Alex had things to talk about. "Call your sister tonight, okay?" he asked Alex. "Or else she'll drive me crazy wondering how you are."

"Yes, I'll call," Alex assured them.

When she shut the door behind them, Spencer let out a breath and collapsed onto the couch. "I feel like I could sleep for a decade."

Alex glanced at the clock. "Well, it's five o'clock on a Friday and I don't work tomorrow. So let's get pizza, have a beer, and then sleep until...at least noon."

He rolled his head to face her and curled a loose piece of hair around her ear. "Okay."

Alex kneeled on the sofa beside him. "When do you have to go back?"

"About that…" he muttered.

Her eyes widened a little in alarm. "What?"

"Well, I'm actually on a holiday."

"What holiday?"

"No, a holiday. Errr…sabbatical."

Alex still stared at him.

"Basically, my boss is giving me some extended vacation time. I haven't taken vacation in, well, ever. I wanted to come here and visit you. And I wanted to"—he swallowed—"go back to visit my father."

Her face didn't change for a minute and then her lips parted. "You want to go to England?"

"For a visit."

"Oh—"

"With you."

She shut her mouth so fast, her teeth clacked.

"I wasn't lying about what I said before. I want my father to meet you. I want him to see that moving here and doing what I've been doing for all these years has been worth it, because it made me a man who's loved by you."

Her lips trembled. "Shit, will you please stop saying things like that?" She made a fist and punched him lightly in the shoulder. "I'm tired of crying, you asshole!"

He grabbed his arm. "Hey!"

"Well, then stop!" She wiped her eyes. "Dammit. You're lucky I didn't put makeup on yet or I'd be really pissed."

"Alex."

She stared down at her knees, then up at him. "What?"

"Will you go to England with me before we come back here and start our lives together?"

She swallowed. "I'm a really awful traveler."

"That's okay."

"No, like, I get grumpy and I am bad at packing and I get motion sickness in vehicles and I can barely understand southern United States accents let alone another country's."

He laughed. "You're really selling yourself as a companion."

"I'm worried you'll get so tired of me that you'll dump me in the Thames. Or whatever that river is in England."

"Well, we have a couple of rivers."

"Oh." She looked confused for a minute and it was adorable. "Okay, well, will you promise not to push me overboard into water with the intention of drowning me to get rid of me?"

"Alex, for God's sake."

"Just promise me."

He rolled his eyes. "I won't try to bloody drown you, Sprite."

She took a deep breath and held his gaze. "Yes, Spencer. I'll go to England with you."

He smiled, and kissed her until she squealed.

Chapter Nineteen

Two months later…

ALEX HADN'T BEEN lying. She was probably the worst traveler Spencer had ever seen in his life. He also sort of understood why. Nothing was made for her. She couldn't reach the overhead bin on the airplane. Her feet didn't touch the floor during their flight so she spent most of the time uncomfortably shifting in her seat. Then they hit turbulence over the Atlantic and she spent the rest of the time with her head in the puke bag.

No one saw her in the airport. She was probably a head shorter than most people, and even with him beside her, people bumped into her constantly.

The train from London to Manchester was slightly better, but she still couldn't reach the overhead bin. He tried to lighten the mood by suggesting she carry around her own step stool, but that had earned him a death glare, so he didn't speak up much after that. She fell asleep on his shoulder on the train, and he figured that was good because she'd had a hell of a time on this trip so far.

But she hadn't thrown him into a river yet, so he figured she was at least still a little bit in love with him. He hoped.

He'd grown up in a small flat in Stockport with his father, and their shop was in Manchester, in an area called Cheetham Hill. They were staying at a hotel in Manchester and then would head to Red Fox Auto the next day. He knew his father would be there, and to be fair, that was his father's home turf more than anything.

He woke up Alex when they neared their stop, and she sat with a grumpy look on her face as the train slowed. He wanted to tell her she was adorable, face creased from a wrinkle in his shirt, but he didn't want to get kicked in the bollocks so he kept his mouth shut.

She rubbed her eyes. "So tell me about Manchester again."

"Well," he said, "it's an industrial city north of London. It's not…posh. Uh, it's very diverse, but yet we all agree there is one main battle, and that's red versus blue."

She stared at him.

"Manchester United versus Manchester City."

She hesitated for a minute, and he assumed her sleep-addled brain needed to catch up. "Oh," she said, making a motion with her foot. "Soccer."

"Football."

"Whatever."

"Yes, it's football. I said before but my father is, uh, a staunch Manchester United fan, and that's one of the reasons his shop is the Red Fox and not the Blue Fox."

A smile tugged at her lips.

"What?" He frowned.

"You English and your football." She said the last word with an accent that wasn't remotely like his.

"Your accent needs work."

She rolled her eyes.

When they got off the train, they took a taxi to their hotel, which was in Manchester. Alex gazed out the window, muttering about how the English drove on the wrong side of the road, and she wanted coffee and they better not try to give her tea and a whole bunch of other complaints.

And Spencer...well, it was a little disconcerting to be back in his hometown for the first time in years. What was strange was that it hadn't changed much, not from what he could see. It still smelled the same. The air still felt the same.

He inhaled deeply and leaned his head back on his headrest. Tomorrow, he'd see his dad, and the thought rolled his stomach with a mixture of dread and anticipation.

As if Alex knew, he felt her hand slip in his. He rolled his head to the side to face her. She grinned. "I love you."

"I love you too."

THE COFFEE WAS shit but Alex knew beggars couldn't be choosers. In theory, she knew it was probably decent coffee but it wasn't her coffee and her coffeemaker in her favorite mug, so this was all a little upsetting.

She really needed to work on being a better traveler. She knew when they fell asleep last night that she'd been a royal bitch all day, but her bones were sore and her mouth felt icky. The only thing tethering her to happiness was Spencer. She was doing this for him.

So she really needed to get over herself.

Spencer took her out to a restaurant to give her a "proper fry-up." She was unsure what that meant but went along with it because she needed coffee and food.

So there they sat in a restaurant, her sipping coffee from a beige porcelain mug while Spencer talked to the waiter. They'd been in Manchester for one night and Spencer's accent was already slipping, his vowels drawing out like that night he'd had too much to drink.

She noticed that's the way the cabbie had talked, as well as the people in this restaurant. After Spencer ordered for her and they were left alone, she swallowed a gulp of coffee. "Tell me about why you're talking differently now."

He blinked at her for a moment before chuckling and taking a sip of his own coffee. "Ah, noticed that?"

"Of course I did."

"Well, just like the United States, different parts of England have different accents. Manchester is known for being, uh, more working class. So if you have a Manchester accent, it kind of gives you away a bit. So I worked on it, tried to suppress it and make it some sort of bastardization of a London accent. I kept it up for a long time, and only really slipped if I'd had a lot to drink or I was tired. But being back here, I just…fell back into it."

She drained her coffee and looked around for someone to refill it. Spencer motioned to their waiter, who hurried over with a carafe. "So," she said to Spencer. "Tried to cover your roots."

"Yeah, I was."

"I kinda like knowing there's a roughneck under those posh suits of yours." She grinned over the rim of her full coffee.

"We have to go visit my father after this. Quit smiling at me like that."

The food arrived soon after and Alex stared at the full plate in front of her. Spencer pointed to the various items on it. "You have your sausage and back bacon, as well as some beans. Also some tomatoes, fried bread, and eggs."

She poked at the sausage. She wasn't sure if Spencer was trying to surprise her, but she was no stranger to huge breakfasts. She came from diner country. "Wanna bet I can eat all this?"

Spencer's eyes rounded, and he barked out a laugh. "No, I'm not betting. I've seen you eat. Not sure where you put it, but no way am I betting anything."

She smiled smugly, picked up the sausage, and bit off the end.

THEY PULLED TO a stop on a small road in what Spencer had said was Cheetham Hill, a section of Manchester. The cab driver had looked at Spencer funny when he gave him the address, and Alex saw why now. The street was barely big enough to fit one car, let alone two traveling in opposite directions. As Spencer paid the cabbie, Alex peered out the window. There was a small metal sign swinging gently, the edges rusty, but she could see Red Fox Auto written clearly in crimson. There was a profile of a fox, which looked a lot like the tattoo on Spencer's chest. She opened the door and stepped out, her booted feet splashing in a puddle.

Outside the shop was a rack of tires, and stone steps led up to a glass door, where a handwritten OPEN sign was displayed.

Everything about the street and the shop was a little bit derelict, and Alex smiled. It kinda felt like home.

She heard an engine and turned to see Spencer beside her as the taxi drove away. He looked at the shop through squinted eyes. She reached for his hand and waited for him to speak.

Finally he shook his head and huffed out a small laugh. "It doesn't look any different."

"No?"

"Not really."

A shadow fell behind the door and Alex took a deep breath. Spencer said he hadn't told his father—who went by Michael—that they were coming, that it was better that way if they showed up without notice. She didn't argue.

The door swung open and a large man filled the frame. He wore coveralls with one strap off, a dirty white shirt underneath. He had a lit cigarette dangling from his lips, and his blue eyes narrowed on Spencer as he took a drag and exhaled. Alex thought he looked a little like Jack. But British.

"Comin' in?" Michael said.

"Hey, Pop."

The man grunted and walked into the shop, letting the door fall shut behind him.

Spencer smiled and tugged on Alex's hand. "Let's go."

She followed along dutifully, and they stepped into an office that didn't look much different from the one at Payton. No one was there, and Spencer led her deeper into the building until they reached the back where there were three garage bays.

Michael stood in front of a Toyota with the hood up, fiddling with the engine. An older Indian man sat on a chair in the corner, his feet stretched out in front of him, arms crossed over his chest. His eyes were closed. Was he sleeping?

"Hello, Amir," Spencer said.

The man opened liquid brown eyes, blinked, then closed them again. "Junior."

Alex lifted an eyebrow at Spencer. His cheeks flushed a little. "That's what I was called when I lived here."

She nodded and looked back at Michael, who was now watching her.

"You gonna introduce me?" He addressed his son without taking his eyes off her.

Spencer stepped forward. "This is Alex Dawn, my girlfriend."

The man didn't wipe his hand before he extended it, and Alex wondered if that was on purpose. She took it anyway and shook it with a firm grip. The man seemed pleased and cocked his head slightly.

Then his gaze shifted to Spencer. "When'd you get in?"

"Yesterday."

Michael's jaw rolled as he took in his son. "Glad you stopped in."

Spencer seemed to deflate a little. "I thought we could stay a little bit, take you out to lunch or dinner. Just…visit."

Michael didn't speak for a while, then focused back on the car. "Not sure I got time. My day is booked solid."

"What's Amir doing?"

"He's on his break."

Spencer was clearly working hard to keep himself composed, and oh no, no way was his father being a jackass on Alex's watch.

They'd come all this way to spend time with the grumpy old man. They were going to damn well do it.

She stepped forward and leaned a palm on the car. "Listen, I spent the whole flight here puking my guts out, then having my bones nearly rattle out of my body on a train, all so your son could see the father he hasn't seen in years. So listen up, Pop. We're going to get some lunch, and we're going to talk, and we're going to have a great goddamn time. Then we'll come back here and I'll roll my sleeves up and help you finish your work for the day."

Michael stared at her, his face unchanging, then his gaze swept down her body and back up. "And how are you going to help?"

She pointed at the engine he was working on. "First, I bet the issue with this Toyota is excessive oil consumption, right? Common for this model year. So I can tell you right away what parts you need to fix it, since I just did one of these earlier this year." She pointed to a Chevy truck in the corner. "Then I'm going to replace the tires because they are practically bald from your shitty roads. Then I'm going to organize some of the paperwork in your office because it's a goddamn mess." She crossed her arms over her chest. "You hungry? Because your son wants to have a meal with you, and his mechanic girlfriend wants some fish and chips."

The only indication Michael was still alive was his chest moving with his breaths. They held gazes for a solid minute but Alex refused to look away.

Finally, Michael's lips split into a grin, then he cackled. He was so loud, the man in the corner cracked an eye open, and someone across the street hollered for him to pipe down.

He quieted and, still smiling, looked at Spencer. "And this woman loves you?"

Alex stepped closer to Spencer's side. "Sure as hell wouldn't have traveled all this way for someone I just kinda liked. I'd rather pull my toenails out than fly."

Michael's gaze studied her for another minute, then it shifted to Spencer. "Ya done good, boy."

Spencer puffed out his chest slightly, wrapped his arm around her back, and squeezed her hip. She'd done well too. She'd made Spencer proud. And dammit, she was proud of herself too.

Michael closed the hood of the car he was working on. "Dare's isn't rubbish. Want to eat there?"

Spencer nodded.

His father walked out ahead of them and Spencer turned to her. "You're fucking amazing, you know that?"

Alex grinned and lifted her chin. "Hell yeah, I know that."

Craving more Mechanics of Love?

Be sure to check out the second installment in
Megan Erickson's sexiest series yet!

DIRTY TALK

*When the one you shouldn't want is the one
you can't resist...*

Brent Payton works hard, plays hard, and has earned his
ladies' man reputation. But he's more than just a good
time, even though no one seems to see it. Until a gorgeous
brunette with knockout curves and big, thoughtful eyes
walks into his family's garage and makes Brent want more.

Ivy Dawn and her sister are done with men, all of them.
They've uprooted their lives too many times on account
of the opposite sex, but that's over now. The plan seems
easy until a sexy, dirty-taking mechanic bursts in Ivy's
life and shakes everything up.

Brent can't resist the one person who sees past his devil-
may-care façade, and Ivy finds it harder and harder to
deny how happy he makes her. But she has secrets of her
own and when the truth comes out, she must decide if
she'll run again or if she'll take a chance on forever.

Available Now from Avon Impulse!

An Excerpt from

DIRTY TALK

BRENT PAYTON WANTED some decent music while he was working.

Not this pop-rock crap the radio had been playing but real rock 'n' roll. Hell, he'd take George Thurgood right about now. Some "Bad to the Bone"? Hells to the yeah. That was better than a cup of coffee, which he could really use this Monday morning.

He'd volunteered to spring for an iPod and a docking station so he could play his own music, but his technology-inept father had acted like Brent wanted to buy a spaceship.

So that was out.

"Brent," Cal's voice called from the other bay of their garage at Payton Automotive.

"Yeah?"

"What's this shit on the radio?" his older brother asked. "Turn it down before my ears bleed."

Brent snorted. Cal was grumpy on a normal basis. But now that he'd quit smoking and wore a nicotine patch, he was even more insufferable. So Brent didn't argue and turned down the music.

A truck rumbled into the parking lot, and Brent turned around, squinting to see who it was.

Alex Dawn, the new employee they'd hired a week ago, strolled into the garage, a bandana wrapped around her head, wearing baggy jeans and a tight T-shirt. She held a banana in one hand.

Brent grinned and walked over to where she stood outside the door to the office, looking over the schedule for the day. She peeled her banana and took a bite. He leaned in and inhaled deeply. "I love the smell of estrogen in the morning."

Her lips twitched only slightly before she turned around and socked him in the bicep, hard. The woman could hit.

He howled dramatically and clutched his arm, swinging it limply from the elbow. "I'm injured! I can't work!"

While Alex gazed at him, one eyebrow raised in amusement, he forgot about his injury, grabbed her banana, and bit off half of it.

"You asshole! That's my breakfast!" Alex smacked him in the stomach, and he started laughing, nearly choking on the banana. "I'm so stealing the Snickers you keep hidden in the office."

He straightened in shock. "You wouldn't."

She was smug, the witch. "I would."

"That's war, woman."

She took the rest of the banana out of the peel and then tossed it so it landed on his shoulder. "Then don't mess with my banana."

"That's some grade-D dirty talk," he said, picking the peel off of his shoulder and throwing it in the trash can.

"Will you two quit it and get to work?" his dad, Jack, hollered, sticking his head out of the office door. "It's like you're related."

Brent shrugged and walked over to the minivan to continue rotating its tires. Alex smirked at him from her bay. Brent winked back.

Working with Alex had been rocky at first. She had a chip on her shoulder—which she refused to talk about—and Brent really enjoyed trying to knock it off, which only led to their sniping at each other. But when some asshole customer gave her a hard time because she was a woman, and she told him to shove it—Payton and Sons Automotive didn't really have that customer-is-always-right policy—Brent developed a newfound respect for her. When Brent backed her up in front of said asshole, she began giving him some respect in return. And so they'd fallen into this brother-sister type relationship that was actually kinda fun. Brent didn't really have friendships with women and especially not women he'd never fucked.

And the thing about Alex was…he didn't want to fuck her. It wasn't because she wasn't hot, because she was. But the chemistry between them was…lacking. Which surprised Brent. Because he was like hydrogen; he reacted with everyone.

Brent worked quietly for the rest of the morning, singing to himself when decent music came on, taking care of the minivan before moving on to the next job.

He was draining oil from an old Toyota when he heard voices from the front of the garage. He spotted Dick Carmichael talking to Alex. She pointed toward the back room, where Cal had disappeared. The Carmichaels had been coming to the shop since before Brent had started working there. Dick was a retired accountant, and his wife still cut hair in an add-on at their house.

"Can I help you, Dick?" Brent asked as he walked closer.

The man turned to him. "Hey, Brent. Uh, no, that's fine. I'll just wait for Cal."

"Oh, well if you need—"

Dick waved him on. "It's fine. You can get back to work. I'm sure you want to break for lunch soon." He patted him on the shoulder, like he was a kid, and chuckled. "Your dad always says that's your favorite part of the day."

Brent tamped down the irritation. First, whatever Cal could help him with, Brent could too. Second, yeah, Brent liked eating a hell of a lot, but that didn't mean he didn't do his job.

So he nodded and walked back to the Toyota. He didn't look up when he heard Cal return, when Dick spoke with Cal about some work he wanted to do to his car—work that Brent would probably be assigned to, but he wasn't Cal, the responsible one.

Nor was he Max, their younger brother, the first of them all to become a college graduate.

Brent was the middle brother, the joker, the comic relief. The irresponsible one.

Never mind that he'd been working at this shop since he was sixteen. Never mind that he could do every job, inside and out, and fast as fuck.

Never mind that he could be counted on, even though no one treated him like that.

A pain registered in his wrist, and he glanced down at the veins and tendons straining against the skin in his arm, where he had a death grip on a wrench.

He loosened his fist and dropped the tool on the bench.

This wallowing shit had to stop.

This was his life. He was happy (mostly) and free (no ball and chain, no way), and so what if everyone thought he was a joke? He was good at that role, so the typecasting fit.

"Why so glum, sugar plum?" Alex said from beside him as she peered up into his face.

He twisted his lips into a smirk and propped a hip on the counter, crossing his arms over his chest. "I knew you had a crush on me, sweet cheeks."

She narrowed her eyes, lips pursed to hide a smile. "Not even in your dreams."

He sighed dramatically. "You're just like all the ladies. Wanna piece of Brent. There's enough to go around, Alex; no need to butter me up with sweet nicknames—"

A throat cleared. And Brent looked over to see a woman standing beside them, one hand on her hip, the other dangling at her side, holding a paper bag. Her dark eyebrows were raised, full red lips pursed.

And Brent blinked, hoping this wasn't a mirage.

Tory, Maryland, wasn't big, and he'd made it his mission to know every available female in the town limits and about a ten-mile radius outside of that.

This woman? He'd never seen her. He'd surely remember if he had.

Gorgeous. Long hair so dark brown it was almost black. Perfect face. It was September and still warm, so she wore a tight striped sundress that ended mid-thigh. She was tiny, probably over a foot smaller than he was. Fuck, the things that little body made him dream about. He wondered if she did yoga. Tiny and limber was his kryptonite.

Narrow waist, round hips, big tits.

No ring.

Bingo.

He smiled. Sure, she was probably a customer, but this wouldn't be the first time he'd managed to use the garage to his advantage. Usually, he just had to toss around a tire or two, rev an engine, whatever, and they were more than eager to hand over a phone number and address. No one thought he was a consummate professional anyway, so why bother trying to be one?

He leaned his ass against the counter, crossing his arms over his chest. "Can I help you?"

She blinked, long lashes fluttering over her big blue eyes. "Can you help me?"

"Yeah, we're full service here." He resisted winking. That was kinda sleazy.

Her eyes widened for a fraction of a second before they shifted to Alex at his side and then back to him.

Her eyes darkened for a minute, her tongue peeked out between those red lips, and then she straightened. "No, you can't help me."

He leaned forward. "Really? You sure?"

"Positive."

"Like, how positive?"

"I'm one hundred percent positive that I do not need help from you, Brent Payton."

That made him pause. She knew his name. He knew he'd never met her, so that could only mean she'd heard about him somehow, and by the look on her face, it was nothing good.

Well, shit.

He opened his mouth, not sure what to say but hoping it would come to him, when Alex began cracking up next to him, slapping her thighs and snorting.

Brent glared at her. "And what's your problem?"

Alex stepped forward, threw her arm around the shoulder of the woman in front of them, and smiled ear to ear. "Brent, meet my sister, Ivy. Ivy, thanks for making me proud."

They were both smiling now, that same full-lipped, white-teethed smile. He surveyed Alex's face and then Ivy's, and holy fuck—how did he not notice this right away? They almost looked like twins.

And the sisters were looking at him now, wearing matching smug grins—and wasn't that a total cock-block? He pointed at Alex. "What did you tell her about me?"

"That the day I interviewed, you asked me to re-create a Whitesnake music video on the hood of a car."

He threw up his hands. "Can you let that go? You weren't even my first choice. I wanted Cal's girlfriend to do it."

"Because that's more appropriate," Alex said drily.

"Excuse me for trying to liven it up around here."

Ivy turned to her sister, so he got a better glimpse of those thighs he might sell his soul to touch. She held up the paper bag. "I brought lunch; hope that's okay."

"Of course it is," Alex said. "Thanks a lot, since *someone* stole my breakfast." She narrowed her eyes at Brent. Ivy turned to him slowly in disbelief, like she couldn't believe he was that evil.

Brent had made a lot of bad first impressions in his life. A dad of one of his high school girlfriend's had seen Brent's bare ass, while Brent was lying on top of his daughter, before the dad ever saw Brent's face. That had not gone over well. And yet this impression might be even worse.

Because he didn't care about what that girl's dad thought of him. Not really.

And he didn't *want* to care about what Ivy thought of him, but, dammit, he did. It bothered the hell out of him that she'd written him off before even meeting him. Did Alex tell her any of his good qualities? Like…Brent racked his brain for good qualities.

By the time he thought of one, the girls had already disappeared to the back room for lunch.

"Do you think we hurt his feelings?" Ivy picked at a stray piece of lettuce hanging out of her sandwich.

She didn't meet her sister's eyes, not even when Alex started making choking sounds across from her at the small table in the back of Payton and Sons Automotive.

"E-excuse me?" Alex stuttered.

Ivy bit her lip and lifted her gaze to her sister's. Alex had talked a lot about Brent, and while there was an underlying platonic affection to her words, most of her talk was complaining about how much of a pain in her ass he was. Maybe Alex hadn't been looking at Brent close enough during their conversation out in the garage, but Ivy had been. She'd noticed the flash of frustration over his face when they'd shut him down.

What made her pause was that it seemed like frustration directed at himself, not at her.

Crap. Ivy dipped her gaze back to her sandwich. This would not do. She and Alex had basically stamped a big red X over all dicks—literal and figurative—for a good long time. They'd already moved twice to get away from men who had ruined their lives. Tory was supposed to be where they settled in, got their lives straight, and raised Violet.

Ivy's defense mechanism was to immediately be cold to Brent. She could have gotten bees with honey, but she didn't want bees. Or honey. Or whatever. So she was all stinger.

She and Alex didn't need men. The two of them and Violet would be just fine.

And yet at this moment, Ivy couldn't stop thinking about Brent. Alex hadn't warned her that he looked...like *that*. Like six-feet, two-inches of hotness straight out of a Mechanics of Your Dreams calendar. Jesus. That dark hair, those full lips that smirked, those slate eyes that did nothing to hide the fact that this man was trouble with a capital T.

"Iv-eeeeee." Alex drew out her name in that way only big sisters could do when they planned to interrogate.

Ivy poked the wheat bread of her sandwich. "What?"

"Why are you concerned about Brent's feelings?"

She didn't know. Honestly and truly, she didn't know, but she couldn't forget that momentary flash of emotion that passed over his face before he covered it with a smirk. "I don't know; he's your coworker and—"

"I know he's basically sex on legs, Ivy, but he knows it. And I'd be hard-pressed to find a woman who hasn't taken a ride in this town."

Ivy pressed her lips together, chastising herself for letting her soft heart show. She needed to focus on finding a job and raising her daughter. Those were her priorities. Not going toe-to-toe with some cocky hot guy. "You're right; forget I said anything." Ivy held up her index fingers and crossed them in an X. "No men."

"Ick," Alex spat.

"Gross," Ivy said.

Alex grinned at her, and Ivy returned it, sipping from her iced tea. "So, work going okay?"

"Yeah, I like it here. Cal's fair. Brent's fun to work with. Jack's still a hard-ass but I think he's warming to me."

Alex had told Ivy that Brent and Cal's dad was a brick wall of gruff and stubborn. "Good."

"Violet off to school okay?" Alex asked.

Ivy's daughter was in first grade at White Pine Elementary School in the Tory school district. They'd moved in time for her start at the beginning of the school year. "Her teacher called me again, saying Vi cried on and off this morning." Ivy knew moving was hard on her, but they hadn't had much of a choice. "I hate this."

Alex squeezed Ivy's hand where it rested on the table. "It's school. You're not torturing her. She'll get used to it."

Ivy's stomach rolled, thinking about it. "I hope."

"She's a good kid. She just needs time."

Ivy sighed. "I guess."

"Alex," a deep voice said from the doorway. Ivy craned her head to see a man who looked a lot like Brent but…wasn't Brent.

"Yeah?" Alex answered.

The man nodded at Ivy. "I'm Cal." He turned to Alex. "Sorry. I know you're eating lunch, but got that customer of yours out front from last week. I tried talking to her, but she likes you better."

Alex laughed. "Greta Sherman?"

"That's the one."

She balled up her empty sandwich wrapper. "I'll be back in a couple of minutes," she said to Ivy.

Ivy looked down at her half-eaten lunch. "I can leave—"

"Nah, I'll be right back. You finish eating."

Alex tossed her trash into the can on the way out.

Ivy took a sip of her tea and picked at her sandwich. She'd spent all morning on the computer, applying for jobs in and around Tory. It wasn't necessarily a mecca of job opportunities, but Alex had found a place she fit in, and the pay wasn't bad. Ivy had some savings, but it wasn't going to last forever, and she wanted to pull her weight in the little family they'd created.

Her résumé was a bit slim. She had a high school diploma but no college degree, having spent her early twenties raising Violet. Her job options in Tory were working as a secretary for a lawyer, selling furniture at a department store, or being a nanny.

None was appealing.

But at least they all paid.

The chair across from her squeaked, and she lifted her gaze, opening her mouth to tell Alex about her job options.

Except Alex wasn't sitting across from her.

Brent was.

He leaned back in his chair, feet up on the table and crossed at the ankle. He held a packet of peanuts and tipped it so a couple fell into his mouth. He chewed, steel eyes on her.

She clenched her jaw shut.

He swallowed. "You looked like you were going to say something."

"Sure I was. To Alex. But you're not Alex."

"No, I'm not. But I'm a great listener."

"I'm sure," she said drily.

His lips quirked. "Want to hear about what other things I'm good at?"

"Not particularly."

"Because I can do this thing with my tongue—"

Good God. "I don't do this."

"Don't do what?"

She waved a hand between them. "This. Flirting."

He raised his eyebrows. "Babe, I haven't even begun to flirt."

She took a deep breath to calm her rising blood pressure. "Don't do that either."

"Jesus! Now what?" His exasperation might have been cute if she still had a heart.

"Nicknames."

"Babe?"

"My name is Ivy. I-V-Y. Three letters. Two syllables." Even she wanted to cringe at how much of a bitch she was being.

He was studying her now, his face a little less amused and more…thoughtful. She didn't like thoughtful Brent. Amused, flirting Brent? Harmless. Thoughtful Brent, who tried to look deeper? Dangerous as hell.

He ran two fingers over his lips and then dropped his hand to the table, cocking his head. "You're just thorns everywhere I touch, aren't you?"

She froze at his words, like a deer in headlights because yes—yes, she was a whole lot of thorns because she'd learned long ago they were necessary to protect all her soft parts.

Brent wasn't done, though; his voice was softer when he spoke again. "You born that way, or something make you that way, Ivy?"

She swallowed. Yep, Brent Payton was dangerous in a sexy-as-hell package. His words were seeping past those thorns, hitting all the spots where she was weak. So she gathered herself and clenched her fists at her sides. "You're just acting like this because I'm the first woman who hasn't fallen at your feet."

He laughed at that. "Fallen at my feet? Nah, there are plenty of women who've told me to go to hell. My percentage is good, though. Maybe eighty-twenty." He grinned that shit-eating grin. "But you got me curious now. I wanna keep prodding until I find a place that isn't a thorn. How long do you think that'll take me?"

Shit, no; that's exactly what she didn't want. With those eyes that were smart and trouble at the same time.

She swallowed and straightened her spine. "You'll never get close enough."

He cocked his head. "No?"

"No."

He hummed a little and leaned back in his chair again. He threw a peanut in the air and caught it in his mouth. Then he chewed, with those steel eyes daring her to look away. "Guess I gotta plan my attack better next time, huh? You better work on those defenses."

She heard Alex's voice as her sister made her way back to the lunchroom. Ivy smiled and lifted her chin. "Who says I'll be the one who needs defense?"

He laughed sharply, like he was surprised. "Oh, babe, bring it."

She gritted her teeth. "Ivy."

"Babe. I call it as I see it, and you're definitely babe."

Ivy growled.

He smiled, and then he was up out of his chair and walking out the door as Alex made her way in. Her eyes trailed Brent as he retreated to the garage.

Alex turned to Ivy, eyes concerned. "Was he bothering you?"

Bothering didn't even touch it. "No, he's fine. Nothing I can't handle."

Alex shrugged. "I can talk to him—"

"Alex, I swear, it was nothing, and even if it was, I could handle it."

Her sister eyed her and then stole a bite of her sandwich. "Fine; now eat. You're getting skinny."

"Quit mothering me."

Alex pointed to the sandwich with raised eyebrows, and Ivy glared at her as she took a bite.

And keep reading for an excerpt from the

first book in the Mechanics of Love series

DIRTY THOUGHTS

Some things are sexier the second time around.

Cal Payton has gruff and grumbly down to an art...all
the better for keeping people away. And it usually works.
Until Jenna Macmillan—his biggest mistake—walks into
Payton and Sons Automotive all grown up, looking like
sunshine and inspiring more than a few dirty thoughts.

Jenna was sure she was long over the boy she'd once loved
with reckless abandon, but one look at the steel-eyed Cal
Payton has her falling apart all over again. Ten years may
have passed, but the pull is stronger than ever...and this
Cal is all man.

Cal may have no intention of letting Jenna in, but she's
always been his light, and it's getting harder to stay all
alone in the dark. When a surprise from the past changes
everything, Cal and Jenna must decide if their connec-
tion should be left alone or if it's exactly what they need
for the future of their dreams.

Available Now from Avon Impulse!

An Excerpt from

DIRTY THOUGHTS

CAL PAYTON SIGHED and braced himself as the opening guitar riff of "Welcome to the Jungle" reverberated off the walls of the garage. Sure enough, several bars later, his brother, Brent, began his off-key rendition, which didn't sound much different from his drunken karaoke version.

Which, yes, Cal had heard. More times than he wanted to.

He growled under his breath. Brent kept screeching Axl Rose, and if Cal wasn't stuck on his back under this damn Subaru, he'd be flinging a wrench at Brent's head. "Hey!" Cal yelled.

There was a blissful moment of silence. "What?" Brent's voice came from somewhere behind him, probably in the bay next to him at the garage.

"Who sings this song?"

"Are you kidding me?" Brent's voice was closer now. "It's Guns N' Roses. The legendary Axl Rose."

"Yeah? Then how 'bout you let him sing it?"

There was a pause. "Fuck you." His brother's footsteps stomped away. Then the radio was turned up, and Brent started singing even louder.

Cal blew out a breath and tapped the socket wrench on his forehead, doing his best to tune out Brent's increasingly loud voice. Cal vowed to buy earbuds and an iPod before he murdered his brother with a tire iron.

He turned his attention back to the exhaust shield he was fixing. The customer had complained of a loud rattle when his car idled. Sure enough, one of the heat shields covering the exhaust system under the car was loose. It was an easy fix. Cal used a gear clamp to wrap around the pipe of the exhaust system to prevent the shield from making noise.

It didn't necessarily have to be done, but the Graingers were long-time customers at Payton and Sons Automotive. And they always sent those flavored popcorn buckets at Christmas. He and Brent fought over the caramel while their dad got the butter all to himself.

He finished tightening the hose clamp onto the pipe and then banged around the exhaust system with the side of his fist. No rattle.

He slid out from under the Subaru and patted it on the side. He squinted at the clock, seeing it was almost quitting time. Their dad, who owned half of the shop— Cal and Brent split ownership of the other 50 percent— had already gone home for the day.

Cal put away the tools he'd used, purposefully ignoring Brent as he launched into a Pearl Jam song. Cal rubbed his temple, wiping away the bead of sweat he could feel rolling down his face. The back room had a small table and a refrigerator, so Cal made his way there to get a water.

In the summer, they kept the large doors of the garage open, but the air was thick and humid today. The American flag outside hung like a limp rag in the still air.

Cal wore coveralls at work and usually kept them on to protect his skin from hot exhaust pipes and any number of sharp tools lying around. But as he walked back to the lunchroom, he stripped his upper body out of the coveralls so the torso and arms of the clothing hung loose around his legs. Underneath, he wore a tight white T-shirt that still managed to be marked with grease and black smudges from the workday.

In the back room, he grabbed a bottle of water from the refrigerator and leaned back against the wall. After unscrewing the cap, he tilted it back at his lips and chugged half the bottle.

After the Graingers came to pick up their Subaru, he was free to head home to his house. Alone. That was a new luxury. He used to live with Brent in an apartment, and it was fine until he realized he was almost thirty years old and still living with his younger brother. He was tight with his money, which Brent teased him about, but it'd been a good thing when he had enough to make the deposit on his small home. It had a garage, so he could store his bike and work on it when he had free time.

Which wasn't a lot, but he'd take what he could get. If his father would quit dicking him around and let him work on motorcycles for customers here, that'd be even better. But Jack Payton didn't "want no bikers" around, ignoring the fact that his son rode a Harley-Davidson Softail.

Cal's phone vibrated in the leg pocket of his coveralls. He pulled it out and glanced at the caller ID. It was Max, their youngest brother. Cal sighed and answered the call. "Yeah?"

"Cal!" Max shouted.

"You called me."

"What's going on?"

"Workin'."

"You're always working." Max huffed.

Cal took another sip of water. "That's what people do."

"Hey, I work."

"You play dodgeball with a bunch of teenagers." Cal knew Max did a hell of a lot more than that at his physical education teaching job at a high school in eastern Pennsylvania, but it was fun as hell to get him worked up. Cal smiled. One of the first times that day.

"Hey, I had to hand out deodorant and condoms to those teenagers this year, so don't give me that shit," Max said.

"Condoms?"

"Yeah, they're kinda liberal here," Max muttered.

"Huh," Cal said, scratching his head. They sure never handed out condoms in school when he was a teenager.

"Anyway," Max said.

"Yeah, anyway, what'dya need?"

"How do you know I need something?"

"Why else do you call?"

"I want to hear your pleasant voice?"

Cal grunted.

"I just wanted to know if you had any plans for your birth—ouch!" There was rustling on the other line, some mutters, and a higher-pitched voice in the background. Then Max spoke again. "Okay, so Lea punched me because she said I'm doing this wrong."

Cal smiled. Lea was Max's fiancée, and she was a firecracker.

"We wanted to come visit you and take you out for your birthday. All of us." Max cleared his throat. "And you can bring a date too. If you want."

A date. When was the last time he'd introduced a woman to his family? Hell, when was the last time he'd had a date? "The five of us should be fine."

"So that's okay? To celebrate? I mean, you're turning thirty, old man."

Cal let the *old man* comment roll off his back. "Yeah, sounds good." He paused. "Thanks."

Max seemed pleased, chattering on about his neighborhood and how he was enjoying being off work for the summer. Cal drank his water and listened to his brother ramble. Max hadn't always been a happy kid. Cal had tried his best after their mom left the family shortly after Max was born. Their dad was pissed and bitter and immersed himself in working at the garage. So as the oldest brother, Cal scrambled to hold the reins of his wild brothers.

He hadn't done such a great job, he didn't think. His brothers survived in spite of him, not because of him, he was sure. Brent was still a little crazy, and it had taken Lea to straighten Max out in college. Cal tried not to dwell on his failure and instead appreciated that at least they were all alive and healthy.

It was why he valued his own space so much now. His alone time. Because he'd been a surrogate father at age six, and he was fucking over it.

Although, by the time he hung up the phone with Max and slipped his phone back into his pocket, he had a warm feeling in his gut that hadn't been there before his brother had called.

He was flipping the cap of the water in his fingers and finishing the last of the bottle when Brent poked his head in the back room. "Hey."

Cal raised his eyebrows.

"Someone's asking for you."

Cal tossed the empty bottle in the trash. "The Graingers?"

"Nope, they just came and got the Subaru and left. This is a new customer."

Cal threw the empty bottle in the recycling bin, turned off the light to the back room, and followed his brother out to the garage. "We're closing soon. Is it an emergency? Are they regulars?" He pulled a rag out of his pocket and began to wipe his dirty hands. He thought about washing them first in case this customer wanted to shake hands.

Brent didn't answer him, didn't even look at him over his shoulder.

And that was when a small sliver of apprehension trickled down his spine. "Brent—"

His brother whirled around and held his arm out as they walked past a Bronco their dad had been working on. "I think it's better if you take this one."

Cal squinted into the sun and when his eyes adjusted to the light, her legs were the first thing he saw. And he knew—he fucking knew—because how many times had he sat in class in high school staring at those legs in a little skirt, dreaming about when he could get back between them? It'd been a lot.

His eyes traveled up those bare legs to a tiny pair of denim shorts, up a tight tank top that showed a copious amount of cleavage, and then to that face that he'd never, ever forget as long as he lived.

He never thought he'd see Jenna MacMillan again. And now, there she was, standing in front of his garage next to a Dodge Charger, her brunette hair in a wavy mass around her shoulders.

Fuck.

OKAY, SO ADMITTEDLY Jenna had known this was a stupid idea. She'd tried to talk herself out of it the whole way, muttering to herself as she sat at a stoplight. The elderly man in the car in the lane beside her had been staring at her like she was nuts.

And she was. Totally nuts.

It'd been almost a decade since she'd seen Cal Payton, and yet one look at those silvery blue eyes and she was shoved right back to the head-over-heels *in love* eighteen-year-old girl she'd been.

Cal had been hot in high school, but damn, had time been good to him. He'd always been a solid guy, never really hitting that awkward skinny stage some teenage boys went through after a growth spurt.

And now…well…Cal looked downright sinful standing there in the garage. He'd rolled down the top of his coveralls, revealing a white T-shirt that looked painted on, for God's sake. She could see the ridges of his abs, the outline of his pecs. A large smudge on the sleeve drew her attention to his bulging biceps and muscular, veined forearms. Did he lift these damn cars all day? Thank God it was hot as Hades outside already so she could get by with flushed cheeks.

And he was staring at her with those eyes that hadn't changed one bit. Cal never cared much for social mores. He looked people in the eye, and he held it long past comfort. Cal had always needed that, to be able to measure up who he was dealing with before he ever uttered a word.

She wondered how she measured up. It'd been a long time since he'd laid eyes on her, and the last time he had, he'd been furious.

Well, she was the one who'd come here. She was the one who needed something. She might as well speak up, even though what she needed right now was a drink. A stiff one. "Hi, Cal." She went with a smile that surely looked a little strained.

He stood with his booted feet shoulder width apart, and at the sound of her voice, he started a bit. He finally stopped doing that staring thing as his gaze shifted to the car by her side and then back to her. "Jenna."

His voice. Well, crap, how could she have forgotten about his voice? It was low and silky with a spicy edge, like Mexican chocolate. It warmed her belly and raised goose bumps on her skin.

She cleared her throat as he began walking toward her, his gaze teetering between her and the car. Brent was off to the side, watching them, with his arms crossed over his chest. He winked at her. She hid her grin with pursed lips and rolled her eyes. He was a good-looking bastard but irritating as hell. Nice to see *some* things never changed. "Hey, Brent."

"Hey there, Jenna. Looking good."

Cal whipped his head toward his brother. "Get back to work."

Brent gave him a sloppy salute and then shot her another knowing smirk before turning around and retreating into the garage bay.

When she faced Cal again, she jolted, because he was close now, almost in her personal space. His eyes bored into her. "What're ya doing here, Jenna?"

His question wasn't accusatory. It was conversational, but the intent was in his tone, lying latent until she gave him reason to really put the screws to her. She didn't know if he meant, what was she doing here at his garage, or what was she doing in town? But she went for the easy question first.

She gestured to the car. "I, uh, I think the bearings need to be replaced. I know that I could take it anywhere, but..." She didn't want to tell him it was Dylan's car, and he was the one who had let it go so long that she swore the front tires were going to fall off. As much as her brother loved his car, he was an idiot. An idiot who despised Cal, and she was pretty sure the feeling was mutual. "I wanted to make sure the job was done right, and everyone knows you do the best job here." That part was true. The Paytons had a great reputation in Tory.

But Cal never let anything go. He narrowed his eyes and propped his hands on his hips, drawing attention to the muscles in his arms. "How do you know we still do the best job here if you haven't been back in ten years?"

Well, then. Couldn't he just nod and take her keys? She held them in her hand, gripping them so tightly that the edge was digging into her palm. She loosened her grip. "Because when I did live here, your father was the best, and I know *you* don't do anything unless you do it the best." Her voice faded. Even though the last time she'd seen Cal, his eyes had been snapping in anger, at least they'd showed some sort of emotion. This steady blank gaze was killing her. Not when she knew how his eyes looked when he smiled, as the skin at the corners crinkled and the silver of his irises flashed.

She thought now that this had been a mistake. She'd offered to get the car fixed for her brother while he was out of town. And while she knew Cal worked with his dad now, she'd still expected to run into Jack. And even though Jack was a total jerk-face, she would have rather dealt with him than endure this uncomfortable situation with Cal right now. "You know, it's fine. Don't worry about it. I'll just—"

He snatched the keys out of her hand. Right. Out. Of. Her. Hand.

"Hey!" She propped a hand on her hip, but he wasn't even looking at her, instead fingering the key ring. "Do you always steal keys from your customers?"

He cocked his head and raised an eyebrow at her. There was the smallest hint of a smile, just a tug at the corner of his lips. "I don't make that a habit, no."

"So I'm special, then?" She was flirting. Was this flirting? Oh God, it was. She was flirting with her high school boyfriend, the guy who'd taken her virginity, and the guy whose heart she'd broken when she had to make one of the most difficult decisions of her life.

She'd broken her own heart in the process.

His gaze dropped, just for a second, and then snapped back to her face. "Yeah, you're special."

He turned around, checking out the car, while she stood gaping at his back. He'd...he'd flirted back, right? Cal wasn't really a flirting kind of guy. He said what he wanted and followed through. But flirting, Cal?

She shook her head. It'd been over ten years. Surely he'd lived a lot of life during that time she'd been away, going to college, then grad school, then working in New York. She didn't want to think about what that flirting might mean, now that she was back in Tory for good. Except he didn't know that.

"So, you think the bearings need to be replaced?" Cal ran his hand over the hood. From this angle, all she saw was hard muscle covering broad shoulders, shifting beneath his T-shirt.

She shook herself and spoke up. "Yeah, it's making that noise—you know, that growl."

He nodded.

The only reason she knew was because she'd spent a lot of weekends and lazy summer afternoons as a teenager, lying in the grass, getting a tan in her bikini while Cal worked on his car, an old black Camaro, in his driveway. She'd learned a lot about cars and hadn't forgotten all of it. She wondered if he still had that Camaro.

"Want me to inspect it too?" Cal was at the passenger side door now, easing it open.

"What?"

He pointed to the sticker on the windshield. "I can do it now, if you'd like. You have to get it done by end of next month."

She opened her mouth to tell him sure, but then she'd have to give him the registration and insurance card, and then he'd know it was Dylan's car. "No, no, that's all right."

He frowned. "Why not?"

"I just…"

He opened up the passenger side door and bent inside.

"What are you doing?" She walked around the car, just as he pulled some papers out of the glove box. She stopped and fidgeted with her fingers, because he'd know in three…two…

He bent and tossed the papers back in the glove box. "I'll have it for you by end of the day tomorrow." He started walking toward the office of the garage.

He had to have seen the name, right? He had to have seen it. She walked behind him. "Cal, I—"

He stopped and turned. "Do you need a ride?"

"What?"

"Do you need a ride…home, or wherever you're going?"

She shook her head. "I'm going to walk across the street to Delilah's store. She'll take me home."

His gaze flitted to the shop across the street and then back to Jenna. He nodded. "All right, then."

She tried again. "Cal—"

"You picking it up or your brother?"

The muscle shift in his jaw was the only indication that he was bothered by this. "I'm sorry, I should have told you…"

He shook his head. "You don't owe it to me to tell me anything. You asked me to fix a car—"

"Yeah, but you and Dylan don't like each other—"

That muscle in his jaw ticked again. "Sure, we don't like each other, but what? You think I'm going to lose my temper and bash his car in?"

Uh-oh. "No, I—"

He shook his head, and when he spoke again, his voice was softer. "You didn't have to keep it a secret it was his car. I'm not eighteen anymore. I got more control than I used to."

She felt like a heel. And a jerk. She wasn't the same person she was at eighteen, so she shouldn't have treated Cal like he was the hothead he'd been then. "Cal, I'm so sorry. I—"

He waved a hand. "Don't worry about it, Sunshine."

That name—it sent a spark right through her like a live wire. She hadn't heard that nickname in so long, she'd almost forgotten about it, but her body sure hadn't. It hadn't forgotten the way Cal could use that one word to turn her into putty.

He seemed as surprised as she did. His eyes widened a fraction before he shut down. "Anyway"—his voice was lower now—"we close tomorrow at six. Appreciate it if you'd pick it up before that." He jingled the keys and shot her one more measuring look, and then he disappeared into the garage office, leaving her standing outside the door, her mind broiling in confusion.

She should have known Cal Payton could still knock her off her feet.

About the Author

MEGAN ERICKSON grew up in a family that averages five foot five on a good day and started writing to create characters who could reach the top kitchen shelf.

She's got a couple of tattoos, has a thing for gladiators, and has been called a crazy cat lady. After working as a journalist for years, she decided she liked creating her own endings better and switched back to fiction.

She lives in Pennsylvania with her husband, two kids, and two cats. And no, she still can't reach the stupid top shelf.

Discover great authors, exclusive offers, and more at hc.com.

Give in to your Impulses . . .
Continue reading for excerpts from
our newest Avon Impulse books.
Available now wherever e-books are sold.

GUARDING SOPHIE
A Love and Football Novella
By Julie Brannagh

THE IDEA OF YOU
Ribbon Ridge Book Four
By Darcy Burke

ONE TEMPTING PROPOSAL
An Accidental Heirs Novel
By Christy Carlyle

NO GROOM AT THE INN
A Dukes Behaving Badly Novella
By Megan Frampton

An Excerpt from

GUARDING SOPHIE
A Love and Football Novella
by *Julie Brannagh*

Hearts beat and sparks fly when two
people find shelter in each other.

Seattle Sharks wide receiver Kyle Carlson needs
to escape and Noel, Washington is the perfect
place for him to do it and figure out his next
step. He likes the seclusion and predictability
of the small town . . . until the biggest surprise
of his life turns up in the local grocery store.

She swallowed hard. She looked down at her hand clasped securely in his. There was so much to say, but for once, she'd like to spend a couple of hours sitting on the couch with nothing more pressing to do than enjoy herself.

"I have to tell you this," he said. "I'm kinda into you. I have been since we were in school." He let out a long breath. "Are you okay if we take this slow?" He peered at her through a mop of dark, shoulder-length waves. His full lips twitched into a shy smile. "I don't want to screw it up," he confessed.

It was probably a huge line he'd used with women before, but hearing something so bashful coming from the normally confident, handsome, funny Kyle charmed her. Even if it wasn't original, it worked. She licked her suddenly dry lips. "I like you too."

"That's good to know," he said. He squeezed her hand.

"I wonder how things would have been different if I'd gone to the prom with you instead."

"You were a bit unavailable in those days."

"Yeah. It wasn't working, no matter how hard I tried to convince myself it was. Of course, then I met Peter, and that was even worse." Maybe she should change the subject. No one wanted to hear about the train wreck that was her love life. She still had a tiny flicker of hope in her heart that things could be different.

Somehow, law enforcement would keep her ex away from her, she'd meet a man she wanted to be with and who wanted to be with her in return, and her life would be happy. She didn't have to plan her entire future in the next ten minutes.

"I've had some sketchy relationships over the years too," he said. They stared at each other for a minute or so, and he grinned at her. "How about that movie? What would you like to watch?"

She'd rather spend the evening talking with him and continuing to catch up on the past ten years, but maybe he preferred the relative safety of a shared activity that would not require baring one's soul. They had plenty of time to explore each other's thoughts and dreams. Maybe sitting on the couch holding hands was the best medicine for both of them right now.

"That's a good question," she said. "Do we watch something we've seen before, or do we take a risk?"

"What's your favorite movie?" he said.

"*Pitch Perfect*," she said.

He clicked the TV on, hit the Amazon Instant Video icon, and located the downloadable movie. "I know I'm supposed to say something like I love the *Fast and Furious* franchise more than anything," he confided. "Don't tell anyone, but I own the *Pitch Perfect* DVD. It's in Bellevue."

"You're not a *Fast and Furious* fan?"

"Don't let it get out," he joked.

"That's aca-awesome, Kyle."

They watched the bar on the screen as the movie downloaded for a few seconds.

"I'll bet you sing along too," he said.

" 'Titanium' is one of my favorite songs," she assured him. "And I sing 'Since U Been Gone' in the car. At least I did when I *had* a car."

"We can sing it in my car." He moved closer to her on the couch as the download ended. "Want something to drink before I click Start on the movie?"

"No, thank you. I'm fine," she said.

"You are, aren't you?"

She laughed as he moved closer.

"I have one more thing to confess," he said as he reached out to cup her cheek in his hand. He slowly rubbed his thumb against her jaw. Her heart was going as if she'd chugged a four-shot latte, and the memories came rushing back. She remembered a thousand nights of football games, pizza, and hanging around on the beach with her friends. She remembered Kyle as a laughing teen with wavy, tumbled dark hair, sparkling dark eyes, and the confidence of someone who believed life held only good things for all of them. She thought that charmed life would go on forever.

They weren't high school students anymore. They'd both had their share of joy and pain as they'd ventured into the adult world. The stakes were higher now, especially since they'd confessed a mutual interest. The pain in her heart, if this did not work out, would be a momentary annoyance compared with the anguish she would feel if she exposed Kyle or his family to danger as the result of her unhinged, vengeful ex.

"What if he finds me?" she whispered. His couch wrapped them in a cocoon of overstuffed comfort.

"We'll deal with that later," he whispered back. "I've wanted to kiss you for years now, Sophie. I think you want to kiss me too."

An Excerpt from

THE IDEA OF YOU
Ribbon Ridge Book Four
by Darcy Burke

In the fourth sexy and emotional novel
in the Ribbon Ridge series, movie star
Alaina Pierce just wants peace and quiet after
a tabloid scandal that rocked Hollywood . . .
but a hot and steamy affair with a gorgeous
Archer brother is the perfect distraction.

Evan Archer rounded the larger of his parents' two garages and was immediately hit by the smell of smoke and the peal of an alarm. He instinctively pressed his hands to his ears and looked up at the apartment on the second floor of the garage. Smoke billowed from an open window. Despite the excruciating sound, he ran toward the door, threw it open, and vaulted up the stairs. The door at the top, which led to the apartment, was open. The acrid scent of smoke assaulted his lungs as the scream of the alarm violated his ears.

A woman stood beneath the alarm madly waving a towel.

Evan strode to the dining table situated in front of the windows and pulled a chair beneath the smoke detector. He said nothing to the strange woman, but nevertheless she moved out of his way. He stepped onto the chair and promptly pulled the battery from the alarm. Blessed silence reigned. He closed his eyes with relief.

"Thank you," she said, draping the towel over her shoulder. "I am so sorry about this. Who are you?"

He didn't look directly at her but recognized her immediately. "You're Alaina Pierce."

"I know who *I* am. Who are *you*?" There was a guarded, tentative look in her eyes. He universally sucked at decoding emotional expression, but that was one he knew. Probably because he'd seen it in the mirror so much when he'd been younger.

He jumped down off the wooden chair and returned it to the table. "I'm Evan Archer. Are you staying here?"

"Yes. Sean didn't tell you?"

"Nope." Evan hadn't seen his brother-in-law today, but that wasn't unusual. He and Evan's sister Tori lived in a condo in Ribbon Ridge proper, while Evan lived fifteen minutes outside the center of town with their parents in the house they'd all grown up in. "Should he have?"

"Maybe not. My being here is a secret."

Then it made perfect sense that he hadn't told Evan. He was terrible at keeping secrets. "I suck at secrets." And knowing when to keep his mouth shut.

"I see. Well, do you think you could keep me a secret?"

Maybe. If he didn't make the mistake of blurting it out without thinking. "I guess."

"Hey," she said with more volume than she'd used before. "Would you mind looking at me so I can see if you're telling the truth?"

He forced himself to look straight at her. She was beautiful. But not in the glamorous movie star way he'd expected. She wore very little makeup, not that she needed any at all. The color of her skin reminded him of rich buttermilk, and her hazel eyes carried a beguiling sparkle. They were very expressive and probably her defining feature. Along with that marquee smile he had yet to see.

"Do you have a superpower that allows you to detect lies?"

Her mouth inched up into an almost-smile. "Yes, I do. It's a side effect of being ridiculously famous."

"Good to know. I was only moderately famous, so that's a skill I don't possess." He was also fairly lousy at lying. How could he recognize it in someone else? He looked away from her, settling his gaze on the still-smoky kitchen. "I'll do my best not to expose your secret."

An Excerpt from

ONE TEMPTING PROPOSAL
An Accidental Heirs Novel

by Christy Carlyle

Becoming engaged? Simple.
Resisting temptation? Impossible.

Sebastian Fennick, the newest
Duke of Wrexford, prefers the
straightforwardness of mathematics
to romantic nonsense. When he meets
Lady Katherine Adderly at the first ball
of the season, he finds her as alluring as
she is disagreeable. His title may now
require him to marry, but Sebastian can't
think of anyone less fit to be his wife, even
if he can't get her out of his mind.

"I take it you have something you wish to say to me, Your Grace."

He still hadn't released her. She was warm and smelled heavenly, and the grip of her hand grounded him. Here and now. That's what mattered. Not the past. The past was a broken place of mistakes and regret.

The April evening had turned chilly and Seb finally let her go to remove his evening jacket and settle it over her bare shoulders.

She pulled the lapels together across her chest.

"Is it to be a long discussion, then?"

Seb reached up to lift the coat's collar to cover more of her exposed skin, but he found himself touching her instead, stroking the soft warm column of her neck and then resting his hand at the base of her throat, savoring the feel of her speeding pulse against his palm. His heartbeat echoed in his ears, as wild and rapid as Kat's, and the longer he touched her, the more the sounds merged, until he could almost believe their hearts had begun to beat as one.

He shook his head. That sort of romantic drivel led only to misery.

But he couldn't bring himself to stop touching her. And

he couldn't deny he wanted more. Leaning down, desperate to know if her flavor was as sweet as her scent, he pressed his mouth to her forehead.

"Your Grace?" she whispered, the heat of her breath searing the skin above his necktie.

He pulled back and lifted his hands from her, remembering who he was, who she was. He was a master at guarding his heart and avoiding intimate moments. She was the woman who'd thrown over multiple suitors during each of her seasons.

"We must speak to your father."

Even in the semidarkness, he could see her green eyes grow large. "You've changed your mind?"

Excitement hitched up her voice two octaves, and Seb wished he'd changed his mind, that he wouldn't have to disappoint her, or her sister and Ollie. If he hadn't wasted all his reckless choices in youth, he might allow himself a bit of freedom now. But controlling his emotions, regimenting his behavior, clinging to logic and order—that had seen him through the darkest days of his life. Control had been his salvation, and he was loathe to let it go.

"No. But Ollie tells me that he and Lady Harriet—"

"Plan to elope."

"You knew?"

"She just told me when you walked off with Mr. Treadwell, and I fear they're quite determined."

He jumped when she touched his arm, her exploring fingers jolting his senses, until each press, each stroke along his collar and then up to the edge of his jaw, made him ache for more. She caressed his cheek as he'd touched hers in the conservatory before sliding her hand down to his shoulder, gripping him as if to brace herself.

"Won't you reconsider my suggestion, Your Grace?"

When she lifted onto her toes and swayed toward him, a flash of reason told him to push her away, to guard against her feminine assault. But the thought had all the power of a wisp of smoke and dissolved just as quickly when he reached to steady her and found how well she fit in the crook of his arms.

He'd been a fool to drag her onto the balcony and touch her like a man without an ounce of self-control.

"If you're going to let me hold you this close, you should call me Sebastian."

"If we're to be engaged, you should call me Kitty."

He hadn't agreed to the engagement and still loathed the notion of a scheme. And yet . . . he couldn't deny the practicality of it. It would forestall Ollie's ridiculous plan to elope, satisfy the Claybornes and allow the young couple to marry, and, best of all, it would keep all the spirited misses eager to make his acquaintance—as his aunt had so disturbingly put it—at bay.

"I'm afraid you'll always be Kat to me. Never Kitty."

"Very well. Is that your only condition?"

His skin burned feverish. He loathed lies. Hated pretense. And yet he loathed nothing about holding Kat in his arms. With her velvet-clad curves pressed against him and her thighs brushing his own, he found himself tempted to agree to her subterfuge. Almost.

"I have two more."

"Go on."

"We end it as soon as we're able." If holding her melted his resolve this thoroughly, what sort of wreck would he be after weeks in her company? "You can jilt me if you like. However you wish to do it. And we tell my sister the truth of what we're doing and why. Pippa's far too clever not to see through a falsehood."

"Agreed, Your Grace."

He caught the flash of white as she smiled and moonlight glinted off the curve of her cheeks. Pleasing her stirred an echo of pleasure in him, and it disturbed him how much he wanted to see her smile again, wanted to bring her pleasure, and not just for a moment.

Lifting a hand to caress her cheek, Seb drew Kat in close, dipped his head, and took her mouth in a quick mingling of chilled flesh and warm breath.

An Excerpt from

NO GROOM AT THE INN
A Dukes Behaving Badly Novella
by *Megan Frampton*

In Megan Frampton's delightful
Dukes Behaving Badly holiday novella, a
young lady entertains a sudden proposal of
marriage—to a man she's only just met!

1844
A coaching inn
One lady, no chickens

"Poultry."

Sophronia gazed down into her glass of ale and repeated the word, even though she was only talking to herself. "Poultry."

It didn't sound any better the second time she said it, either.

The letter from her cousin had detailed all of the delights waiting for her when she arrived—taking care of her cousin's six children (his wife had died, perhaps of exhaustion), overseeing the various village celebrations including, her cousin informed her with no little enthusiasm, the annual Tribute to the Hay, which was apparently the highlight of the year, and taking care of the chickens.

All twenty-seven of them.

Not to mention she would be arriving just before Christmas, which meant gifts and merriment and conviviality. Those weren't bad things, of course, it was just that celebrating the season was likely the last thing she wanted to do.

Well, perhaps after taking care of the chickens.

The holidays used to be one of her favorite times of year—she and her father both loved playing holiday games, especially ones like Charades or Dictionary.

Even though he was the word expert in the family, eventually she had been able to fool him with her Dictionary definitions, and there was nothing so wonderful as seeing his dumbstruck expression when she revealed that, no, he had not guessed the correct definition.

He was always so proud of her for that, for being able to keep up with him and his linguistic interests.

And now nobody would care that she was inordinately clever at making up definitions for words she'd never heard of.

She gave herself a mental shake, since she'd promised not to become maudlin. Especially at this time of the year.

She glanced around the barroom she was sitting in, taking note of the other occupants. Like the inn itself, they were plain but tidy. As she was, as well, even if her clothing had started out, many years ago, as grander than theirs.

She unfolded the often-read letter, suppressing a sigh at her cousin's crabbed handwriting. Not that handwriting was indicative of a person's character—that would be their words—but the combination of her cousin's script and the way he assumed she would be delighted to perform all the tasks he was graciously setting before her—that was enough to make her dread the next phase of her life. Which would last until—well, that she didn't know.

Sophronia was grateful, she was, for being offered a place to live, and she didn't want to seem churlish. It was just that she had never imagined that the care and feeding of poultry—not to mention six children—would be her fate.

Which was why she had spent a few precious pennies on a last glass of ale at the coaching inn where she was waiting for the mail coach to arrive and take her to the far reaches of beyond. A last moment of being by herself, being Lady Sophronia, not Sophy the Chicken Lady.

The one without a feather to fly with.

Chuckling at her own wit, she picked her glass up and gave a toast to the as yet imaginary chickens, thinking about how she'd always imagined her life would turn out.

There were no members of the avian community at all in her rosy vision of the future.

Not that she was certain what her rosy vision of the future would include, but she was fairly certain it did not have fowl of any kind.

"All aboard to Chester," a voice boomed through the room. Immediately there were the bustling sounds of people getting up, gathering their things, saying their last goodbyes.

"Excuse me, miss," a gentleman said in her ear. She jumped, so lost in her own foolish (fowlish?) thoughts that she hadn't even noticed him approaching her.

She turned and looked at him, blinking at his splendor. He was tall, taller than her, even, which was a rarity among gentlemen. He was handsome in a dashing rosy-visioned way that made her question just what her imagination was thinking if it had never inserted him—or someone who looked like him—into her dreams.

He had unruly dark brown hair, longer than most gentlemen wore. The ends curled up as though even his hair was irrepressible. His eyes were blue, and even in the dark gloom, she could see they practically twinkled.

As though he and she shared a secret, a lovely, wonderful, delightful secret.